continued . . .

D0029694

"Lucy Richardson is a funny, smart, and resourceful sleuth, a librarian fresh from Boston finding a better life on the scenic Outer Banks of North Carolina. Is it so wrong to be jealous of her charming lighthouse library? Her quaint and possibly haunted apartment? That hint of new romance? Well, even if it is wrong, I'll still want to steal Charles, the splendid cat, and then eat all the gooey pecan tarts from Josie's Cozy Bakery. Then I'll demand the next book in this well-written and entertaining new series."

—Mary Jane Maffini, author of the Charlotte Adams Mysteries

By Book or by Crook

A LIGHTHOUSE LIBRARY MYSTERY

Eva Gates

AN OBSIDIAN BOOK

OBSIDIAN
Published by the Penguin Group
Penguin Group (USA) LLC, 375 Hudson Street,
New York, New York 10014

USA | Canada | UK | Ireland | Australia | New Zealand | India | South Africa | China
penguin.com
A Penguin Random House Company

First published by Obsidian, an imprint of New American Library,
a division of Penguin Group (USA) LLC

First Printing, February 2015

ISBN 978-0-451-47093-5

Printed in the United States of America
10   9   8   7   6   5   4   3

For my number one fan, Alexandra Delany

AUTHOR'S NOTE

The Bodie Island Lighthouse is a real historic lighthouse, located on the Cape Hatteras National Seashore on the Outer Banks of North Carolina. It is still a working lighthouse, protecting ships from the Graveyard of the Atlantic, and is open to the public. The lighthouse setting and grounds are as wonderful as described. It is not, however, a library. Nor is it large enough to house a collection of books, offices, staff rooms, two staircases, or even an apartment.

But it is large enough to accommodate my imagination. And I hope the reader's also.

Chapter 1

Only in the very back of my mind, in my most secret dreams, did I ever dare hope I'd have such a moment.

Too bad it was being ruined by the cacophony of false compliments and long-held grievances going on behind me.

The party was a private affair, a viewing of the new collection for staff and board members of the Bodie Island Lighthouse Library, as well as local dignitaries and community supporters, before the official opening tomorrow. We were celebrating the arrival of a complete set of Jane Austen first editions, on loan for three months.

Jane Austen. My literary idol. So close.

I tried to block out everyone and everything and concentrate. I rubbed my hands together. Perspiration was building inside the loose white gloves. That, of course, was the purpose of the gloves: to keep human sweat and other impurities off the precious objects.

I took a deep breath, closed my eyes. And I touched the worn leather cover.

I imagined I could feel the very power of the words themselves coming up through my fingers.

"Incredible," a voice beside me said.

My eyes flew open. I snatched my hand back, embarrassed to be caught in a moment so emotional, so *personal*.

"Go ahead, honey," Bertie said, with a laugh. Her eyes danced with amusement. She understood. "Open it."

"Am I allowed to? I wouldn't want to damage anything."

"These books are precious, to be sure. But they'll be put back in their cabinet as soon as the party's over. And they've been cherished, cared for, and thus aren't as fragile as some would be at that age. Enjoy, Lucy. Enjoy. But don't spend too long here. I have people I need you to meet."

The head librarian touched my arm lightly, gave me another smile, and went back to her guests.

I turned the heavy cover, flipped pages with shaking hands, and was soon gazing in awestruck wonder at the frontispiece of the first volume of *Sense and Sensibility*, by "A Lady." A Lady all the world now knew to be Miss Jane Austen. An illustrated first edition, printed in London in 1811. I closed my eyes again and breathed. The scent was of old paper and aging leather, carrying with it memories of the foggy streets of London, the sound of horse's hooves rattling across cobblestones, the gentle rustle of skirts and petticoats, and the crackle of fire.

All I wanted to do was to gather the volume into

my hands, spirit it away to a cozy corner with a good reading lamp, and curl up to spend the rest of the night simply enjoying it. Reading it, smelling it, touching it. To be lost in Austen's delightful pastoral England. A world of balls and dances. Of men in handsome uniforms and women in beautiful gowns. Romance and laughter—as well as foolishness and heartbreak. Sense versus sensibility.

With a sigh, I remembered that I had duties. They might be informal ones, but they were still duties.

I closed the book, returned it to its place, slipped off the gloves, and laid them back on the table for the next person to use. I pasted on my fake smile, turned, and stepped forward, ready to plunge into the party.

I was almost knocked off my feet as an excessively thin man shoved me aside. His tiny black eyes blazed with lust as bright as the flashing light on the top of this historic lighthouse. The tip of his tongue was trapped between small browning teeth, and a spot of drool touched the corner of his plump lips. To my horror, he extended an ungloved hand toward the book.

"Excuse me," I said in what I hoped was my best librarian tone. "Those books are extremely valuable. You must put on the gloves. Please don't lean over them like that."

His nose might have been made for peering down at uppity young librarians. "Excuse me," he said with an accent I'd last heard when Prince William visited America. "I am well aware of the proper storage and handling of books. I am, in fact, quite disappointed in Bertie for agreeing to house the collection in this"—he waved his hand as if encompassing not only the crowded room but also the lighthouse we were standing in, the Outer Banks, the moist sea air, and the waves crashing against the sand dunes, maybe even North Carolina itself—"place."

"This is a library," I said. "The proper place for books. Besides, Miss Austen lived near the sea. Her entire country is bound by the sea. I'm sure her books are delighted to be breathing salty air once again."

He sniffed. As well he might. I do have a tendency to get carried away sometimes.

"You," he said, still peering down his long, patrician nose, enunciating each word carefully, "must be the new girl."

His tone wasn't friendly or at all welcoming. But if I was going to get on here, in my new job, my new life, I'd pretend he'd intended it to be. I shoved my hand forward. "Lucy Richardson. I'm the new assistant librarian. Pleased to meet you, Mr. . . ."

He barely touched my outstretched fingers. "Theodore. Everyone knows me as Theodore. At your service, madam. If there is anything you need to know, young woman, about the handling and collection of rare books, you may call on me to enlighten you." He dug in the pocket of his tweed jacket, which emitted a strong aroma of pipe smoke, and pulled out a small square of paper. "My card. Now, if you'll excuse me." He turned away from me. I waited until he was pulling on the gloves and left him to examine the books in peace. I put the card in my pocket without reading it.

"Don't you mind Theodore, honey." My aunt Ellen slipped her arm around me. "We call him Teddy.

Drives him nuts. He's just plain old Teddy Kowalski from North Carolina. He was born about ten miles from this very spot, over in Nags Head. Teddy was a smart little tyke; I'll give him that. Always had his head in books when the other boys were tossing balls around. He went to Duke and got a degree in English literature, and came home pretending to be an English lord or some such nonsense."

I laughed. "Did you know him when you were children?"

"Sakes no! He was a couple years ahead of Josie in school."

"How old is he?"

"Thirty-five."

"Really? I would have put him in his fifties." I glanced at the display table. Theodore was bent over *Pride and Prejudice.* He'd propped a pair of reading glasses on his nose.

"He deliberately tries to give that impression. See those glasses? Plain glass. He thinks they make him look more professorial."

"Fool," I said.

Bertie appeared at my side. "Don't take him for that, Lucy." My new boss's tone was serious. Almost warning. "Teddy has airs and pretentions, but he knows everything there is to know about eighteenth- and nineteenth-century English literature. He's a serious collector, or at least he would be if he had the money. A word of warning: always check his bags when he leaves, and if he's wearing a big coat, make him open it. He'll protest, act affronted, but . . ."

"Are you three going to stand here chatting all night long? You need to introduce Lucy. Everyone's simply dying to meet her." It was Josie, my cousin. If I didn't love Josie so much, I'd hate her. She was everything I am not. Strikingly beautiful, with long, glossy hair bleached by the sun, a pale face full of dancing freckles, cornflower blue eyes that seemed to always be sparkling, perfect white teeth. As proof that life was never fair, Josie was model tall and model thin (except for the generous breasts—more unfairness!). The irony was compounded by the fact that she was the owner and chief baker of the best bakery in the Outer Banks, if not the entire state of North Carolina. Thinking of Josie and her business, I snuck a glance at the dessert buffet she'd catered. I felt a pound settling onto my hips. Hips that definitely did not need further poundage.

"Josie's right, as always," Aunt Ellen said. "You best be meeting folks. Making friendly."

"Come on," Bertie said, "I'll introduce you."

As its name suggests, the library I now worked in was situated in a lighthouse—a fabulous old lighthouse on Bodie Island, part of the Outer Banks of North Carolina. The minute I'd entered the building—long before that; the minute I'd first seen it from the road when I was a child on vacation—I'd loved it. What an imaginative, absolutely perfect place to house a library. All round whitewashed walls, iron spiral staircases going up . . . and up . . . and up, tall windows in thick walls overlooking the marsh on one side and the sand dunes of the shore and the storm-tossed ocean on the other. The shorter back staircase went up only one level, to where the rare and valuable books were housed. The general collection was accessible from the main staircase and filled three floors. Fiction was on the first, as was some nonfiction, with children's books on the second and Charlene's office and her research materials on the third level.

Above that, another turn on the spiral staircase to my own room. Small—pokey really—but absolutely perfect for sipping a cup of tea, reading, gazing out at the ocean, and daydreaming. And worrying that I'd made the worst decision of my life.

From there, the staircase had another hundred or more winding steps to reach the top of the lighthouse. Beyond my room, the stairs were seldom used in this day of electric, computer-programmed lamps.

Since I'd started work here all of four days ago, I figured I'd lost enough weight on those stairs that I could indulge in one of Josie's Cozy Bakery's gooey pecan tarts.

Music, Mozart at the moment, came quietly from the sound system, and the room was full of the low buzz of conversation.

Outside, night was falling, bringing with it a heavy ocean mist carried on a cool wet wind. Inside, we were warm and dry, bathed in soft yellow light. The partygoers were women mostly, with a few husbands dragged along. I smiled to myself at the thought that some of the husbands had probably been persuaded to come only upon hearing that the catering was by Josie's Cozy Bakery. Everyone wore their almost-best, like proper Southern fund-raisers. Colorful summer dresses and heels, primarily, and a few pantsuits, all accented by tasteful and expensive jewelry. Most of the men were in open-necked shirts, but a few wore a jacket and tie.

The majority of the interior lights had been switched off, leaving only a scattering of wall sconces to illuminate the room. Electric, of course. Candlelight would have been perfect, but this was, after all, a public place and a library at that. The alcove against the back wall, where generations of lighthouse keepers had sat to record the weather and the temperament of the ocean, ships passing, and the routine of lighting and extinguishing the great lamps, was now the central display area. Tonight the Austen collection took pride of place. That area was brightly lit and protected by a red velvet rope, warning anyone who wanted a closer look that red wine and gooey pecan tarts did not go well with nineteenth-century paper. When the display opened tomorrow for the public, the rope would mean "Keep back."

"Ronald's been on vacation." Bertie tipped her head toward a short man in his mid-forties pouring himself a glass of wine at the circulation desk that had been converted into a bar for the party. Thick white hair hung in curls around his collar, and he wore shiny black loafers, sharply ironed gray trousers, a crisp white dress shirt, and a giant yellow polka-dot bow tie. "You haven't had a chance to meet. Come on, I'll introduce you. He's the children's librarian and we're very, very lucky to have him." We hadn't taken more than a step before Bertie gripped my arm and jerked me to a halt. "Too late! He's fallen into her clutches." Bertie whirled around. "Who else do you need to meet?"

I craned my neck to see over her and the crowd of

partygoers. A stately Southern matron, of the sort I—a born-and-bred New Englander—imagined them to be, was waving her finger in Ronald's face. He smiled and nodded, but I couldn't help but notice that his eyes were jerking around the room, looking desperately for an escape. And not finding it.

"Who's that with him?" I asked Bertie.

She dropped her voice. "Mrs. Peterson, one of our most active patrons. She's a newcomer, meaning she might have been born on the Outer Banks, but her grandparents were not. Her husband, however, is a member of one of our oldest families. She thinks Ronald should be her children's personal librarian and reading instructor. She'd just love to have him on her staff. If not for the minor fact that they have no staff, because her husband lost all of his family's money when he sank every penny into a Canadian gold-mining exploration company that turned out not to have a speck of gold in the ground. Poor Ronald. Mrs. Peterson took his vacation as a personal insult. You don't have to worry much about her, honey. She hasn't the slightest interest in adult books. I doubt she's read a single book since high school. When I announced that I'd been able to secure a visit of the Austen collection, Mrs. Peterson actually said, out loud"—here Bertie put on a very good imitation of a snooty, high-pitched voice—"'But why would anyone be interested in such *old* books?'"

We left Ronald, looking increasingly desperate under the barrage of Mrs. Peterson's verbal assault, to his own devices.

"Where's Charles?" I asked, referring to one of my favorite library employees.

"Banished to the closet by the staff break room for the duration of the party."

"How's he taking that?"

"If you listen closely you can hear the howls of indignation from here." Charles (named in honor of Mr. Dickens) was the library cat. A gorgeous Himalayan with a black face and expressive blue eyes in a ball of long, tan fur that must weigh a good thirty pounds (I wondered if he frequented Josie's Cozy Bakery), Charles was particularly loved by the library's younger patrons. "Mrs. Peterson is allergic to cats. Or so she says. She's starting to make noises about her dear little Dallas coming home from the library with watering eyes."

Aunt Ellen chimed in, "If she dares to suggest you get rid of Charles, I'll . . . I'll do something."

"I'm sure you will," I said. I smiled at my aunt.

"Let me finish introducing Lucy," Ellen said to Bertie. "You have your guests to see to."

"True. Although I'd prefer to spend my time with you two." Bertie straightened her shoulders and waded into the crowd.

"So, you're the new one, are you? Let's have a look at you."

"Excuse me?" I blinked. A woman was standing much too close, intruding into my private space, staring boldly into my face, her eyes dark with hostility. I'd never seen her before. The amount of product in her hair, teased and sprayed into a stiff helmet in a shade of red not known to nature, competed with her perfume. Her fingernails were the color of the wine in the glass she gripped in her right hand. Her dress was lower cut than suited her turkey-neck throat and chest and she tottered on stiletto sandals with straps the thickness of dental floss. She had to be well into her sixties, and not going into old age gracefully. She exhaled alcoholic fumes into my face. The party was just getting under way. She must have had a couple of drinks before arriving.

"Diane, I don't think . . ." Aunt Ellen said.

"I don't care what you think. A *librarian*. A *young* librarian. Just what we need in this town. Another one of *them*." She spoke as if "librarian" were another word for "ax murderer." I had absolutely no idea what she was going on about. I was quite proud to be a librarian.

"At least," Diane said, with a snort, "she's not very *pretty*."

That hit a sore spot. I might not be a beauty like my cousin Josie, but I didn't consider myself to be a total dog, either.

"I can't imagine where she got that dress. Her mother's closet, perhaps?"

Another direct hit. I'd bought this dress especially for this party. It cost considerably more than I could afford, but I wanted to make an impression. Apparently I had. But not the impression I was hoping for. The dress was new, but the clerk in the store told me the vintage look was back in style. It was pale yellow, with a square-cut neckline, close-fitting bodice, tightly cinched patent leather black belt above a flaring skirt, and a stiff petticoat that ended sharply at the knees. The shoes were also new, of the same color and material as the belt, and turning out to have been a mistake. My aching feet were reminding me that I should stick to ballet flats and sports sandals.

"Diane, you're creating a scene." Mr. Uppiton, the chair of the library board, took the woman's arm.

She shook him off. She took a hefty swig of her wine. "No, Jonathan, you're the one who made a scene. You think the whole town isn't talking about you? About how this place, this library, is more important to you than our marriage of thirty years?"

All around us the buzz of polite conversation died as people turned to look. Diane Uppiton's face was turning as red as her hair and nails. Her eyes filled with water that threatened to spill over and ruin her heavily applied makeup.

In the sudden silence, I could hear a ghost screaming from the depths of a castle dungeon. Or it might have been Charles the cat, expressing his opinion at being locked in the closet.

"Our marriage," Mr. Uppiton said, with a sniff, "was a mistake from the beginning. I finally came to realize that. I decided to take the blame for its demise myself, to allow you to leave with some medium of dignity. Dignity that you, my dear, clearly have forsaken."

Stuck-up jerk. He was speaking louder than he needed to, and although he was trying to look concerned, the corners of his mouth were in danger of curling upward. He, I realized, was playing to the audience, and thoroughly enjoying every minute of it. My sympathy shifted and I felt very sorry for Mrs. Uppiton.

"Our marriage"—the tears began to flow—"was my world. I gave you my youth, my beauty. My life. But you, nothing mattered to you more than this cursed library. Nothing."

"In a library, at least, one can have silence," Mr. Uppiton said, with the exaggerated sigh of a martyr. A few people tittered, more in embarrassment than in enjoyment of the joke. But Mr. Uppiton looked pleased with himself indeed.

"Come along, honey." Bertie plucked the wineglass from Mrs. Uppiton's fingers and passed it to the closest person. Me.

Unfortunately that had the result of turning Mrs. Uppiton's attention back to me. "You." She stabbed one of those potentially lethal nails in my direction. "Stay away from my husband."

"That's soon-to-be-ex-husband, I'll remind you," he sniffed.

She ignored him. "Do you hear me? I know your kind."

I refrained from mentioning that about the last person I'd ever want to get close to (shudder) was Mr. Uppiton. The crotchety old jerk, he'd made it plain to everyone who'd listen—and many who didn't want to—that he didn't like me and didn't want me in the job. I was, according to him, a flighty debutante. I figured he meant "dilettante," but wasn't about to point out the difference.

"And you," she said, spraying spittle all over her husband's face, "you'll get what's coming to you. See if you don't. I'll dance on your grave yet."

"Come along now," Bertie cooed. "Let's dry those tears."

"Really, my dear," Mr. Uppiton sniffed as his sobbing wife was escorted to the ladies' room. "Credit me with a medium of taste." I suspect he meant "modicum." Again, I declined to correct him.

Since starting work here, I'd come to realize that Bertie had eyes in the back of her head. As she led Diane away, without even glancing over her shoulder she shouted, "Charlene, don't you dare touch that CD player!"

The reference librarian leapt away from the machine, a look of total innocence on her face.

Charles reminded us he was still trapped in the closet.

Chapter 2

I'd been worried about getting to know everyone who was someone at the Lighthouse Library.

Now everyone knew me. Although they all pretended they hadn't actually been listening to that ugly confrontation.

The partygoers turned back to their drinks and conversation. There was a sudden rush on the bar and the dessert buffet. Mr. Uppiton looked quite pleased with himself, but I sensed the majority of the room was not on his side. Most of them were women of a certain age. The right age to be dumped by a longtime husband in favor of a pretty young girl.

Not that that girl was me.

Mr. Uppiton had been the first to arrive for the reception, and he'd come alone. He was the library chair, and had stalked into the lighthouse as if he owned the place, ordering the lighting in the alcove to be adjusted, demanding that more room for the bar be created, even though we had no place to put the printer. He'd disapproved of the collection of vocal jazz CDs Bertie had selected for tonight's background music, and took a stack of Mozart and Beethoven out of his cavernous, ever-present briefcase. Bertie whispered to me that if she'd chosen Mozart, Mr. Uppiton would have produced Diana Krall.

His love of the library, Bertie had warned me on my arrival, was sometimes a bit . . . excessive.

You'd think he and I would get on well. I also loved libraries, and had loved this one in particular since I'd first seen it when vacationing on the Outer Banks. But no, Mr. Uppiton was also a stickler for numbers, and if the library budget didn't allow for another staff member, no matter how desperately one might be needed, that was all there was to it. That Bertie had found the money to employ an extra staffer through our busiest time of year, the summer, by going directly to the town council, was of no consequence to Mr. Uppiton.

The door opened, bringing in a gust of cold, wet fog, and all thoughts of seeking new employment come fall, of library budgets and board members, even of Jane Austen and that first edition of *Sense and Sensibility* so tantalizingly close, fled.

"Your Honor!" Mr. Uppiton boomed. "So glad you could make it." He pushed and shoved his way across the room to get to the new arrival. He pumped the man's hand with an excess of enthusiasm, not giving him the chance to wipe sea spray and mist off his face and hands first. "Welcome, welcome to our little sobriety."

"Is that anything like a soiree?" Josie whispered to me. "Love, love, love that dress, by the way. It is absolutely perfect on you. Next time you wear it, I've got a brooch that'll be a perfect match. You really do need to wear bright colors more often, Lucy. You're a winter, you know."

"Oh, good. The mayor's here," Bertie said. "I was hoping he'd come."

"What'd you do with Diane Uppiton?" Josie asked.

"Left her reapplying her makeup. I suggested she go home, but she would have none of that. I could hardly tie her up and carry her out the door over my shoulder, now, could I? I'll make sure she doesn't try to drive home. Poor thing. Despite her rudeness, I do feel sorry for her."

I scarcely heard her. I stood, fixed to the spot, as Mr. Uppiton dragged the mayor around the room, introducing him to everyone of importance and ignoring those who were not. That the mayor of such a small town would probably know everyone quite well didn't seem to matter to our library chair.

"And now how about a look at our piece of resistance?" Mr. Uppiton boomed, once the mayor had a bottle of beer in his hand and had managed to dry off somewhat.

"Your what?"

"He means, of course, the Austen collection," Bertie said. She held out her hand. "Welcome, Connor. It's nice to see you."

"Wouldn't miss it," he said. "It's a real coup for the library, and for the town, that you were able to get it here, Bertie. My congratulations."

Mr. Uppiton tried to edge the mayor away from our little group, but Bertie stood firm. "First, I'd like to introduce you to our newest librarian. This is my assistant . . ."

"Lucy," he said, with a huge smile. "It's been an awful long time."

My heart pounded in my chest. Connor McNeil. Even handsomer than I remembered.

"You know each other?" Mr. Uppiton said.

"Sure do. Lucy and I were kids together. Right, Lucy?"

I found my tongue at long last. "I'm surprised you remember me, Connor. I was only a summer visitor and it was a long time ago."

"I remember all our visitors. Wouldn't be much of a mayor if I didn't." His eyes were the color of the ocean on a sunny day, and as welcoming and friendly. "But you I remember in particular. Very fondly."

My face has a horrible habit of showing exactly what I'm feeling at any given moment. Waves of heat were rising. My petticoat crinkled noisily as I wiped my palms on my skirt. Josie was looking at me, her beautiful eyes full of questions. Aunt Ellen had a slight smile on her face. Most of the onlookers nodded politely.

Mr. Uppiton chafed at losing his moment in the spotlight. "This way, Mr. Mayor," he said, extending his arm in a flourish. "Theodore Kowalski, get out of the way and let His Honor have a look."

Throughout the party, every time I'd glanced toward the alcove, Theodore had been bent over the books, peering through his plain-glass spectacles, ungraciously allowing others close enough to have a look and practically shoving them aside when he figured they'd had long enough. At least he kept the gloves on and turned the pages carefully and with the reverence they deserved.

Connor's lips moved. "We'll catch up later," they seemed to say. And then he allowed Mr. Uppiton to escort him to the Austen collection.

"There's a story here," Josie whispered, "and I'm going to get to the bottom of it."

Connor McNeil. The first boy I'd ever kissed. I'd been fourteen years old. The first summer I'd been allowed to visit Aunt Ellen and Uncle Amos without my parents or bothersome brothers. A beach party, a roaring bonfire shooting sparks into the night air, laughing kids, waves crashing on the unseen shore, a blanket of stars overhead.

A walk along the beach in the dark. A kiss.

It had been a light kiss, an innocent fourteen-year-old girl and a well-brought-up fifteen-year-old boy.

I went home to Boston the next day, vacation over. But that kiss remained, all these years later, the best kiss I had ever had. I'd spent the whole year dreaming of him and had been shattered the next summer when I came back and heard that his father had found him a summer job in Ocracoke on a fishing charter boat.

Connor had been a cute boy. He'd grown up to be a handsome man. Dark hair, curling now in the damp mist, lovely blue eyes, prominent cheekbones, good skin with a trace of stubble breaking through.

"Lucy?"

I shook my head. "Sorry—what was that?"

"I said, 'I'm going into the back to replenish the buffet. Do you want anything?'"

"I think I'll have one of those pecan tarts after all." I plunged through the crowd. I like the occasional glass of wine, but tonight I was sticking to mineral water; I knew I needed to keep my wits about me when meeting a room full of strangers. Influential strangers at that. I had nobly kept my distance from the buffet table, but seeing Connor again had thrown me for a loop and I told myself I needed sustenance in order to keep calm. Chocolaty, nutty, gooey sustenance.

Heck, the tarts were quite small. Two wouldn't hurt. And since I hadn't had a serving of fruit all day, I'd better take one of the lemon squares at the same time. By the time I finally made up my mind I had a nice little pile of treats on my plate.

I found a place against the wall and stood, munching happily, watching the room. Ronald had been backed into a corner by Mrs. Peterson, who was still talking and gesticulating wildly. Theodore was attempting to shrink his six-foot frame in order to slink around Connor and Mr. Uppiton and get back at the books. Connor was nodding at whatever Mr. Uppiton was saying, and all the while his eyes moved around the room. He caught me watching, gave me an almost imperceptible wink. I ducked my head, heat rushing back into my face. Josie, helped by Charlene, was bringing out more food. Aunt Ellen chatted to a group of Friends of the Library, and Bertie stood by the door, greeting latecomers as they arrived.

Mrs. Uppiton had returned. She'd scrubbed her face, dried her eyes, and slathered on another layer of mascara and eye shadow. She was, I noticed, heading directly for the self-serve bar. Her head was high and she pointedly did not look at her husband as she passed.

"Nice party," a deep voice said.

I turned around and came face-to-face with a man I'd noticed when he'd entered the room. Who wouldn't? Since he'd made a beeline for Josie, I—telling myself I was not at all disappointed—had tried to pay him no further attention.

He held out a massive paw. I choked down a piece of pecan and offered my hand. It was swallowed up, like a minnow disappearing into a whale's mouth. "Butch Greenblatt," he said.

"Pleased to meet you. I'm . . ."

"Lucy, the new assistant librarian. I made a point of finding out." His smile was full of white teeth and a healthy dose of humor.

I smiled back.

Josie slid up beside him. She playfully bumped her hip against his, and he put his arm around her shoulders. I tried not to groan in disappointment. Another Josie conquest. Since I'd arrived in North Carolina, we hadn't had much of a chance to talk, but I'd thought she was dating a chef, some guy named Jake. Apparently Jake, like so many men before him, had been discarded.

"I see you two have met," she said. "I'm glad."

I gritted my teeth. Jodie attracted men like her pecan tarts attracted flies if left uncovered on a hot, sunny day. I'd just have to get used to it if I wanted to live happily in the Outer Banks.

She slipped out of Butch's arm and glanced at the wineglass in his hand. His fist was wrapped around the stem and it looked as if it was about to snap in two. "I do believe there's a beer or two in the fridge. Can I get you one?"

Relief crossed his face. "That would be great. Yes, please."

She laughed. "Be right back."

He watched her go, a smile on his face.

"You're good friends with my cousin," I managed to choke out.

"More than friends, I hope."

"How nice." I glanced around the room, seeking escape. Right now, a visit to the dentist would be a welcome escape.

"I'm expecting my brother to pop the question any day now. If he doesn't, I'm going to do it for him. He'd be a fool to let that girl go."

"Your brother?"

"Yeah. He's a cook—a chef, I guess I should say. Back in Nags Head after ten years learning the ropes in New York City. He's opened a restaurant of his own. Jake's Seafood Bar. It's already being called the best fish place on the Outer Banks. Course that's my mom saying that, but others will be, too, soon enough."

Josie was back. She plucked the wineglass out of Butch's paw and placed a bottle of the Outer Banks Brewing Station's stout in its place. He nodded his thanks.

"The reviews of the restaurant have been great," Josie said. "We're so excited! Oops, looks like we're running out of napkins."

"Have you been there yet?" Butch asked me.

"I haven't been much of anywhere. There's so much to do. Settling in, getting familiar with the job."

"Perhaps you'd like . . ."

"Butch, my boy! I've something I want to talk to

you about. You know that nephew of mine? Keeps getting himself into trouble. I figure you're the one to give him an awful good talkin'-to. You don't mind if I borrow this big fellow for a few minutes, do you, little lady?"

Butch threw a smile over his shoulder as he allowed himself to be led away.

I glanced at my watch. Seven forty-five. My feet were killing me, and it felt as if my smile were pasted on my face with superglue. Bertie had said she had an important announcement to make at eight, something to do with the Austen collection. Even I didn't know what that was. Surely everyone who was interested would be here by now. All the people I'd met since starting the job had arrived, except for . . .

Curses! As if my thoughts had summoned her themselves, the door flew open, bringing in more cold, damp air, along with the one person I was hoping I wouldn't see. Louise Jane McKaughnan. Wanna-be librarian. Louise Jane had volunteered at the library a few times, filling in here and there for vacations, and she thought that qualified her for a full-time position. That Louise Jane had neither education in library science nor any experience other than shelving books and checking them out seemed not to matter to her one bit. She wanted the new job, and she had no qualms expressing her displeasure at it being given to—*horrors*—an outsider. I slunk behind a cabinet displaying books of nautical charts and a scale model of an eighteenth-century sailing ship, wondering whether I could hide out here for the rest of the night.

Until Butch was free, anyway.

Bertie, as could be expected, greeted Louise Jane warmly, as if they had not exchanged bitter words behind the head librarian's closed office door only this morning. Louise Jane pointedly ignored her, and marched into the room as though she were a general leading her forces into battle.

In her wake followed not an army, but Poor Andrew MacGillacuddy. No one ever called Andrew just "Andrew," and certainly not Mr. MacGillacuddy. He was always Poor Andrew. For reasons unknown to everyone in town, Poor Andrew adored Louise Jane and trotted in her wake, begging for scraps of attention. Louise Jane treated him with mild contempt, when she could be bothered to notice him at all.

From my hiding place I heard Andrew say, "Can I get you something to drink, Louise Jane?" in a high-pitched, almost pleading voice. Andrew was close to six feet tall, but I'd have been surprised if he weighed more than a hundred and fifty pounds soaking wet. Which, come to think of it, he was right now. A lock of blond hair flopped over his forehead and he lifted a hand to push it back. His eyes were a nice shade of pale blue, and would have been attractive if not for the look of intense adoration they had when looking at Louise Jane. Which they almost always did. Then those longing eyes would put a six-week-old puppy to shame.

"Get me a beer," she snapped. "Good. There he is." She headed straight for the alcove, where Connor was still standing beside the collection, exchanging greetings with patrons.

But it wasn't Connor she was intent on cornering. I saw a look of alarm cross Bertie's face and came out of hiding to join her. "Oh no. Not now. Not here," she muttered.

"I have a bone to pick with you, Mr. Uppiton," Louise Jane bellowed. Once again, conversation ground to a halt and heads turned. Connor blinked in confusion. "Is there a problem, Miss McKaughnan?"

"There sure is. As Mr. Uppiton knows full well. This can't be allowed to continue." Andrew tiptoed up to her and held out a glass full of frothy beer. She snatched it out of his hand and swallowed half of it in one go.

Bertie pushed her way through the crowd. I'd never seen such a look of pure anger on her face. In addition to her job as head librarian of the Lighthouse Library, Bertie was a yoga instructor. She practiced its calming rituals every day.

Knowing, fearing what was about to happen, I followed in my boss's wake.

"I agree with you, Louise Jane," Mr. Uppiton said. He also was almost shouting, playing to the crowd once again. "I'm grievously disappointed in Bertie. I thought she had more sense."

"Obviously not," Louise Jane said. "That job was promised to me. Me!"

Andrew's head bobbed in agreement. Partygoers whispered questions to each other.

"It's a total waste of library funds," Mr. Uppiton said. "And not included in this year's budget."

"My great-grandfather manned this very lighthouse. His dedication was nothing short of heroic. My grandparents, God rest their sainted souls, built this town. My mother raised funds for the restoration of the lighthouse."

"As I recall," Aunt Ellen whispered in my ear, "Jane McKaughnan put on an enormous garden party. By the time she'd paid to have her grounds groomed and fountains installed to make it a suitable venue, rented a tent and a hundred chairs along with silver cutlery and crystal wineglasses, paid for a live string orchestra, and booked caterers for a full afternoon tea, with champagne, about ten dollars remained for the lighthouse fund."

I chuckled, despite myself.

"It's not as if the girl has any real community library experience, anyway," Mr. Uppiton said, addressing the crowd. Louise Jane grinned maliciously beside him. "A *university* librarian. Totally useless."

"Quite right, Mr. Uppiton. I've said all along—haven't I, Andrew?—that what we need here is someone from a true Bodie Island family. Someone who knows the history of the land, someone in whom the blood of the old families runs in . . ."

"This is not the time nor the place." Connor attempted to get a word in.

"What we need," Mr. Uppiton thundered, "is no further unnecessary expenses. About all this girl from. . . . from . . . Boston . . . is needed for is to make tea for Bertie and to shelve books."

"That's enough." Bertie pushed her way through the crowd of onlookers. Her whole body shook and a vein pulsed in the side of her throat. "I hired Lucy, who just happens to be a highly qualified librarian with a master's degree, no less, because she is sorely needed here."

"I'll admit she has the education," Mr. Uppiton sniffed, "but really, Bertie, you have to learn to control your spending. Why, you could have hired Louise Jane here for a fraction of the cost."

"I could have hired a trained donkey for a fraction of the cost. But I need a librarian, not a trained donkey."

A couple of people tittered. Was Bertie—calm, sensible Bertie—calling Louise Jane a donkey?

"Hey," Louise Jane said.

"But that's beside the point. We don't have the funds in the budget. You shouldn't have hired anyone. As I have said . . ."

"Over and over and over," Bertie said. "Fortunately, hiring staff is my responsibility."

"As head of the library board, it is within my power to call a special meeting of the board to overturn your decision."

Bertie stepped forward. "You. Would. Not. Dare." She punctuated every word with the poke of a long, thin finger into his chest.

He sniffed. "Really, my dear. I will do whatever is necessary to maintain the integrates of this library and its funding."

Charlene laughed. Mr. Uppiton threw her a ferocious glance, and she was overcome by a coughing fit.

"Most of the board seems to be here," he said. "I call an emergency meeting for tomorrow night. We will vote on terminating the position of assistant librarian and putting a moratorium on any further hiring."

"Hey," Louise Jane protested. "That's not what I meant."

Bertie's yell drowned her out. "You pompous

jerk! How dare you override my authority in this manner. I won't stand for it."

"You," Mr. Uppiton said, "have no choice. Now, where were we, Your Honor? I believe we were discussing my idea for installing a contemplative fountain on the library grounds."

Bertie, however, wasn't finished. Her face was flushed with rage. "If you fire Lucy," she said, loudly enough for everyone to hear. "I will not be responsible for my actions."

"A threat?" Mr. Uppiton raised one eyebrow theatrically. "How childish of you, Bertie."

"That's enough," Connor said. "You're deliberately goading Bertie, Jonathan. This is a party to celebrate the Austen collection and all of Bertie's hard work in securing it for us. Now, I, for one, haven't had any of Josie's delicious squares yet, and there seems to be plenty of wine still left at the bar."

People moved away and conversation resumed, as everyone pretended not to have been caught listening.

The party went downhill from there.

The hands of the big clock over the door touched eight, but Bertie didn't make her announcement. Instead, she slipped into a dark recess behind the shelf labeled Morrison–Proulx and stood alone, taking deep, calming breaths while gathering her arms in swooping motions to her chest. No one made a move to leave. No doubt they were all waiting to see if there would be any more excitement.

I decided I needed a chocolate-chip cookie to settle my nerves. Two chocolate-chip cookies.

Would Mr. Uppiton go through with his threat? I

couldn't bear to lose this job. Without a job I had no place to live on the Outer Banks. Aunt Ellen would offer to take me in, of course, and insist that they had plenty of room. Which they didn't. Once their children moved away for college and jobs, she and Uncle Amos had bought their dream home: a small, perfect seaside house. I couldn't stay there for long without becoming a burden. Even worse than being homeless and jobless, I'd lose access to the Austen collection. I saw my dream of taking those books, one at a time, up to my tiny, circular room high above the crashing waves, disappearing.

On a more practical level, I didn't know what I would do then. Where would I go if I couldn't find a home or a job? I couldn't bear to go back to Boston. To my brothers' told-you-so sneers, to my father's absentminded pat on the head, to my mother telling me that she was glad I'd come to my senses. Finally.

As I stood by the buffet, worrying and stuffing food into my mouth, a path opened in front of me, and I could see all the way to the far side of the room into the alcove. The precious books were temporarily alone. Even Theodore had gone in search of sustenance or further gossip.

No, there he was. Heading not for the drinks and company, but for the back stairs. The stairs that bypassed the main rooms and gave access only to the private collection. Where we kept rare and valuable books.

I put down my half-finished cookie and took a step forward.

"Don't worry about him, Lucy. He's all talk and no action. He'll back down tomorrow."

At first I thought Butch was talking about Theodore. Then he continued, "If I know Bertie, and I do, your job's safe."

I peered around his shoulder. It was much too high to actually look over. I thought I saw the soles of Theodore's shoes disappearing up the curving stairs. "I need to . . ."

"My brother's working flat out to make his restaurant a success," Butch said. "I want to give him all the business I can. Are you free tomorrow evening?"

"Tomorrow? You mean for dinner?"

"Yes, I mean for dinner." He smiled at me. His eyes were a deep brown speckled with flakes of gold. Someone bumped him from behind and mumbled, "Sorry." Butch stepped closer to me. He smelled of beer and aftershave and delicious male hormones. "You don't have any other plans, I hope."

Oh, my gosh. This amazing man was asking me out. On a date. My face began to burn.

"You do eat, don't you?" A smile touched the edges of his mouth.

Flames shot into my cheeks. "Of course I do. Eat, I mean. I'd enjoy trying your brother's restaurant."

"Good." He took a sip of his beer. His eyes were focused on me, not glancing around, not seeking someone more interesting. I enjoyed the attention. Although in the back of my mind I was aware of Connor, moving easily through the room, exchanging greetings with everyone. "Josie tells me you're from Boston. What brings you our way?"

I told Butch about vacationing on the Outer Banks when I was a kid. How much I'd always loved it. I said I was bored with my job at the Harvard Library and wanted to make a change. I'd come here to get away, to spend time with my favorite aunt and uncle in my favorite place in all the world. To have space and time and the support to make some decisions about the direction I wanted my life to take.

I didn't think this was the time or the place to go into the *real* reason I'd fled Massachusetts so abruptly.

The day after I arrived, I told Butch, Aunt Ellen had invited her best and oldest friend to tea, knowing full well that Bertie had long been searching for an assistant librarian for the Lighthouse Library. Not even realizing I was undergoing a job interview, by the time tea ended, I had an offer of employment. Just for the summer, to begin. If it worked out, it could become permanent.

Only, I hastened to add, because of my qualifications and experience. I didn't mention how Bertie had touched my hand when she left and said that she didn't really give a fig for my master's degree. It was the passion for books and the obvious joy I found in reading that I expressed with every word I spoke that convinced her I'd be perfect for the Lighthouse Library. And that the Lighthouse Library would be perfect for me.

"Speaking of which," I said. "Bertie was planning some sort of big announcement at eight. It's well past that now, isn't it?"

Butch glanced around the room. He was tall enough that he could see over everyone's heads. "I don't see her. Maybe she's getting ready."

At that very moment a piercing yell filled the room. Then came a solid thud on the floor over our heads. People stopped talking, looked up, faces full of confusion.

The thud was followed by a moment of silence, broken only by Charles screaming to be released, the soft music, and the sound of wind rattling the windows and pushing against the solid, round walls of the lighthouse.

After a moment's hesitation, Mrs. Peterson's voice rang throughout the room. "Primrose, on the other hand, is such an advanced reader that I fear the school library simply can't rise to her level. Of course, we'd love to send her to a *better* school, but until that happens, Ronald honey, I'm hoping you . . ."

Then we heard a piercing scream and a cry of "He's dead!"

Chapter 3

We all stood rooted to our spots, mouths open in surprise and shock, looking at one another as though waiting for someone to tell us what was going on.

Everyone except for Butch. He was halfway across the room, sprinting for the back stairs, before I'd had time to close my mouth.

Without conscious thought, I ran after him. My first thought had been for *Sense and Sensibility*, *Emma*, *Pride and Prejudice*, and Jane Austen's equally wonderful but lesser-known books. Had someone slipped into the party in an attempt to steal them? Were they now being carried through the damp mist by a scoundrel with no knowledge of the proper care of old papers and nineteenth-century binding?

The scream had sounded like a woman's, and I'd noticed that Bertie was no longer attempting to calm herself behind Toni Morrison's works. Was she heroically fighting off the thief?

As I ran, I glanced around me. Josie was frozen in the act of arranging the few remaining cookies and squares on the buffet table. Aunt Ellen held a tray of dirty plates and glasses. People began murmuring questions to each other.

Connor fell into step behind me. "Where does that staircase lead?"

"The private collection."

Ronald abandoned Mrs. Peterson in midsentence. He strode into the center of the room and lifted his arms, drawing everyone's attention to himself. "Ladies and gentlemen. Remain where you are. Officer Greenblatt has gone to investigate. Charlene, why don't you stand at the bottom of the stairs, and ensure no one else goes up?"

Louise Jane was with Mrs. Fitzgerald, second in command on the library board, close to the back staircase. She waved an empty glass in the air, explaining that she didn't mean the assistant-librarian job should be *eliminated*. Only that it should be given to her. Andrew hovered at her elbow, his head bobbing like a PEZ dispenser. Daffy Duck, perhaps. In a quiet area beneath the curve of stairs, Mrs. Uppiton had cornered one of the few unaccompanied men at the party. She was batting her overly made-up eyelashes at him while he leered down the front of her dress.

I glanced at the Austen collection as I darted past. Everything appeared as it should.

The back stairs don't go all the way to the top of the lighthouse. They end in a small round room that's not open to the general public, where we keep the oldest and rarest of our collection for viewing by appointment. That room would be where Bertie was likely to keep the surprise she'd been planning to unveil at eight o'clock.

Like the main lighthouse stairs, these are spiral and made of black iron, curving around and around, leading up into the darkness. I could see the bottoms of Butch's shoes above me and could hear the pounding of Connor's feet below.

I burst into the rare-books room. The walls were lined with old bookshelves. There was no window at this level, so no danger of sunlight touching the papers. The center of the room was filled by a gorgeous antique secretary, the warm, aged oak polished to a brilliant gloss, with a high back of pigeonholes and multiple drawers. A tall, modern desk lamp, now switched off, stood nearby for close examination of old handwriting or worn and fading print. The single yellow bulb in the ceiling cast a weak light that did not reach the corners. Not that the room, being round, had many corners.

The secretary's drawers were closed, but the desktop stood open, propped up by the sliders on either side. It held a single book, no more than four inches square and an inch thick. A notebook, leather cover worn and faded with the passage of many years and many hands. I'd never seen it before.

I paid it little attention now.

Mr. Uppiton lay in the center of the room, on his stomach, his arms outstretched. A puddle of dark liquid spread out from his upper body, and the unexpected scent of beer filled the air. He was very still. His right hand appeared to be reaching toward the massive book next to him, which lay faceup, open to a page showing an eighteenth-century map of the New England coast. Butch crouched over him, fingers to Mr. Uppiton's neck.

Before I could stop myself, I took a step forward, intending to pick up the book and check its spine for damage. Shards of glass were scattered on the floor, sparkling in what little light there was.

"Stay back," Butch said, his voice not light and flirty as it had been only moments ago, but full of cool authority. "Connor, call nine-one-one. We'll need police and an ambulance. Although the ambulance needn't hurry. He's dead."

I sucked in a breath.

Butch rose slowly to his feet. Connor left the room to make the call. These walls were made of solid stone, many feet thick in places. Cell phone reception was spotty to nonexistent. Only as I watched him go did I notice Bertie, standing against the far wall in the dark shadow between two bookshelves.

She was holding something in both hands. The neck of a broken bottle. Her hands opened and the bottle fell to the floor with a crash.

None of us said anything for a long time.

Then Butch took one step toward her. "Albertina James," he said. "You're under arrest for the murder of Jonathan Uppiton."

She said nothing, looked at him through wide, shocked eyes.

"You can't be serious," I shouted. "That's absolutely ridiculous. Bertie wouldn't hurt a fly."

"They're on their way," Connor said, slipping back into the room.

"Then we'll wait," Butch said, his eyes fixed on Bertie. "Right here."

Soon sirens pierced the silence of the room and the night, heading our way, getting closer.

Bertie snapped out of her empty-eyed stare. She gave her head a good shake and said, "No, Officer Greenblatt. I didn't kill anyone. I found him"—she gestured—"like that."

Butch pointed to the broken glass on the floor. It was from a beer bottle, small neck, brown glass. "Looks like the murder weapon to me. How'd you happen to be holding it?"

"I came into the room to get Miss Austen's notebook."

A notebook? A Jane Austen notebook? "What notebook?" I asked.

Butch threw me a look. "I don't think that's relevant right now."

"Sorry."

"I came into the room. Then I saw him. Right there." Bertie's hand quivered as she pointed. Her face was very pale, ghostly, almost, in the dim light. "I thought he'd fallen. I knelt down to see if I could help. Then I saw . . . I don't remember picking up the bottle. I guess I must have."

"Librarian's instinct," I told Butch. "There are valuable books and papers in this room. Spilled liquid could ruin them."

"So could a man's blood," Butch said.

Outside, sirens screamed. We could hear the buzz of excited conversation below us, whispered questions, and shouted demands for information. Then boots on the staircase, and suddenly the room was full of men and women and equipment.

A man, late forties with a crew cut above a square face and lantern jaw and cold, unfriendly eyes, approached us.

"Detective Sam Watson," Butch said.

Detective Watson glared at me. "Who are you?"

"Lucy Richardson. Assistant librarian?" My voice squeaked.

"You the one who found the body?"

"No."

"You the one who killed him?"

"Me! Certainly not."

"Then I don't want you here. Downstairs, now. You, too, Mr. Mayor, unless you want to confess."

Connor didn't dignify that with a response. "Come on, Lucy. I'll help you down."

In the four days I'd been working here, I might have dashed up and down these stairs, as well as the main ones, a hundred times. Tonight I was grateful for the offer of assistance. Connor held out his arm and gave me an encouraging smile. But the smile didn't reach his eyes.

I glanced across the room at Butch. He was huddled with Sam Watson, talking in a low voice. He pointed toward Bertie and I heard only one word: "threatened."

So Butch was a police officer. I felt awful as I realized I'd been so busy talking about myself, trying to cover my nervousness in the unusual situation of being flirted with by such an intensely masculine creature, that I hadn't even asked him about himself. His accent was definitely Outer Banks—that's about all I knew. I heard my mother's voice as clearly as if it were she, not Connor, who had a gentle hand on my arm. "Really, Lucille. A lady never beats a gentleman at tennis. And she certainly never monopolizes the conversation to talk about herself!"

Behind us, I heard Watson telling Bertie she wasn't under arrest. "At this time," he added ominously. She was not to leave Dare County. In the meantime, she was to wait in her office to be questioned.

Connor and I descended the stairs. A female police officer followed, her hand gripping Bertie's arm.

Clearly no one had been told what was going on, as we were assaulted from all sides when we reached the bottom. I heard cries of:

"What's happened?"

"Why are the police here?"

"Is someone injured?"

"I saw them taking Bertie away. Is she under arrest?"

Mrs. Fitzgerald had collapsed into a wingback armchair and was calming her nerves with a small golden fan. And a large glass of red wine.

I opened my mouth to speak, but Connor gave my arm a warning squeeze. "The police will let us know what's happening in due course. In the meantime, I suspect they'd prefer if we remain here. Josie, do you have any more of those delicious pecan tarts? Perhaps you'd better put on another pot of coffee. I'm sure the police would enjoy a hot cup on a cold, wet night. Mrs. Peterson, Josie could use a hand with the coffee."

We all practically jumped out of our skins as the CD player started up and the not-at-all-subtle voice of Jay-Z blared into the room.

"Charlene!" Ronald yelled. "Turn that blasted thing off."

She turned a knob, and the sound diminished fractionally. "Turn it off, please, Charlene," Connor said.

"And I mean off—don't just turn the sound down. Perhaps we can enjoy your musical selection when the police have left. Thank you."

Blessed silence. Even Charles the cat had been shocked into muteness. The effect was, unfortunately, only temporary, and he soon reminded us of his sad predicament. Charlene was our reference librarian. As hardworking as they came, smarter than your average whip, she'd spent five years in England working among the sainted bookshelves of the Bodleian Library at the University of Oxford. She'd returned home to the Outer Banks when her mother fell ill and needed care. As well as a love of medieval literature, somehow in England Charlene had found a love of twenty-first-century American rap music. She was, Bertie had told me, with a sad shake of her head, on a mission to introduce the staff and patrons of the Lighthouse Library to her passion.

That the staff and patrons had been introduced and found the music not entirely to their taste was seen by Charlene as merely an obstacle in her road.

But right now I had more important things to think about than Charlene's appalling taste in music. I studied the faces of the people in the room. No one stood out as looking guilty or anything other than confused.

Under Connor's politely delivered orders and calm Southern charm, people began to relax. "If the mayor isn't upset, then nothing to worry about," I heard someone say. People headed back to the buffet table (I wondered if Josie had an inexhaustible supply of cookies and squares) and the bar. Aunt Ellen began bringing out fresh coffee and mugs.

She placed them on the table and then slid up to me. "The door to Bertie's office is closed and an unfriendly policewoman is standing outside. What's happening? Is Bertie ill?"

I glanced at Connor. He was crouched by Mrs. Fitzgerald's chair, talking to her softly. "I can't say. But it . . . doesn't look good."

"Jonathan!" Diane Uppiton let out a full-throated cry. "Where's my Jonny?" She dashed for the stairs.

Connor leapt to his feet and intercepted her. "Mr. Uppiton is . . . indisposed. . . . Why don't you have a seat, Diane? I'll get someone to join you momentarily."

This time his calming words had no effect. "He's not here. Jonny!" she yelled. "Where's Jonny? And where's Bertie? She had something to do with this, I know it! She threatened my husband. I heard her. You all heard her!"

The crowd gasped. Shouted questions flew across the room. People demanded to know what was going on. Diane Uppiton shoved Connor aside. She began to cry, and black makeup dripped down her cheeks. "I have to get to Jonny. Oh, my darling Jonny."

Sam Watson appeared, as if in a puff of smoke, at the bottom of the iron staircase. Butch Greenblatt, a badge hastily pinned to his shirt, was beside him.

"Let me through," Diane declared.

"Threats," Watson said. "What's this about threats?"

"That . . . that woman, threated Jonathan. In this

very room, no more than half an hour ago. We all heard her."

People began to mumble in agreement.

"What woman?" Watson asked.

"She means the head librarian, Albertina James," Butch said. "I heard her myself."

"That's ridiculous." I pushed my way forward. "Bertie and Mr. Uppiton had an argument—that's all. People make threats all the time that they never carry out. Sure, Bertie was angry. She . . ."

I felt a soft hand on my arm. "Lucy," Aunt Ellen said, "You are not helping."

"But . . ."

"No 'but.' Come with me. Have a seat."

I glanced over my shoulder at the police. Watson was watching me, his gaze not friendly. Butch was also looking at me. I might have been mistaken, but I thought I saw a touch of pity in his hazel eyes.

Chapter 4

Detective Watson took a brief statement from everyone at the party and told them they would be interviewed in detail at a later time. And then they left, some dragging their heels and shaking their heads, some seemingly eager to spread the news far and wide, and some reluctantly, hoping, probably, to stay to watch the body being removed. Diane Uppiton, weeping and calling out for Jonny, had been led away by the man she'd been talking to earlier.

Only Mrs. Peterson seemed unaffected by the dramatic change in events. Once the police took control and Ronald was no longer needed to maintain order, she resumed her favorite (only?) topic of conversation. "Now, Charity, on the other hand, needs a bit more encouragement than the other girls. She'd rather be kicking that soccer ball around than doing her schoolwork. I have no idea why on earth she's so fond of that useless endeavor. What do you suggest we do, Ronald, to . . ."

"Mrs. Peterson," he said, his voice full of strain.

"You'll have to excuse me. I believe Detective Watson is trying to attract my attention. Must be my turn to be interrogated." He gave her a wan grin. Watson was nowhere to be seen. "Tomorrow I'll look up a line of YA sports–related books. Something designed specifically to attract young people who need extra encouragement." Then, without waiting for Mrs. Peterson to excuse him, Ronald simply walked away.

I tried to give him an encouraging smile, but I don't think he even noticed me. Mrs. Peterson huffed loudly and looked around the room. Seeing as how everyone else was heading for the door, she followed. "Norma, honey, wait up there. I'm sorry we didn't get a chance to chat earlier, but I've been meaning to ask about your idea for that summer camp. My Dallas would . . ." A gust of wind slammed the door shut behind her.

Josie was being told she could not clean up or even throw out the garbage. She didn't like that. "I need my coffeemaker, my serving trays. I have a business to open tomorrow."

"I'm sorry, Josie," Butch said. "The forensics people will want to check it all over."

She threw her hands up. "There's no evidence to be found in my coffeepots, I can assure you."

"Please, Josie. Go home. Do you want me to call Jake to come and get you?"

"No."

"Let's go." Aunt Ellen put her arm around her daughter. "The sooner we get out of the way, the sooner the police can finish up here."

I eyed the remains of the buffet. Then I poured

coffee into a mug, added a hefty dose of cream and the three spoonfuls of sugar I knew Bertie liked, tossed the last two cookies onto the saucer, and carried it out of the main room.

The stern, unsmiling policewoman guarding Bertie's office barked at me to turn around.

"I'm sure Bertie would love a cup of coffee," I said as liquid sloshed over the rim of the mug onto my hand.

"You can't go in there."

"Can I leave this with you to give to her?"

"No."

I turned. And almost spilled hot coffee on Detective Watson. The man walked on cat's feet. He took the mug and plate from my hands. "Thanks. Didn't have time to finish my supper." He looked into my face for a long time. He said nothing. I felt blood rushing into my cheeks.

"I hope," I said, trying to keep my voice confident, as if I belonged here, which I did, "you won't be handling the Austen collection."

"What's that?"

"We have a full collection of Jane Austen first editions. That's the reason for tonight's reception. They're on display in the alcove in the main room. I won't have them handled by inexperienced people." A sudden thought filled me with horror. "You can't even think about dusting them for fingerprints."

"Jane Austen. Didn't she write that movie my wife's so fond of? Some English thing with fancy accents and long dresses."

I didn't bother to explain. "Yes."

"Are her books valuable?"

"Literally priceless. The first one was printed in 1811. This collection is of incomparable quality."

"That so?"

"We don't own it. It's on loan here for three months." My chest swelled with pride, even if just a tiny bit. Despite the chaos and my fears for Bertie and the library, I had remembered my duty to protect the collection.

"I'll dust 'em if I have to."

My chest deflated.

"We won't be releasing details of the murder at this time," he said. "I expect you to keep whatever you saw upstairs to yourself. Think you can do that?"

"Of course I can." I tried to look offended at the very idea I'd been planning to spread the story far and wide.

"Make sure of it." Watson nodded to the policewoman, and she opened the office door.

I hurried back to the main room, intending to stand guard over the Austen collection all night if necessary. Only the library staff and the police remained. "Bertie didn't do it," I said to Butch.

He gave me a long look. Upstairs someone shouted for him, and Butch hurried away.

"They're saying Bertie has been arrested," Ronald said to me. "I can't believe it."

"That's ridiculous," Charlene said.

"Ridiculous, yes. Arrested, no. At least I don't think so. Watson's in her office now. It'll all be cleared up soon."

"Are they sure it was murder? Maybe he had a heart attack, fell, and hit his head?"

"I saw him, Ronald." I shuddered at the memory. "I think he was stabbed."

"What do you suppose Mr. Uppiton was doing on the private level, anyway?" Charlene asked.

"I've no idea."

Charlene glanced around the room, taking in the discarded wineglasses, dirty mugs, half-eaten baking, crumpled paper napkins illustrated with colorful sketches of overfull bookshelves, matching paper plates scattered with crumbs. The room was quiet—too quiet. The partygoers had left, the music had ended, and even the police were temporarily elsewhere. Outside, the wind had dropped and waves no longer pounded the distant shore.

The deep silence reminded me of Charles. Even the library cat had gone quiet.

"Guess the party's over," Charlene said. "Still, no reason we can't have some music." She went to the CD player and swapped discs. Jay-Z again.

I left her to it. Might as well annoy the police.

I stuck my head around the corner and peered down the hall. The policewoman guarding Bertie's office had gone. A plaintive cry came from behind the closet door.

I slipped in and closed the door behind me. I suspected Detective Watson wouldn't be pleased at having Charles disturbing his crime scene. The cat's food bowl was empty, but the litter box was definitely not.

"Whew," I said. "I'll get that cleaned out for you." Charles wound himself around my ankles. I dropped to the floor, stretched my legs out in front of me, and arranged my stiff skirt and petticoats. He climbed into my lap, rolled over, and presented his belly for scratching. I rubbed the soft, deep fur, and he began to purr.

What, I thought, *will happen to the library—to my job—if Bertie is jailed?*

I shoved the thought away. My job was not the important thing here. In the short time I'd worked for Bertie, I'd found her to be a kind, thoughtful woman, passionate about her library, her yoga practice, and the Outer Banks. Bertie had not murdered anyone. Of that I was positive.

Who, then, had killed the odious Mr. Uppiton?

My mother's voice sounded in my tired, confused head. *Curiosity killed the cat, and I swear, Lucille, it'll be the death of you, too. A lady does not concern herself with other people's affairs.* My mother, one of the Gossip Queens of Boston, continually amazed me with her ability to entertain two totally contradictory thoughts at the same time.

Footsteps in the hall. They stopped at the closet door. I held my breath.

"We're finished here," Watson said. "For now. Tomorrow I'll want to pay a call on everyone who was at this shindig."

"Need any help with that?" Butch.

"I might. You definitely heard Bertie James threaten Uppiton?"

"Loud and clear. Everyone heard it. And then, not half an hour later, she's standing over the body with the murder weapon in her hand. Looks pretty open-and-shut to me."

"Perhaps."

Butch's voice softened. "Then again, plenty of

folks here tonight seemed to be arguing with that guy. It might be premature to accuse anyone."

"She's a well-known member of this community," Watson said. "Friends in high places. I intend to have an airtight case when I arrest her. If I do."

I bit down on my tongue to keep from crying out. Charles yelped as I dug into the tender skin of his belly.

"What's that?" Watson said.

"Cat. The library cat—Charles is his name, friendly thing—was locked in that closet during the party."

"Has the room been searched?"

"Did it myself earlier. Nothing but the cat and some cleaning equipment."

"Cats. Can't stand them myself." The men's voices faded away.

I lifted Charles off me, ignoring his protests, and clambered to my feet. I opened the door and stuck my head out. The hall was empty. I could hear Watson telling Ronald and Charlene the library would be closed until further notice.

I knocked lightly on the office door and then opened it. "Bertie?"

She sat at her desk, her head in her hands. Her office was very small, no room for much more than a desk, a chair for her and one for visitors, and the locked cabinet where she kept budget and staff papers. The floor was dark wood, old and worn, stained in places, the walls white. Behind the desk, she'd hung a large poster of a woman performing Downward Dog on the beach, the sun rising over the ocean.

Her desk was, as always, neat and tidy. The black-eyed computer monitor looked out of place in this historic room.

"You okay?" I asked.

Her face was pale, the bags under her eyes dark, the lines around her mouth deep. She tried to force a smile. She failed. "Isn't this a mess? What would Miss Austen think?"

"Can I get you something? Coffee? Water?"

"No, but thanks, anyway. I didn't kill Jonathan."

"I know that."

This time she did smile. "Thank you, honey. I needed to hear that."

She got to her feet. "As I am not under arrest but was ordered not to leave Dare County, I'm going home."

"Do you have any idea who would have wanted him dead?"

Bertie lifted her thick, hand-knitted shawl off the coat stand in the corner. She wrapped it tightly around herself, as if seeking warmth. "You were there, Lucy. Tell me: who didn't want to kill him?"

Chapter 5

Watson was momentarily nonplussed when telling me I could go home, and being informed that I *was* home.

"I live here. Upstairs. Fourth floor."

"In the lighthouse?"

"Yes, in the lighthouse." Was the man obtuse?

"Lucy's rooms are accessible only by the staircase that goes all the way to the top," Butch said. "She won't be in the way of our people, or the crime scene."

"How do you know where her rooms are?" Watson asked.

"I know the layout of this lighthouse. I've been coming here since I could crawl up those stairs on my chubby knees."

"Okay," Watson said. "You can stay. If you promise not to go up the back stairs and to stay out of our people's way. We'll be working here most of the night."

"Promise," I said.

Watson walked away, leaving me with Butch. He

shifted from one big foot to another. "I'm sorry this had to happen."

"Not as sorry as Mr. Uppiton is." I wished I could swallow the words. "That was insensitive of me."

"It's okay. Everyone deals with these things in their own way. I meant, I'm sorry we didn't get to finish our conversation. I was enjoying getting to know you, Lucy."

I flushed. I wanted to say something, but my fat tongue twisted itself in knots.

"I'll have to cancel our dinner."

"Dinner?"

"At Jake's? Tomorrow? Unless we can wrap this up mighty fast, I won't be able to get away."

"Oh. Dinner. Right."

He reached out one hand and touched my shoulder. For such a large man, his touch was light and delicate. I wanted to melt into his arms.

I resisted.

"I'll help you upstairs."

"No, I'm okay." I hesitated. "Actually, maybe you can. I'll take Charles—can't leave him locked up all night. And you"—I glanced into the alcove—"can bring up the Austen collection."

"What?"

"I won't leave those books down here all night. Unprotected."

"We're the police, Lucy. We won't steal your books."

"Maybe not. But people are tramping in and out, and . . ."

I broke off at a movement at the door. Two men were attempting to wrestle a stretcher through the narrow entrance. A large black bag rested on it. I swallowed.

"Oookay," Butch said, "I see your point. Let's get those books moved."

Between us we got Charles, his few possessions, and the collected works of Jane Austen up the twisting black iron stairs to the fourth floor. I tossed Charles into the bathroom so he couldn't escape while my back was turned, and then cleared off my small desk by simply sweeping books and papers onto the floor. Butch put the Austen collection down with, I was pleased to see, the care and reverence it deserved.

"Good night, Lucy," he said. And he left.

I closed the door behind him and leaned my back against it. I kicked off my shoes. So much had been happening that I'd forgotten how much my feet hurt. Now that I was alone, they were reminding me.

I was pleased I'd had the foresight to make my bed and tidy my room before going to the party. I'm not normally known for my housekeeping abilities; after all, I didn't know people actually made beds until I went away to college. I thought everyone's sheets tucked themselves in. And clothes bounded willingly onto hangers and into closets, makeup spills magically disappeared, and the carpet had a self-operating vacuum.

Okay, I'm not quite that sheltered. I knew the maid did those things. I just never appreciated that it was *work*. When I visited the Outer Banks on summer vacation, I was expected to do the same chores as my cousins. But somehow, being on holiday at the beach, wrapped in the loving, chaotic embrace of

Aunt Ellen and Uncle Amos's home, chores seemed more like play than work.

My accommodations on the fourth floor of the Bodie Island Lighthouse were small but absolutely perfect. I had one room, plus the bathroom. The whitewashed walls curved with the structure of the lighthouse. Cheerful watercolors by local artists, a variety of Outer Banks scenes, added bursts of color. The iron daybed, painted a glossy white, was tucked in a corner, covered in a thick quilt of yellow and red flowers and mounds of sage pillows. I'd picked wildflowers this morning and popped them into a vase on my bedside table, on top of my TBR pile. To Be Read—all the books awaiting my undivided attention. The heap seemed to grow every time I looked at it.

More of my TBR pile was stacked on the seat nestled into the window alcove. My favorite thing in the room, the seat was tiny and perfect, covered in cushions matching those on the bed. The room had only one window, long and thin, with a spectacular view over the marshes to the pure, unspoiled national refuge beaches and the sea. The walls were four and a half feet thick at this level, the window about three feet wide, making a perfect one-person reading recess. Although I was four stories up, with no one between my refuge and the open sea, the windows came with heavy curtains. Down below, this might be a busy library, but it was still a working lighthouse, and the first-order Fresnel lens maintained the rhythm of 2.5 seconds on, 2.5 off, 2.5 on, and 22.5 seconds off. At night, the thousand-watt bulb could be seen forty miles out to sea, warning ships to veer away from the coast, as danger lay to the south.

Now the storm was breaking and a sliver of moonlight shone on wave-tossed black water. Lights from ships far out to sea blinked on the horizon. I pulled the curtains to as the lamp came on and brilliant white light flooded my room.

I had a small area for entertaining: a couple of comfortable wingback chairs around a low coffee table. Plus, a work area with a desk, and a minuscule kitchen. The kitchen, just a microwave and toaster oven, a sink, a bar-sized fridge, and a round table with two chairs, was tucked into a back corner.

I let Charles out of the bathroom and unzipped my dress. The phone rang. I mostly made use of a landline here; cell reception in these stone walls was poor and unreliable. Bertie had told me if I kept the iPhone on the window seat, it might receive calls, and if I wanted to talk, it helped to open the window and lean out.

My first thought was *Mother*. She'd heard about the murder and was calling to order me home. I glanced at the display. A local call.

"Hello?"

"Lucy, it's Connor. "

"Oh, Connor. Hi."

"I know it's ridiculously late to be calling, but I wanted to check up on you. I'm sorry I didn't have a chance to say good-bye, but Detective Watson hustled us out of the library so fast, my head's still spinning. Are you okay?"

"I'm fine."

"You saw the body. That can be upsetting."

"You found it, too, Connor. I should probably ask if you're okay." I sat on the edge of my bed and wiggled my toes to bring some life back into them.

A deep chuckle came down the line. "I will admit I poured myself a stiff bourbon as soon as I got in. I wasn't really expecting you to answer. I'm surprised the police let you stay."

"I'm under orders to remain in my room. That will not be a problem. I have absolutely no desire to poke around downstairs." An image of Mr. Uppiton popped unwelcome into my head. Mr. Uppiton, lying on the floor. Dead. I shuddered and gathered a couple of cushions into my lap.

"Bertie?"

"They let her go home, too. They didn't arrest her . . . but . . . I think they might be planning to."

"I'll call the chief in the morning. I can't interfere, of course, nor would I want to, but I'll try to find out what's going on. In the meantime, if you need anything, please call me."

"Thank you."

"I'll let you go now. You must be exhausted. Are you . . . uh, free for dinner, say Saturday?"

"Dinner?"

"Dinner. Jake Greenblatt's opened a new restaurant. I've been wanting to try it out, but haven't had the chance yet. Traditional Outer Banks cooking, they tell me."

I struggled with my decision for a bit. Butch had invited me to dinner tomorrow at the exact same restaurant. But he'd canceled, saying he'd be busy with this murder investigation. "I'd like that."

"Good night, Lucy,"

"Night." I hung up.

I flopped back onto the bed. Charles jumped up and lay on my chest. *Wow!* Two dinner invitations in one night. That was a new one for me. It was unlikely Connor wanted a *date*, as in "date." He was just being friendly to the newest resident. Looking for my vote, probably.

The newest resident.

I liked the sound of that.

Of course, if my mother had her way, it would be back to Boston for me.

You might not think that moving to the Outer Banks, North Carolina, to become a librarian, living a stone's throw from my aunt's house, was a terribly rebellious thing to do.

But it was to my mother.

For almost as long as I'd been aware, my family had intended that I would marry Ricky. Richard Eric Lewiston III, that is. Ricky was the son of a Boston family so old-money they almost matched the stature of my father's family. Richard Eric Lewiston Jr. is my dad's partner in the law firm of Lewiston, Richardson, and a bunch of other old white guys. The company had been established by Richard Eric Lewiston I and my grandfather. Ricky's a junior associate in the firm, and everyone knows he'll be the Lewiston on the door and the letterhead when his father retires.

Ricky and I grew up closer than brother and sister. Certainly closer that I'd ever been to my three older brothers. We went to everything together—the best schools, drama camps, music lessons (Ricky reasonably proficient on the piano; me managing to make the instrument of Beethoven sound like I was, in our teacher's immortal words, playing the bagpipes), tennis lessons, country-club youth events. My mother, I often suspected, intensely disliked Ricky's mother, Evangeline. Evangeline, you see, was as old-money as the Lewistons and the Richardsons. Mom and Aunt Ellen's family was not. They could trace their lineage back only to their dad, who'd been a fisherman. He never knew his own father, who had run out on the family days after my grandfather was born.

Mom intended that I would marry Ricky. Evangeline, for some reason, always seemed rather fond of me. Perhaps she, no fool, had an eye to keeping it in the family, or as close as could be. My dad, frankly, didn't much care about anything other than the law or golf. Or his evening bottle of Laphroaig behind the study door. Mr. Lewiston went along with whatever Evangeline wanted.

I've never dated, which seems a pretty awful thing for a thirty-year-old to confess. With Ricky, I've gone to plenty of country-club dances, weddings, or birthday parties of the relatives in one of our families or the other, even out for dinner or a movie now and again. But a date, with hours of trying to decide what to wear, sweaty hands, wondering whether he'd be content with a good-night kiss or want something more? Nope.

Perhaps that one stroll on the beach and light kiss with Connor was such a precious memory because it was the only one of the like I've had. *Perhaps,* I thought, *I'll find out tomorrow if the feelings have continued all these years.*

After high school, Ricky headed off to Harvard for a law degree and I went to Northeastern for English lit. I'm sure Mom would have preferred I stay at home to arrange my trousseau, but that was a fight she wasn't prepared to wage. I loved dorm life and made girlfriends I still have, but somehow I never even considered going out with another guy. That would have been cheating on Ricky. What Ricky got himself up to at Harvard, I can only guess. After all, everyone at the country club knows better than to leave their daughters alone with his father, and you know what they say about the apple falling not too far from the tree.

I'd always loved books, everything about books, from the feel of crisp new paper to the smell of the binding and the look of neatly ordered rows of print. But it was at Northeastern that my love of great literature grew to a passion beyond bounds. And, as with all passions, so did my determination to spread the word. On graduation I applied, without telling Mom, to Simmons for a master's of library science.

Mom wasn't too thrilled—all that education! But even she had to admit that if I had to have a—shudder—career, librarian was at least a feminine occupation, and probably not too taxing. I graduated top of my class, and then, degree proudly in hand, I applied for a job at the Harvard Library.

To no one's surprise more than mine, I got the job. And I loved every minute of it.

Ricky and I continued on our preset path. He studied for his law degree and worked on the *Harvard Law Review*. He articled at a firm belonging to a friend of the family and then joined Lewiston, Richardson.

We continued to attend country-club parties and family weddings together. We even took Caribbean and Mediterranean cruises with our mothers. (In a nod to some modernity, Ricky and I were allowed to share a suite.) In Boston we maintained our own apartments, although we would occasionally spend the night together in one or the other's place.

As the years ground on, I found Ricky increasingly boring, and I am sure he found me much the same. My mother was getting worried that nothing was happening, and began dragging me to wedding and baby showers and the nuptials of friends of friends of friends. Meanwhile, my brothers married, and their wives began throwing me pitying glances when they thought I wasn't looking.

Friends, and some enemies, began to whisper that they had seen Ricky in the company of one woman or another. Conversations in restaurants and coffee shops abruptly ended when I returned from the restroom. Worse, I was losing enthusiasm for life. I still enjoyed my job, but found I had little time, between the rounds of weddings and family obligations, to bury myself in a nineteenth-century classic or a modern mystery.

Then the big day came. Ricky asked me out to dinner. Nothing unusual in that. We went to one of the most exclusive and expensive restaurants in Boston. Nothing unusual in that, either. Ricky liked to spend money, and he liked to be seen spending it. We had a pleasant dinner, and then Ricky ordered champagne without asking if I wanted it. Which I didn't. The champagne and two crystal flutes arrived on a silver platter. A small box, wrapped in silver paper with a big blue bow, sat beside it on the tray. The tuxedo-clad waiter was grinning so hard, he wasn't much more than a row of white teeth.

My heart sank into my stomach. And there it sat. Beside the salad of baby greens, the sole, and the asparagus.

The waiter poured the champagne and departed, still grinning.

And then, to my horror, and the amusement of the staff and other diners, Ricky picked up the silver box and dropped to one knee in front of my chair. He opened the box.

A row of diamonds, each one carat or more, glittered on a background of blue velvet. And to me, at that moment, the diamonds looked like stars dragged out of the sky, captured and imprisoned.

"Lucille," Ricky began.

"No," I said.

Ricky usually didn't hear me when I spoke. Tonight was no exception. "Will you do me the great honor of being my wife?"

I pushed my chair back. Somehow I got to my feet, although my legs didn't seem to want to hold me up. "No."

"I've loved you since . . . What?"

"No. Ricky. I'm sorry, but I am not going to marry you. I'm . . . I'm leaving Harvard. I'm leaving Boston. I have to— I . . . Good-bye."

I ran out of the restaurant, past openmouthed waitstaff and wide-eyed diners. I spotted a woman from the club, one of my mother's friends, her eyes sparkling with pure delight. I had no doubt what would be this week's topic of conversation across the tennis net.

My iPhone began ringing before I so much as made it back to my apartment. Mom. I didn't answer.

The next morning, I went into my boss's office and handed in my resignation. She was, she said, sorry to see me go. Although not entirely surprised.

Ricky had texted me once, the day after the incident. Something about understanding, time to think, being there when I came home.

I suspect, reading between the lines, as well as the obvious fact that he didn't bother to come in pursuit of me, Ricky was more relieved than anything else. I never paid much attention to the gossip at my mother's clubs or her afternoon bridge parties, but it was hard not to know that the Lewiston family was having trouble maintaining the life to which they had become accustomed. Something about bad investments and Richard Eric Lewiston Jr.'s gambling problem. Ricky, I suspected, was being pressured into marrying me in order to get an injection of funds into the family.

Unknown to Evangeline, I didn't have any money other than from my wages. Not one red cent was left to my brothers or me in my grandfather's will. My grandmother left me her favorite silver tea service— the sort of thing you see gathering dust and tarnishing at every antiques fair in the East. My parents are only in their fifties, active and healthy, so it will be a long time indeed before I can expect to come into any money.

Regardless of everything, that I didn't love Ricky,

how boring I found him, how boring I knew our life together would be, I might have drifted into accepting his proposal if he'd said something like, "Wanna make our parents happy and get married?" But the whole champagne–silver box–down-on-his-knees thing reminded me that if I married Ricky, for the rest of my days I'd be trapped in a life of social expectations. He and I just weren't on the same page anymore.

Apart from two suitcases of summer clothes, my favorite beach sandals, and a few dishes and beloved knickknacks, I dumped all my possessions in my parents' house (phoning first to check with Maria that Mom was out) and drove my teal Yaris to the Outer Banks, intending to cry on the shoulder of my favorite aunt. But Aunt Ellen isn't one for weeping, and instead she arranged for her best friend to meet me over sweet tea and sandwiches.

Among my other possessions, I'd filled the back-seat of the Yaris with two huge boxes. One of Signet Classics and another of mystery novels.

Now I took a book off the top of the bedside pile. *The Moonstone* by Wilkie Collins. One of my absolute favorites.

I laid out Charles's litter box on the bathroom floor and prepared myself for bed. I clambered up onto the daybed and snuggled deep into the pillows and duvet. One of my projects at the library was to set up a book club. Bertie had said I could have a free hand with the type of books we were going to read. I'd originally decided on a mystery club, but now, with so much interest in the Austen exhibit, I was thinking classics might be fun. For the first book, we could combine the two. *The Moonstone*, written in

1863, is often called the first detective novel and laid out many of the tropes that have become standard for that genre. The author, Wilkie Collins, was a friend of Charles Dickens.

My own Charles curled himself in a ball at my side and purred.

I opened the cover of the book. I ran my finger across the paper. I let out a deep, contented sigh and began to read. "I address these lines—written in India—to my relatives in England."

I put down the book.

Someone murdered Jonathan Uppiton. In this very building.

I was here alone, a woman in the dark, a long way from any houses or streets, but I didn't fear for myself. Not only was the lighthouse full of police, but Mr. Uppiton's murder seemed a personal thing. Someone had been after him, and probably not a crazed killer (as is often found between the pages), but someone who knew Mr. Uppiton personally.

The police suspected Bertie of the killing. I knew she was innocent. Any woman who'd provided me with this perfect refuge couldn't be a killer.

How much effort would the police put into seeking the real killer, now that they had their prime suspect? Would they pin it on Bertie and then head off to the doughnut shop to congratulate themselves on a job well done?

What evidence did they have against her?

One: she was found in the room with the body.

Meaningless. Someone had to come across the body sometime, and Bertie, more than anyone else at the reception, had reason to go upstairs.

Two: she had the murder weapon in her hands. *Irrelevant.* Any librarian worth her horn-rimmed glasses would instinctively pick up a bottle leaking liquid. I would have done so myself. I did, come to think of it, reach to pick up the map book, and was yelled at by Butch for my troubles.

Three: she'd been heard threatening Mr. Uppiton.

And what had she been angry about? Me. Bertie had been trying to defend me.

Bertie was suspected of murder. And it was all my fault.

I closed *The Moonstone.*

Here I was, in my gorgeous lighthouse aerie, living above a library, a classic novel in my hands, the rest of my beloved books only an arm's reach away. Not to mention a full collection of Jane Austen first editions on my desk. And I couldn't concentrate.

For once I couldn't lose myself in the pages of a book and leave all my troubles until another time.

I put the book back on the side table.

If Bertie was in trouble because of me, then it might be up to me to get her out of it.

Chapter 6

The next thing I knew, a stabbing pain pierced my chest.

I was being murdered in my own bed. The killer had followed me upstairs after all, probably armed with the same weapon he'd used to fell poor Mr. Uppiton.

"Meooooow!"

My eyes flew open. Gigantic round blue orbs stared back at me.

I screamed. The blue eyes blinked and the pain stopped.

Sunlight touched the edges of the drapes, and Charles had been kneading my chest, telling me it was time to rise and shine.

I threw off the covers and sat up. I would rise, but I was certainly not going to shine. Charles made a dash for the food bowl, now empty, on the kitchen floor. I was sure I'd filled that bowl before getting into bed.

I glanced at the bedside clock and almost screamed

a second time. Nine-thirty! Unpardonably late for work.

Then I remembered. It was unlikely anyone would be worried about what time the library opened today. If the police would even allow it to open.

Some detective I was. I'd fallen asleep in the midst of trying to solve a murder.

I fed Charles, cleaned his litter box, and then showered quickly and pulled on jeans and a loose cotton top and sneakers. Before putting on my librarian uniform, I wanted to see what was happening downstairs. I ran a comb through my hair, stuffed the unruly black curls into a crooked ponytail, and left my apartment.

As I descended the stairs I heard voices below. I stopped and listened. These were spiral stairs; sound traveled straight up, but anything above the second or third twist couldn't be seen without tilting your head all the way back.

Detective Watson. "What have you got?"

A long pause. He was on the phone, standing by the open door where he could get reception.

"Okay. I need the rest of that info ASAP. Yes, I know. Same old story, always too busy. Give it to me when you can." The door slammed shut.

"The lab?" Butch said.

"They pulled fingerprints off the bottle. Match the ones we took last night from Bertie James."

"No surprise there. We saw her holding it."

"Yeah. There were also a couple of smudges under hers."

"Could be anyone. The beer was kept in the fridge

in the break room. Josie brought bottles out when needed and put them in a cooler that anyone could get into. It was an open bar, no bartender. People sometimes go through the lot, looking for the coldest or another brand. They fetch drinks for friends."

"Yeah, I know. You know these people, Greenblatt. Tell me about Bertie James. Type to fly off the handle at the slightest provocation, is she?"

I clattered down the stairs. "Morning, gentlemen."

Butch gave me a smile, but Watson's eyes narrowed as he wondered how much I'd overheard.

"When can we open the library?"

"Not today," Watson said. "Tomorrow, maybe. You, and only you because you live here, can use the main floor if you have to, but don't go up the back stairs."

"Okay."

Watson gave me a long stare. "New to town, are you?"

"I arrived last week. Although I've been coming here every summer for as long as I can remember."

"Any murders the summers you were here?" He asked, watching me too carefully to be serious.

I blinked. "What?"

"Amos O'Malley's her uncle," Butch explained.

"Is that so?" Watson walked away.

He was joking. Wasn't he?

Without so much as a good-bye to Butch, I fled. I knew what my shaking nerves needed. I drove into Nags Head, fully conscious of the speed limit. It wouldn't do, not now, to be pulled over for speeding. The summer season was swinging into high gear, and the roads in Nags Head were full of RVs, camper trailers, and cars loaded down with beach chairs, pillows, and excited kids.

I wanted to enjoy the drive, but thoughts of yesterday wouldn't be banished. I tried to envision the scene at the reception. What had been happening moments before we heard that thud and then Bertie cry out?

I'd been talking to (flirting with?) Butch. Couldn't ask for a better alibi than that.

Josie and Aunt Ellen can't be suspects.

Josie had been at the buffet table, laying out yet another round of treats, with Aunt Ellen helping her. Moments before they would have been in the staff break room, where the food and drink were assembled.

Connor? I'd seen him, doing the rounds of the room, chatting with everyone. I couldn't swear he hadn't slipped out for a couple of minutes.

Ridiculous to even think of the mayor doing something like that.

I pounded the dash in frustration. I simply didn't know enough to speculate.

Josie's Cozy Bakery was located in one of the numerous, unattractive strip malls that line the Croatan Highway as it runs through the towns of Kitty Hawk, Kill Devil Hills, and Nags Head, part of which forms Bodie Island. Bodie Island, however, is not actually an island. Apparently it was at one time, but shifting sands and constant movement of the ocean filled in a section of the channel. Still, it has the feel of an island, a long, thin island where you can see water on both sides at higher elevations. These higher elevations are mainly found in buildings, as it's pretty darn flat.

I pulled off the highway into the mall. The line outside Josie's Cozy Bakery spilled out the door and curved past the neighboring beachwear store and art gallery. As I cruised through the lot, wondering if I'd be able to find a place, a gleaming silver Lexus with Ontario plates pulled out of a spot, and I snagged it.

I'd take that as a good omen for the remainder of the day.

I took my place in the line, breathing in the delicious scents of warm pastry, hot cinnamon, and rich coffee, all mingling with fresh, salty air off the ocean. The line was long but it moved swiftly, and I was soon through the doors.

Josie had decorated the place as Seattle coffee bar–meets–Outer Banks fishing shack. The service area was all glass and chrome, everything polished to a high gloss. Stocky white mugs and thick glasses were stacked against the beige walls, the display case stuffed full of mouthwatering delights. Espresso machines hissed and spat clouds of sizzling steam. In the seating area, the chairs were upholstered in a nautical blue-and-white print, the tables made from recycled barrels or wooden tea chests. Large, framed photographs of sailing ships and lighthouses decorated the walls. I recognized the distinctive white with three black bands of my lighthouse. The picture had been taken at night, from behind the building, looking out over the marshes to the sea. The ocean looked dark and foreboding, the rotating light at the top offering guidance and protection to men in ships.

"Lucy. Over here!" Aunt Ellen waved at me from

a table tucked into a back corner. Bertie was with her, as were Ronald and Charlene. They had full mugs and plates of scones or muffins in front of them. I waived in return and pointed to the cash register.

The young man behind the counter was short and chubby, with a mass of cheerful dreadlocks tied back with a red-checked bandanna.

"A large nonfat latte and a low-fat blueberry muffin," I ordered. I hesitated, and then boldly threw caution to the wind. "No, make that latte with whole milk, and give me a raspberry and white chocolate scone." Heck, I'd almost been accused of murder this morning. Might as well live on the wild side.

Aunt Ellen and the library staff scooted over to make room for me while Charlene found a spare chair.

"Is this a meeting?" I asked. I held my mug to my nose and breathed in deeply. Heaven.

"Not intentionally," Ronald said. "But where else would you expect to find us if we can't get into the library?"

"How are you doing?" I asked Bertie. The lines of strain were deep on her face and the customary sparkle was gone from her eyes.

"Okay, I guess. I've been ordered to report to the police station at one."

"That doesn't mean anything, right?" I said in an effort to be positive. "They want to talk to everyone who was there last night."

I felt warm hands on my shoulders and turned to see Josie standing behind me. "Morning, sweetie," she said. She was dressed in tattered jeans and an overlarge T-shirt. A long, plain gray apron was tied around her slim waist, and her hair was dotted with flecks of flour. She looked, as she always did, sexy as all get-out.

One of her baristas, wearing a blue-and-white-striped apron with JOSIE'S COZY BAKERY stamped across the front and the stylized logo of a croissant curling around a lighthouse, brought over a stool and a mug of black coffee. Josie dropped onto the seat and drank deeply. "I've got only a couple of minutes, Mom. We're run off our feet back there. What's up?"

"You arrived in good time, Lucy," Ellen said. "We're about to have an impromptu council of war."

"About . . . about Mr. Uppiton?"

"Yes. Bertie has to be at the police station in Nags Head at one o'clock. Amos will accompany her."

I let out a sigh of relief. In his younger days my uncle Amos had been one of the top defense attorneys in the state. He was slowing down a little, doing more family law work, and taking only the criminal cases he found interesting. With Amos on her side, Bertie had nothing to worry about.

Or so I told myself.

"Amos had to be in court this morning, otherwise he'd be here. He's cleared his schedule for the rest of the day."

"What's happening at the library, Lucy?" Bertie asked.

"Watson said we might be able to open tomorrow."

"Good. What about the Austen collection?"

"I took it upstairs with me last night. It's safe."

Some of the tension left her face. "I knew I could

trust you, Lucy." She touched my hand. I gave hers a squeeze in return.

"As important as those books are," Aunt Ellen said. "We have more important things to worry about right now."

"The notebook," Bertie said. "Is it safe also?"

"Sorry, I don't know. They haven't allowed anyone to go up to the rare-books room to check."

"If they've . . ." Bertie began.

"*Bertie,*" my aunt said, "forget about the books. You have perfectly competent staff to handle that. Let's talk about the matter at hand. Jonathan Uppiton."

The table fell silent. We concentrated on our caffeine, sugar, and fat. Around us, people laughed and chatted and placed their orders. No one paid any attention to the table in the corner. Bankers—what some of the local residents call themselves—were busy in the summer and would be at work by now. Most of the people in the bakery at this time of the morning were visitors. They wouldn't have read the morning paper, and if they had, they wouldn't recognize us as central characters in last night's drama.

"I guess the first question," Josie said, "is who would want him dead?"

Not one of us looked at Bertie.

"A great many people," Ronald said. "He was a thoroughly nasty old man."

"I'd like to know," I said, "what he was doing upstairs. If he was there before Bertie came to get the notebook, then he went up alone. Why would he do that?"

"To gloat over the notebook and plot how to get Bertie removed as head librarian," Charlene said.

"Except that he was obviously not alone," Aunt Ellen said. "Where was everyone? Think, people. The room was full and we were all busy, but let's try to remember if anyone wasn't in the room a few minutes before Bertie went up to get the notebook."

"I was talking to Butch."

"Mom and I were restocking the pastry table. We had just brought out a fresh coffee urn and tray of lemon squares."

"I was where I can always be counted upon to be," Ronald said. "Being lectured by Mrs. Peterson about the virtues, numerous as they are, of her five daughters."

"So you're Mrs. Peterson's alibi?"

"No. I'm not. She excused herself to go to the ladies' room a few minutes before the ruckus broke out. I tried to hide by talking to someone else, but the old bat . . . pardon me, our valued patron, tracked me down on her return."

"You can't seriously be thinking that Mrs. Peterson killed Jonathan?" Bertie asked.

"We have to seriously think of everyone who was at that reception," Aunt Ellen said, her voice turning hard. "Someone did. And unless a member of a biker gang or a mafia hit man snuck into the reception unnoticed, it was one of the members of the library community."

We let out a collective breath.

"So, think, people. Who else left the room shortly before eight o'clock?"

Dead silence.

"Okay, if we can't say who left the room, the question becomes who didn't?"

"I just don't know," Josie said. "Sure, I noticed people now and again, but to be positive that so-and-so was in the room the entire time in question? Impossible." She threw her hands up.

"How long a time frame is that, anyway, do you think?" Charlene asked.

A round of shrugs. "Ten, fifteen minutes, maybe," Aunt Ellen said. "No more than that."

"About the only person I can testify for was Butch," I said. "I was talking to him for a long time."

"So I noticed," Josie said, with a sly grin.

"Just being friendly. Hey, I remembered something! I saw Theodore heading up the stairs."

"Excellent," Aunt Ellen exclaimed. "When was that?"

I thought hard. "Not long after Bertie had that argument with Mr. Uppiton. I checked the clock. It was after eight, and I remember wondering when Bertie was going to make her announcement. I saw Theodore sneaking up the stairs. I was about to go ask him what he thought he was doing when . . . well, I got distracted. I'd completely forgotten until now."

"You have to tell the police that, Lucy honey," Aunt Ellen said. "Call them soon as we're finished here. See, everyone? Keep trying to remember. You never know what's important." When they were first married, Ellen worked in Uncle Amos's single-person law office, helping him set up his practice. Obviously what she'd learned there had stuck.

"Which brings us back to . . ." Josie's voice drifted off. "Oh, dear."

As one, we turned to see what had caught her attention. Detective Watson and Officer Greenblatt were coming through the doors. They saw us and left the line.

"Y'all having a little conclave?" Watson asked.

"We're enjoying a late breakfast," Aunt Ellen said. "In a public place."

"Getting your stories straight?"

"I do not care for that implication, Detective." Aunt Ellen rose to her feet and glared down at the six-foot-tall detective. She could stretch her five foot four to a considerable height.

Butch threw a pleading glance at Josie and an embarrassed smile at me. He shifted from one foot to the other.

Watson pointedly checked his watch. "I believe we have an appointment soon, Ms. James."

"I'll be there."

"Good."

At that moment the couple at the table next to ours got up. They crumpled their napkins and gathered their dishes to put in the bussing tray.

"Let's sit right here. I'll guard the table," Watson said, "while you go to the counter, Greenblatt. Coffee for me. Black. Oh, and one of those pecan tarts if there are any left."

"I have to get to work." Josie pushed back her stool. "Pecan tarts don't make themselves."

Ronald and Charlene got up also. I stuffed the last piece of scone into my mouth.

We headed en masse for the exit.

"I've an idea," I said to Bertie, as we stepped out into the heat and sunshine and exhaust fumes. "Watson said I could use the main floor of the library. I'll bring down the books, arrange the display, get everything ready for tomorrow. Would that be okay?"

She beamed at me. "Much more than okay. Thank you, Lucy." She'd said almost nothing as we discussed what might have happened last night. She had to be dreadfully worried.

I watched her head for her car, and I was determined more than ever to help this woman who had put so much trust in me.

Chapter 7

On Saturday morning, we were preparing to open the Bodie Island Lighthouse Library on its usual schedule.

I took a deep breath, expecting a stream of chattering patrons to enter. Many of them, I was sure, would come here to see the Austen collection. We had advertised the exhibit extensively throughout the Outer Banks. But a good many would probably be interested in having a peek at a crime scene, too.

They were to be disappointed.

The rare-books room had been cleaned up, all evidence of police activity removed. All evidence of Jonathan Uppiton also, thankfully, removed. A thick chain had been strung across the bottom of the back steps with a sign that read PRIVATE. STAFF ONLY.

In light of the recent murder and ongoing police investigation, Bertie and I had decided to delay the initial meeting of my book group. We wanted to attract readers, not the ghoulish.

Bertie, as well as Ronald and Charlene, had arrived early, anxious to show that the library was back to normal. The four of us had taken a moment to admire the display.

The first-edition books themselves were in a table-top cabinet bought specifically for this purpose. We would take them out if asked, but always handle them ourselves. No ice cream–fingered children or sticky-fingered book collectors would be allowed to touch them. A red velvet rope of the sort found in museums and art galleries was strung across the alcove. It wouldn't keep anyone out, but was intended to serve as a polite warning.

The notebook lay open at the front of the cabinet. It would not be handled, except for every morning when Bertie would turn one page. It's hard for me to describe the feeling I had when I carried that notebook down (after the police told me they were finished). I had been alone in the library, and had slipped on a pair of white gloves and curled up in a deep wingback chair to read it. The handwriting was small, the dark ink fading, the words crossed out in many places, the topic mundane. A chronicle of the day-to-day activity of a woman's life.

But what a woman.

And what a life and legacy.

Surrounding the cabinet, I'd arranged a selection of Jane Austen novels available for circulation, as well as various biographies and critical works. A separate bookshelf was devoted to other greats of nineteenth-century English literature, including the Brontë sisters, Mary Shelley, and Thomas Hardy. Another bookshelf was set aside for contemporary adaptions such as *Bridget Jones's Diary* by Helen Fielding. That display included DVDs: not only film versions of *Pride and Prejudice* and *Sense and Sensibility*, but Austen's life or legacy in movies such as *Austenland*, *Becoming Jane*, and *Clueless*.

Bertie's idea when obtaining the collection had been to use it as a springboard to discuss the ways in which enduring literature still had relevance for today's world.

On the alcove walls, I'd hung a couple of cheap prints of English pastoral scenes. The sort of thing I imagined Miss Austen would have seen in her daily life.

I had done, if I do say so myself, a pretty good job.

"Did you tell Detective Watson about Theodore?" Charlene whispered to me. "About seeing him heading upstairs moments before Mr. Uppiton was killed?"

"Yes." I'd had my formal police interview yesterday, right here in the main room of the library.

"What did he say about that?"

"Nothing."

"Nothing?"

"Nothing at all. I suspect Detective Watson keeps his cards close to his chest."

"Quarter to nine. We need some music to lighten the mood. I'll see what we have."

Bertie might have looked like she was totally calm and back to her normal self, but it was a clear sign of her inner turmoil that she didn't even order Charlene to turn off her musical selection. Thus we were entertained by 50 Cent until it was time to open the doors to the public. I attended to that, while Ronald switched off the CD player. And, I noticed, hid the CD under a stack of back issues of *Library Journal*.

Connor had been one of the first to arrive. He made a big show of greeting Bertie with a kiss on the cheek and gave a spontaneous speech, ensuring that everyone knew it was she who was responsible for the coup of bringing this priceless collection to the Bodie Island Lighthouse Library.

The speech might not have been entirely spontaneous, but it reflected well on him that he was prepared to so publicly declare his support for Bertie.

He admired the display, greeted patrons, and then got into the line at the circulation desk, where I was busy checking out books. Expecting them to be popular, we'd bought additional copies of Miss Austen's books, as well as borrowed what we could from libraries all over the state, but at this rate the shelves would be empty by lunchtime.

When it was Connor's turn, he put a paperback copy of *Pride and Prejudice* on the counter. A scene from the Keira Knightley movie illustrated the cover. "For the daughter of a friend," he said. "She loved the movie but says books are boring. I'm hoping to change her mind."

"Tell her to drop by on Monday afternoon. I'm giving a talk on books to movies especially aimed at young women." That had been Bertie's idea, and I was planning to spend my Sunday watching movies while trying to think of something to say to encourage teenage girls to read.

"I'll do more than that," he said. "In fact, I'll bring her myself. Are you free for that dinner tonight?"

"Uh . . ." I said.

"You close at seven, right? So why don't I pick you up at eight?"

At that moment Connor pitched forward across the counter. The book flew into my lap. A man, with forearms that looked as though he spent his days hauling in fishing nets, had slapped our mayor on the back. "Whoa there, Mr. Mayor," the fellow bellowed. "Don't you be getting friendly with all the lovely young ladies, now. Leave some for the rest of us." He tossed a DVD of *Emma* onto the counter.

"George," Connor said. I handed him the book.

The man chuckled again. "Don't you be tellin' folks that I've taken out that ladies' movie there. My reputation won't stand it, but the wife's at work and she asked me to come in."

"Your secret's safe with me," Connor assured him.

"Can we speed this up a bit?" whined a voice from farther back in the line.

"Eight o'clock," Connor said to me as the fisherman led him away.

"Now that I've got you here, Mr. Mayor, I've been havin' trouble with . . ."

They reached the front door, and Connor stood back to allow his companion to exit. A woman pushed her way past them.

"Louise Jane," Connor said politely. "How nice to see you."

"Humph," she said.

"'Scuse me, 'scuse me." Louise Jane's shadow, Poor Andrew, followed in her wake.

I came out from behind the circulation desk. "Can I help you?"

"I hardly think I need anyone *new* to show me around this library. Is that it?" Louise Jane and Andrew approached the alcove. A couple of older women, tourists judging by their sunburned noses and plaid shorts, were shoved aside.

Louise Jane put her hands on her bony hips and studied the display. The alcove lights had been switched off, as the cabinet had an interior light of its own that lit up the books and the notebook beautifully. She turned to me, her long nose wrinkled in as much distaste as if Charles had been allowed to use the Austen notebook for his litter box. "This is the best you can do?"

"What do you mean? I think it all looks great."

"You would." She opened the cabinet door and stretched her hand toward the notebook.

"Don't touch that!" I intended the words to come out like a command, authoritative, leaving no doubt as to who was in charge. Instead they were more of a squeak.

Louise Jane snorted. Andrew tittered.

She picked up the notebook.

What was I to do? Wrench it out of her hands? Wrestle her to the ground in a fight to the finish? While Poor Andrew kicked at my shins?

"Put that down," said a voice that truly was authoritative.

Louise Jane dropped the notebook. I tiptoed around her, reverently returned the book to its place, and closed the cabinet doors.

"Really, Louise Jane," Bertie said. "I thought you, *of all people*, would know better than to touch an old book with your bare hands."

Louise Jane flushed.

"Louise Jane doesn't need to be lectured by anyone," Andrew said. "Do you, Louise Jane?"

"Of course not. If *she* hadn't made such a fuss about it. Bertie, when I heard the good news, that you'd been released from police custody . . ."

The listening tourists gasped.

"I thought I'd drop by to talk about my job."

"Oh," said Bertie, "you found a new job. How nice."

"I mean, my job here. Now that Jonathan Uppiton is . . . well, no longer chair of the board, obviously you'll be reevaluating his decisions."

"Louise Jane," Bertie said, with a heavy sigh, "this is not the time. Have some respect. The man isn't even buried yet."

The tourists' ears twitched.

"You might be prepared to allow this library to fall into rack and ruin, but I . . ."

Bertie walked away.

People were lined up at the circulation desk, waiting to have their books and movies checked out. Ronald and Charlene were nowhere to be seen, but I stood firmly in front of the display case. I didn't trust Louise Jane not to make another grab for the notebook.

"Don't consider this matter finished." She sailed out of the library like she was on a billionaire's yacht heading for the open ocean. Poor Andrew bobbed in her wake like a rubber dinghy.

Chapter 8

By three o'clock things were slowing down. Those eager to see the Austen books, the murder scene, or both, had left, and the after-work and after-beach traffic was yet to arrive. During the summer months, for the duration of the Austen collection, we would open for extended Saturday-evening hours.

I took advantage of the lull and went to the staff room for a short break. Charlene was our reference librarian, but I'd soon learned that here everyone pitched in to help one another, and she offered to staff the desk for fifteen minutes and keep a watchful eye on the alcove. Charles was curled up on the tattered couch. He opened one eye, no doubt hoping a cat treat would fall from my pocket. The patrons generally adored seeing a library cat here, and the children in particular made a fuss over him when he strolled up to the second level and settled into a beanbag chair or on a child's lap to listen to Ronald read a story. He slept and ate in the break room, and his litter box was kept in the tiny staff restroom, along with the cleaning equipment. He wandered the library at will.

I wasn't accustomed to cats. In our house we had dogs, usually a bichon frise or something equally small and fashionable for Mom, and a German shepherd or something equally manly for Dad. The dogs occasionally even got on.

At first I'd largely ignored Charles, until I took him up to my room the night of the ill-fated reception. Last night, when I'd mounted the stairs at the end of the day, he'd followed. He inspected the kitchen for food, and, finding none (because I'd returned his bowl and bag of kibble to where they belonged), gave me a look of such sheer disappointment that I gave in and trudged back downstairs to collect his things.

And thus, without my intending it, Charles set up housekeeping in my fourth-floor aerie.

Ronald sat at the table, flicking through a children's publisher's catalog, when I came into the staff room. "Still busy out there?"

I plugged in the kettle. "It's slowed down quite a bit. Charlene's watching the store for me."

He glanced at his watch. "The preteen reading group's coming at three-thirty. I'm not looking forward to it. All they'll want to know are did I see the body and was there a lot of blood and were my fingerprints taken."

"Bertie has barely stuck her head out of her office all day. She says she can't face any more questions. Charlene found a couple of people in the act of climbing over the sign saying the upper level is out of bounds. Not to mention Louise Jane picked up the notebook in her bare hands."

"Bertie has got to be worried sick."

The kettle switched itself off and I poured boiling water over a tea bag in a souvenir mug from an ALA conference in Chicago. I've never developed a taste for iced tea. I like it piping hot and fresh. I added my customary half spoon of sugar and stirred. Then I tossed in a heaping one.

It had been a rough day.

"I can't stop thinking about it," Ronald said. "About that night. Trying to remember where everyone was and what they'd been doing."

"Me, too," I confessed.

"If only Bertie hadn't allowed herself to get so mad at Uppiton."

"That's not really fair. He annoyed everyone. Even his wife . . ." I stopped.

"What about her?"

"I can't believe I forgot. So much was going on that evening even before the killing and I had so many new people to meet, it's all somewhat of a blur. Mrs. Uppiton. She threatened her husband. Her soon-to-be-ex-husband, now late husband, that is."

"She did?"

"I heard her myself." I tried to dredge up that horrid scene. She'd accused me of having designs on her husband and then . . . "She said she'd dance on his grave."

"A figure of speech."

"I wonder. I should probably call Butch."

"Not Detective Watson?" Ronald's eyebrows wiggled.

I flushed. "Him, too."

I pulled my iPhone out of my skirt pocket. A spot

next to the wall, near the sink, could get a signal. By now, I had Watson (and Butch) on speed dial. Watson answered with his usual less-than-cheerful greeting. "What is it now, Lucy?"

My information, it seemed, wasn't all that new. Other people had overheard the altercation between Diane and Jonathan Uppiton and reported her threat to the police.

"Thanks for calling," he said, sounding as if he didn't mean it.

We closed the library at seven, and I hurried upstairs to change for my dinner date.

Is it a date? I pulled everything out of my closet while Charles watched. Aside from beach attire, work clothes, and dresses suitable for an evening at Mother's club, I didn't have much. I couldn't wear the yellow dress again.

I tossed a black dress onto the bed. Perfectly suitable for attending a librarian convention.

Charles meowed. I looked at the dress again.

It was unadorned, cut without much shape, but made of excellent linen. If I wore it with the black leather belt that had come with the yellow dress, it would give me some much-needed curves. But stark black seemed so . . . Boston. I eyed a three-quarter-sleeved yellow sweater, cropped at the waist, that I'd bought for something to throw on over shorts if a summer evening turned cool. The sweater would give the outfit a pop of color.

Perfect.

Next I eyed my collection of footwear. Those heels looked back at me.

What the heck? I wouldn't be walking anywhere. Connor was picking me up here.

I called good night to Charles as I sailed out the door on my killer heels. Killer in more ways than one. The cat wished me a good evening. Either that or he was complaining about the quantity of food left out for his supper.

I love libraries at all times, but never more than when they're empty. Empty of people, that is. Then I can imagine the words whispering to each other, sharing stories, making up new ones. Sci-fi chatting to romance; American history exchanging views with Brazilian politics; Vietnamese cookbooks swapping tips with Indian. And my beloved mystery characters listening in on everything, perhaps taking notes.

I had switched off all the main-floor lights, leaving only the ones in the alcove on. The Austen books fairly glowed. The shelves of books intended for circulation were almost empty. That was a good thing. Bertie hoped to introduce Austen to the general reading public as not just some old writer or the inspiration behind a few movies, but as the author of books that could still be enjoyed. Loved, even.

All was quiet. The shelves were straight, everything on the circulation desk neatly laid out waiting for the rush to resume on Monday. Small blue lights glowed on the computers and the printer. The first-order Fresnel lens flashed in its rhythm. The light had been designed to be cast far out to sea, so in here, far below, it didn't get overly bright.

A car turned into the parking lot, the noise of the engine breaking the silence, the headlights breaking the soft twilight. I hurried outside to meet Connor. He got out of his car, a shiny, two-seater blue BMW, and held open the passenger's door for me with a low bow and twinkling eyes. I was glad I'd gone to some trouble to dress nicely. His shirt was open-necked, but he wore it under a sharply pressed gray suit with a thin blue stripe, and shiny black loafers.

On the drive to the restaurant we chatted comfortably about the early success of the Austen exhibit.

Jake's Seafood Bar was located on the west side of the highway, set well back from the road in a large, spacious parking lot. It faced Roanoke Sound and Roanoke Island beyond, where lights all along the shore were coming on against the dusk.

Connor pulled the BMW into a spot near the entrance. I wasn't sure if I was supposed to wait for him to come around and open the door, but decided that was too formal for me in any event, so I leapt out almost as soon as the engine stopped.

As expected, the restaurant was decorated in a fishing motif, and was Outer Banks casual. The dining room was full of laughter, low conversation, soft light, and delicious smells.

"Evenin', Connor," the smiling young waitress said. "I've reserved you a table outside, if that's okay."

"Lucy?"

"That would be perfect." It was a warm evening, and I knew I'd be comfortable in the yellow sweater.

She picked up menus and led us across the busy dining room, through the open glass doors, and out onto a spacious deck. Theodore, the book collector Bertie had warned me about, was at a table by himself, head down, peering through his plain-glass spectacles at the volume propped up against the salt cellar in front of him. As I passed, I took a quick glance at what he was reading. *Moby-Dick*. He didn't look up, didn't seem to notice us as we passed. He shoveled food into his mouth mechanically, as if he were doing so only to add fuel to an engine, rather than eating for the enjoyment of the meal. He was guzzling up a big bowl of seafood bouillabaisse, and I wondered whether he'd purposefully ordered something that didn't have to be cut up. That way he could devote one hand to eating and one to turning the pages.

Diane Uppiton was also here, accompanied by the man she'd been with at the ill-fated reception. Her eyes flicked over me and she pointedly looked away.

The hostess showed us to a table set for two tucked against a wood railing, and told us our waiter would be by shortly.

Once we were seated, I whispered to Connor from behind my menu. "The grieving widow doesn't seem to be so grieving." Diane wore black trousers and a deeply cut blouse in a rather startling shade of red. A heavy red glass necklace plunged into her décolletage, and matching earrings swung at the sides of her neck.

"Despite what Diane had to say at the party, she and Jonathan never exactly had the best of marriages," Connor whispered back. "I can't remember ever seeing them doing anything but sniping at each other. His main interest in life was the library, and she resented it. When she left him, we all wondered why she hadn't done it years ago. Or why he hadn't left her."

"Do you think she stands to inherit anything?"

"I can't say. He wasn't a wealthy man, but he seemed comfortably off. The house they lived in was left to him by his parents, so she had no claim to it. At least, when he was alive."

"She threatened him at the party. I told Detective Watson that, but he said he'd heard it from a lot of people."

"She left him in a fit of temper, and when she calmed down and went back, Jonathan wouldn't take her. He wasn't a nice man, Lucy. I think he rather enjoyed the attention her histrionics brought him and the chance to cut her dead. With what he thought was withering wit and everyone else just thought was mean."

"Can I get you folks something to drink?" the waiter, a handsome young man with bronzed skin, sun-bleached hair, and a Minnesota accent asked.

"Go ahead, Lucy," Connor said. "I'm driving so I'll just have a sweet tea, thanks."

I ordered a glass of Chardonnay.

A soft wind blew off Roanoke Sound to caress my cheeks and ruffle my hair. The patio was illuminated by white globes strung from posts on the railing and the covered area of the outdoor bar. A blaze of lights from Roanoke Island shone on the still waters of the Sound, and the white light of the fourth-order lens of the Roanoke Marshes Lighthouse, a modern reproduction, flashed in the distance.

We looked across the water for a few moments in comfortable silence.

"A lighthouse," Connor said at last, as the Roanoke light flashed, "is a truly marvelous thing."

"Beautiful," I agreed.

"So much more than that. At the Currituck Light they have a saying on the wall I always remember: 'to illuminate the dark space.' That doesn't seem so important in today's world, where there are so few truly dark spaces. Particularly along most of the coast of North America. Lights on the Eastern Seaboard are so bright, some cities scarcely have night anymore. But in the old days, the days before electricity? Imagine being out to sea, in a warship powered only by wind, or a small fishing boat on a cloudy night—no radio, no satellite guidance—with a storm raging all around. And then, in the distance, that flash of light. And you would know you were not alone."

"I see what you mean." I smiled as I remembered my fourteen-year-old self. Part of the reason I'd liked Connor was that he didn't seem at all like the boys back in school. Even then, Connor McNeil thought about things like lighthouses almost as much as he did baseball or fishing. Nice to see he hadn't changed.

"The first lighthouses were buckets of flaming coal or pitch hauled up to the top of a long pole, calling fishermen or sailors home. But these big lights, they were built for the aid of men one would never know. Ships passing in the night, far out at sea. Keeping strangers safe. Because it was the right thing to do. I try to remember that sometimes, when I get caught up in a petty political battle."

"I bet it's not easy," I said, "being the mayor in a small place like this. Everyone wanting to tell you their problems."

"Not easy, no. But I love this place, and I like to think I'm giving something back to the community."

"You've always loved it," I said. "I remember that, from when we were kids. I couldn't imagine having such an attachment to a place. My father's family's lived in Boston since before the Revolution, but he'd move in a shot if he could make more money someplace else."

He smiled. "My family's been here on the Outer Banks since the 1700s. The men went to sea, the women worked at fish plants, down through the generations. Perhaps that's why we have such an attachment to the lighthouses."

"You didn't become a fisherman, though, did you?" Connor's accent was deep and Southern, but there were no rough edges to it. He sounded as if he'd been raised in a plantation house. "What have you done with yourself since that summer? On your way to becoming the mayor?"

"That's a lot of years to cover in one night, Lucy. No, I didn't really fish, other than high school and college summers, working on charter boats. My parents wanted more for me than that. I'm an only child. My mom made sure I concentrated on my schoolwork. You must remember that I was the dorky kid sitting at home on a Saturday night, poring over books, while the other boys rode their bikes through town and took girls to bonfires at the beach."

I blushed and hoped he couldn't see in the soft light. "You took me to a bonfire at the beach."

"I suppose I was a normal kid some of the time. My parents saved every penny they could for my education. That, plus some scholarships, got me into

Duke, and then to med school at UNC. I am, truth be told, a dentist."

"A dentist!"

He laughed. "You sound so surprised. Yes, I'm a dentist. I've cut my practice down a fair amount while I'm mayor, but I still have some hours, to keep my hand in and to serve my regular patients."

We leaned back to allow the waiter to put our drinks in front of us. He recited the night's specials and left us to consider the menu.

"I can never resist she-crab soup," I said. Butch Greenblatt came onto the patio. For a moment I considered crawling into my menu. Butch had invited me to have dinner here with him recently. He had canceled, hadn't he? Nothing wrong with me having dinner with the mayor. Nothing at all.

"Evenin', Lucy, Mr. Mayor."

"Butch," I said, "How lovely to see you. Case all resolved, is it?"

"We've haven't ordered yet," Connor said. "Would you like to join us?"

Nothing awkward about that. Nothing at all.

But Butch didn't seem to mind. "No, thanks. I saw you folks sitting outside and came to say hi. I'm picking up something to go. We're working late down at the station." He glanced around, lowered his voice. "About . . . you know."

"Any developments?"

"A few. Look, this isn't really the time or the place to talk, but a word of advice, Lucy. Don't get too attached to your job, okay?"

"What are you saying?"

"I . . ."

"Hey, look who's here." Josie swung onto the patio in a flurry of flowing blond hair, tiny shorts, and high-heeled sandals. Every man in the place almost choked on his food. "Having a nice dinner? Why are you standing up, Butch? We can find a bigger table."

"I'm not staying, just picking up something Jake prepared for me and the detectives."

"Nice," she said. "Jake doesn't usually do takeout, but anything for his little bro, eh?"

Right on cue, a waitress arrived, bearing a white paper sack. My mouth watered at the scents rising from it. She handed it to Butch; he mumbled goodbyes, threw me a glance, and took his leave.

I grabbed my glass and gulped down a mouthful of wine. I reminded myself that I wasn't dating Butch. I wasn't dating Connor, either. I was having dinner in a public place with a person who happened to be a man. A handsome, single man. A childhood friend. No need to feel guilty.

None at all.

I threw back another mouthful of wine. "Gee, did I interrupt something?" Josie asked. "I didn't mean to. I wouldn't have thought this was the place to conduct police business." She glanced at me with a sparkle in her eye. "Or maybe Butch wanted the chance to talk to you, Lucy?"

"I have no idea what you mean," I said, fighting to keep from blushing. "Why are you here, anyway?"

"Date night. How pathetic is that? Jake's so busy at night getting the restaurant up and running, and I start early at the bakery and work all day; we don't have much time to spend together. I'm going to sit on a stool and watch him cook."

"It'll be worth it, Josie," Connor said. "You have to make sacrifices when you're young if you want to achieve your dreams. I'm proof of that."

"Yeah," she said, with a tinkling laugh. "You're such a crusty old guy, dispensing a lifetime of wisdom to us young'uns. Here's a word of wisdom from me: try the seafood tray. It's to die for."

She wiggled her fingers in a wave and skipped through the doors. Diane Uppiton threw her date, who was gaping at Josie's rear end like a fish on a line, a scathing glare, before calling for another bottle of wine.

I thought about Connor's words for a moment. I'd never sacrificed anything. Everything I'd ever wanted in life had been handed to me. I'd never given a thought to fees for tennis or music lessons or the extra tutoring I needed to get into a good college. I didn't even know how much tuition cost at Simmons or a dorm room at Northeastern. I'd taken my monthly allowance without question and thought I was hard done by if I had to phone Dad and ask for more. My Yaris had been a gift for my thirtieth birthday. I'd been proud of myself, thinking I was proving my independence when I told my parents I'd rent an apartment myself, out of my own salary, rather than letting them buy me a place when I began work.

"Ready to order?" Connor asked, interrupting my thoughts.

"What do you think he meant?"

"Who?"

"Butch. About my job?"

Connor let out a long sigh. "I think, Lucy, he was trying to tell you not to count on Bertie being around much longer."

"You can't mean they're going to arrest her. Charge her with murder? That's preposterous."

"I don't know what the police are thinking, Lucy. But it does look as though, right now, Bertie's their prime suspect."

"That can't be. What about Theodore? Sitting there reading *Moby-Dick* without a care in the world. I saw him go upstairs moments before Uppiton was killed. I told the police that." I leaned across the table. Despite how upset I was, I kept my voice low, and none of the other diners paid us any attention. I had been well trained never to create a scene. The worst sin, in Mother's eyes. "Bertie didn't do it!"

"I know that, Lucy. I also know she needs all her friends around her, and I'm glad you're on her side. I'm going to take Josie's advice and have the seafood tray. A Caesar salad to start. What about you?"

I tried to relax and enjoy a pleasant evening with Connor, but I couldn't get Butch's warning out of my head. An arrest, a trial, maybe even a conviction, would be a nightmare for Bertie and also for the library.

Diane Uppiton laughed uproariously at something her date said. The man glanced around the patio, grinning, seeking approval. His false teeth were too large for his mouth. Theodore, sitting directly under one of the round white lights, turned a page with his left hand while his right wiped the bottom of his bowl with a slice of freshly baked bread.

Maybe it was time I made some sacrifices in life.

Tonight I'd enjoy my dinner. Tomorrow I'd start poking my nose where it didn't belong.

Beginning with Theodore and Diane Uppiton and her companion.

Chapter 9

I was awakened by the tinkling of a bell. It took a few moments for my head to clear and for me to realize, first, where I was (in my lighthouse aerie), and, second, what the noise was.

The doorbell.

I opened one eye. Outside, it was daylight. Charles leapt up on the bed and swatted at my face as if to say, *Aren't you going to answer that?*

I stumbled out of bed, crossed the room, and switched on the camera that was mounted over the door to the outside. It wasn't a security camera, because it didn't record anything, but it had been installed by a previous resident of the fourth floor so he didn't have to run downstairs every time someone hammered on the door to return a book or ask if the library was open (if so, why would the door be locked and the parking lot empty?).

Louise Jane McKaughnan obviously knew about the camera, because she was smiling up at it. In one hand she held a tray bearing two extralarge take-out cups from Josie's, and in the other a small paper bag.

She lifted the bag to the camera and pointed with the cup-bearing hand. Grinning all the while.

I switched the sound on. "Louise Jane."

"Isn't it a beautiful morning, Lucy? It's going to be a real Outer Banks day, just like we had when I was young. I thought you'd enjoy a treat." She smiled.

I glanced around my room. The bed was unmade but everything else reasonably tidy. Connor had driven me home after dinner and walked me to the front door. I didn't suggest he come up, and he did not ask.

Slowly, slowly, I'd thought.

He waited until I was safely inside and the door shut behind me before returning to his car and driving off into the night with a roar of the vehicle's powerful engine.

Expecting to be able to sleep in and enjoy my day off, I'd not gone to bed but had filled the kettle for hot tea, hung up my dress, put on comfortable cotton pajamas, and switched on the computer. I'd worked late into the night, enjoying the sounds of quiet and the distant waves crashing against the shore, and doing some research to advance my admittedly limited knowledge of Jane Austen. Charles had attempted to assist, but after the seventh time I'd removed him from the keyboard and placed him firmly on the floor, he gave up and curled on the window seat for a nap.

"It's a bit early for a social call, Louise Jane," I said, attempting to stifle a huge yawn.

"We Outer Banks girls get up with the sun. I brought coffee and muffins."

"I'll be down in five minutes."

"Don't bother—I know where the spare key's hidden. I just wanted to make sure you were . . . alone." She gave me a long wink that almost turned my stomach.

"Fourth level."

"I know."

I flew into the bathroom, splashed water on my face, stuffed unruly curls into an elastic band, and threw on the first clothes that came to hand. I was not going to be found in my jammies by Louise Jane McKaughnan.

I was pulling a T-shirt over my head when I heard footsteps on the iron stairs and then a knock at the door. I opened it, and Louise Jane tumbled into my apartment. She headed straight for the kitchen, opened a cupboard, took down two small plates, and laid out muffins and scones. All while I was still standing with my hand on the open door. "Make yourself at home."

"Thanks. I will. Josie said you take cream and sugar, so I added that already." She put the cups and plates on the table and pulled out a chair. "I adore this little room. It's just perfect."

Louise Jane was trying hard to be friendly, but the woman had not one iota of warmth. She came across much like a shark smiling from the other side of the aquarium glass. *If this glass breaks, you'll see what I really think of you.*

I accepted a cranberry bran muffin and chastised myself for being mean. Perhaps Louise Jane really did want to be friends.

"Absolutely perfect for a single woman who's just passing through," she finished.

"Where's Andrew today?"

She waved a hand. "Off playing somewhere. We don't *live* together, you know. He's not my boyfriend. We're only good friends. I've found it helps deter unwanted male attention, having Andrew at my elbow. Not something I suppose you'd understand." She bared her teeth at me in what she thought was a smile. "The sea air certainly makes your hair . . . curly, doesn't it?"

"I'm from Boston, Louise Jane. I am not a stranger to sea air."

"Just making a comment. I've heard that older men still like those old-fashioned curls." She openly studied my room. "Everything looks . . . okay. Have you been bothered by anything?"

Other than unwelcome Sunday-morning visitors who knew where the spare key was hidden?

"No. I enjoy the quiet and the dark."

"At night . . ."

"What do you mean?"

She stood up and went to the window. She pulled the heavy drapes aside. Charles hissed at her. "Nasty beast. You really are too soft for your own good, Lucy, letting him upstairs like this. I never could understand why Bertie took him in. Animals have no place in a library."

"I like him." I went over to give Charles an approving pat.

"You would."

The sky was a brilliant, cloudless blue, the sparkling ocean as calm as bathwater. A rusty, red-hulled freighter passed, a distant speck on the flat horizon. Fish crows swooped low over the marshes. Even

Louise Jane had to stop being catty and admire the view. "They say animals have powerful senses."

"True."

"Have you noticed him acting strange at all?"

"What do you mean?"

"Nothing. Just wondering." She walked over to my laptop and wiggled the mouse to get rid of the screensaver—libraries around the world.

The page that came up showed images of Jane Austen, where I'd left my research last night.

"Did you know I'm named after her?"

"No."

"Louise is my grandmother, but my mother always adored Jane Austen, so she added that name in tribute."

If that was true I'd eat Charles's dinner and give him the fresh flounder I'd planned to buy later.

"We've always been great literature lovers in my family. I did a paper on Jane Austen in college. Got an A-plus. My professor desperately wanted me to switch to English lit, but I had to drop out before finishing. We can't all get graduate degrees. My grandmother was ill and she needed me. We've always been awful close."

"This has been lovely, and thanks for the coffee, but I have an appointment soon," I said. "I've . . . I've . . . booked a sailing tour. I'm looking forward to a day on the ocean. Looks like it will be perfect for it, too."

"My greatest interest has always been the history of this area. My family came here in 1764. One of the very first families. What a wild and desolate place it was then. And over all those generations, the Mc-Kaughnans have never even considered living anywhere else. This strip of land is my family. And my family is this land."

"How nice. Will you look at the time?"

"This is a charming little apartment. I hope you'll like it here. Perhaps you won't . . ."

"Won't?"

"Never mind. It's just that, well, they've had trouble getting people to stay here, you know. For more than a few nights." She ran her fingers over the frame above the window seat. Charles hissed and leapt down. He darted into the kitchen and crawled into a corner. "You might want to keep the window closed at night."

The window was set into a white-painted wooden frame with black iron bars outside. The bars presumably were intended to protect one from falling out. The window opened and closed by turning a latch at the bottom. Water and salt streaked the outside of the glass. "I like the breeze. I always keep my windows open at night."

Louise Jane gasped. "No!"

"Why not?" I said, stepping directly into her trap.

"I'm not surprised Bertie hasn't told you. It really isn't my place, but if you're going to live here . . . One of your predecessors killed herself. She threw herself out that window, back in the 1990s, I think it was. A sweet young thing, much younger than you, so you probably have nothing to worry about."

The bars would stop an accident, but they were wide enough apart that a normal-sized woman would be able to squeeze through. If she wanted to. "That's sad, but I'm hardly going to kill myself because someone I don't even know did."

"I'm sure you're right. It's just that . . . well, my grandmother knows the story. A lighthouse keeper brought his young bride here. It was 1872, and the lighthouse was newly built to replace the one destroyed in the War Between the States. He was an older man, much older than her. Too old to be a lighthouse keeper, but so many of the young men had died in the war or never come back." Her voice settled into storytelling mode, and despite myself, I listened. When she wasn't trying to be catty or get in a dig at me, Louise Jane's voice could be deep and calming. A perfect storyteller voice.

"The young bride—Frances was her name—was the youngest daughter of a wealthy family that had lost everything in the war. She wasn't pretty and was too fond of sticking her nose in books, but that didn't matter to potential suitors, because her family had money and land. But when that was gone her parents were forced to marry her off to the only man who would have her.

"He was old and very cruel, and, according to my grandmother, who was told by *her* mother, was one of the ugliest men God ever put on this earth." Louise Jane shuddered, and despite myself I felt goose bumps crawling across my arms. "He brought her to the lighthouse, to this lighthouse, and here she stayed. Until she died. She never came into town, not even to church. Women attempted to call on her, and the old man would turn them away, saying Frances was ill and had to keep to her bed. Eventually they stopped calling. The reverend was the only one allowed into the lighthouse. He would stay for a short while, and when he left he would be seen shaking his head and heard muttering dark words. This is a remote spot now, but back then . . . When the occasional wanderer did pass at night, they said they could hear the terrifying sound of Frances's screams.

"Screams that came, Lucy, from this room. Have you noticed how this room doesn't really fit the design of the lighthouse? It was built after the lighthouse was built. It was built to be Frances's room. Her prison. She would stand at that window, weeping, calling out for someone to help her."

Louise Jane's hand jerked upward, pointing. I almost leapt out of my skin.

"It was a different time, of course. Frances and the lighthouse keeper had been married in the presence of God, in a church, with many witnesses. Although the townspeople's hearts went out to her, no one would help her. Children would ask why no one would help *the Lady*, and their mothers would tell them to hush.

"And then, one day, about a year after Frances had come to the Bodie Island Lighthouse, two men hunting ducks in the marsh spotted her broken, lifeless body. At the bottom of the lighthouse. Right beneath *that window*!"

I jumped. "How awful."

The edges of Louise Jane's mouth curled up. "I debated telling you about this. Andrew said I should keep it to myself. But I thought you deserved to know, Lucy. After all, you're sleeping here. In the very room where Frances went mad. And died. You're an intelligent, educated woman, aren't you?"

I nodded. It was daylight, the twenty-first century. Bright sunlight streamed in the window, the sun played on the calm sea. My room was cheerful, modern, with electric lights, plumbing, Wi-Fi, a telephone. Even a doorbell. But the corners seemed deep and full of shadows. I mentally shook my head. This room didn't even have corners!

"Now, don't get me wrong," Louise Jane continued. "Frances—*the Lady*, she's called now—isn't an evil spirit. Not at all. She was kind in life, or so they say, until she was locked away. She remains kind in death. When she sees a woman, a young—well, almost young—woman living in this room . . . Frances believes she's trapped. And tries to free her. The only way she knows how. The way she freed herself."

It was so quiet up here when the library was closed, high above the sea and the marsh, no one else around. At night, the darkness broken only by the rhythmic flash of the light.

"Well, well, look at the time. I promised to meet Andrew for a hike along the beach before lunch. Fresh air and exercise, there's nothing like it. Are you all right, Lucy? You look awful pale."

"I'm fine," I squeaked.

"If you liked that story, I can tell you plenty more. This lighthouse has seen a lot of things over the years. A lot of strange and terrible things. And about the death of poor Mr. Uppiton—they say ghosts haunt the places they loved most in life, don't they? Don't bother coming down—I can let myself out."

And she left.

Charles rubbed himself against my ankles. I picked him up and stroked the soft tan fur. He purred. "She didn't scare you, did she? Didn't scare me, either. Silly story. Probably isn't even true." I glanced at my laptop. It shouldn't take more than a few minutes to look up legends of the Bodie Island Lighthouse.

Nonsense. "Fresh air and exercise sounds like a good idea," I said to Charles. "After breakfast."

Louise Jane hadn't touched her muffin. I was considering it when my phone rang. I crossed the room, picked it up off the window seat, and glanced at the display. My heart sank. Couldn't put it off any longer.

"Morning!" I trilled. I clambered onto the seat and pressed the phone between my ear and the glass.

"Lucille," Mom said, "I trust you're packing to come home."

"Why would I do that? I'm having a great time here. The weather's been perfect." I'd sent e-mails to my parents and my brothers, telling them about the new job, that I had a place to live. That I was happy. Mom had called a couple of times, and I let it go to voice mail.

"This killing. It was in your very library. I called Ellen, and she told me the police had the investigation well in hand. But that's not what the papers are saying. And you're living right there. I know that lighthouse. It's miles from anywhere!"

"The killing made the Boston papers?"

"No, but I do follow the news from the Outer Banks, you know."

Since when?

Since I moved here, I guessed. Somehow that was nice to know. Although not in this particular instance.

I lost her next words in a burst of static. "I can't hear you too well, Mom. But I'm fine. Why, look at it this way: this is the scene of a police investigation. I couldn't be safer." I peeked out the window, out and down. Way down. Not a vehicle or human being was in sight. A wooden boardwalk wound through the marsh off Croatan Sound at the back of the lighthouse. Later in the morning hikers would be taking the trail and exploring the outside of the lighthouse, but this early I had only gulls and crows for company.

I'm a city girl, born and raised in Boston. Except for idyllic Outer Banks summers, I've lived my whole life surrounded by cars stuck in traffic jams and fast-walking people. But my maternal ancestors were true Bankers, and maybe the love of the ocean and dunes and open places skipped a generation to land firmly on me. When Mom holidayed here, she stuck to the beach, the best restaurants, the shops at Manteo and Duck. And the outlet mall in Nags Head.

Perhaps soon I'd come to miss the city, but right now I was thrilled to live here.

Despite Louise Jane and her stories.

"There is that, at least," Mom said. "Do you get a phone signal way up there?"

"It's not the best, but I'm talking to you now, Mom."

"Keep it with you at all times."

"Yes, Mom."

"I saw Evangeline yesterday."

At last we got to the purpose of the call. "How's she?"

"Brokenhearted. As we all are. Lucy, darling, Evangeline says Ricky has positively thrown himself into his work. He scarcely comes up for air. She hasn't seen him once since . . . since that silly misunderstanding."

"You mean when I told him I wasn't going to marry him? No misunderstanding there, Mom."

"Lucy, darling. You should call him. Let him know you're okay and thinking things over."

"Mom. If Ricky wants to talk to me, he has this number."

"Men can be stubborn sometimes."

A gull swooped past the window, so close I instinctively jumped back. "Looks like I've got company, Mom. Gotta run. It's so busy here today, you wouldn't believe it."

"I love you, dear."

"I love you, too, Mom." And I did. No matter how exasperating she might be at times, I always knew that.

As I finished off my breakfast, kindly provided by Louise Jane, I debated what to do for the day. There was nothing I'd rather do than spend the whole day at the beach, jumping in the waves, reading with my toes stretched out into the surf, but I had to get ready for tomorrow's talk on Austen movie adaptations. Something I didn't know much about. I hoped for a pack of teenage girls so enthusiastic I wouldn't have to say much other than a brief introduction. But just in case they asked questions, I'd brought a couple of DVDs upstairs to watch on my laptop. *Sense and Sensibility* with Emma Thompson, *Pride and Prejudice* with Keira Knightly, *Emma* with Gwyneth Paltrow. I wasn't looking forward to a whole day of movie watching, not when the sun was shining and the beach was so tantalizingly close.

Needs must, as my father would say.

I finished breakfast while reading a critique of *Emma*, prior to putting on the movie. Then I figured a nice walk would get my head in the right place before facing a day reluctantly spent indoors.

"You can't come," I said to Charles, who made no indication of intending to move from the center of the daybed. He yawned and stretched.

I trotted down the stairs, all one hundred of them, and let myself out of the library.

I locked the door and turned. A head popped around the side of the lighthouse. I yelped in surprise.

"Good morning, my dear," Theodore Kowalski said. "Did I give you a fright? Terribly sorry. Didn't mean to."

"Where'd you come from?" The only car in the lot was my Yaris.

"I tied my boat up at the wharf and walked in. The marsh birds are so active in the mornings." A popular nature trail ran from a small, rough wooden dock on the waters of Blossie Creek through the marsh to the lighthouse grounds.

"You're a birder?" I asked, noticing the lack of binoculars, bird book, or anything with which to take notes.

"An enthusiastic amateur." His smile was about

as fake as the English accent he was struggling to maintain in the absence of Harris Tweed and a cravat. Today he wore jeans and sneakers.

"Harrumph," I said.

"Now that I have you here, Lucy, have there been any . . . developments?"

"Developments?"

"The investigation into the death of Jonathan, of course."

"The police aren't keeping me informed."

"I thought you might have picked up something, that's all."

"I haven't."

He smiled at me. I smiled back. "I'm heading out for a morning stroll," I said. "Why don't you let me walk with you? I'd love to see your boat. You can tell me everything there is to know about the birds we see. Back home in Massachusetts, I'm quite a keen birder myself." I crossed my fingers behind my back.

"I don't . . . I don't particularly know their names. I just like to admire them."

"Great." I set off at a comfortable pace. "Let's go, then."

He couldn't very well refuse, now, could he? I looked over my shoulder to see him staring up at the lighthouse. Then he turned and reluctantly followed me to the boardwalk.

Fortunately, I wasn't forced to talk about birds, and Theodore walked beside me in silence.

We reached the water. The only boat tied up to the dock was nothing but a rickety old rowboat that had seen far better days. "You came in that?" I said, unable to hide my surprise.

"It's perfectly seaworthy. I like to be down low, close to the water."

"I guess you're that." Not only close to the water, but sitting in it if an unexpected wave came up. I wouldn't want to trust my life to that thing, not even in the calm, shallow waters of the Croatan Sound on a sunny day. He clambered in, and the boat teetered ominously under his unsteady steps. I hoped I'd be able to remember what I'd learned the year I'd taken a lifeguard course. Theodore dropped onto the seat and picked up the oars.

"Nice talking to you," I said.

He pulled away from the dock. I watched until he was a good distance from shore, moving slowly through the grasses of the marsh. It took a long time. I was surprised that anyone who'd grown up on the Outer Banks could be so useless in a boat.

I walked back to the lighthouse, deep in thought. Had Theodore been sneaking about the library on a Sunday, hoping for a chance to get in and snatch a private peek at the Austen books? Or was he hoping to remove something incriminating the cops hadn't found yet?

Chapter 10

I'd been determined to try my hand at snooping, but over the next few days we were so busy at the library, I didn't have much of a chance. Crowds of eager book lovers poured through our doors as word spread about our exhibit. Most of the books we had for circulation by Austen and her contemporaries had been checked out by Monday afternoon. Ronald had been sent over to the mainland to buy every copy he could lay his hands on from bookstores there. All three branches of the Outer Banks' Island Bookstore sold out of their stock and placed rush orders. My talk on Monday about book-to-movie adaptations was so well attended, we had to temporarily shut the doors and turn people away. As I'd hoped, the audience was already so informed about the movie adaptions that I didn't have to say all that much. Connor McNeil brought his friend's daughter, a tall, thin girl dressed all in black, with hair dyed the color of midnight, excessive black make-up, black fingernail polish, and numerous strangely placed piercings. She confessed to the group, almost in tears, that she saw herself as a modern-day Kitty Bennet. The middle child, always seeking a place of her own between the more accomplished older sister and overly indulged youngest.

Connor stood at the back of the room against the wall, his soft eyes focused on his niece. He caught my eye and gave me a thumbs-up.

By Tuesday, tour buses were pulling into our parking lot to disgorge entire book clubs from as far away as Tennessee, DC, or Florida.

Ronald tried valiantly to keep his full program of summer holiday activities for children and preteens going, as well as drive all over the state searching for Austen books, and help to handle the crowds. Charlene's academic work was pretty much pushed aside, along with two visiting English grad students who were here to examine old records as part of their dissertations on the impacts to shipping along this coast during the Civil War. They were stuffed into the rare-books room—which the police had kindly allowed us to use once again—with the door closed while Charlene answered questions about Miss Austen's life and times.

At the end of the day on Tuesday, Bertie called a staff meeting.

Charlene dropped into a chair. "The word 'chaos' was invented to describe this afternoon." Charles jumped onto her lap and gave her a nudge of encouragement with his right paw. "I had no idea this exhibit would be so popular."

"Some of the parents were asking me when you're going to give that talk again, Lucy," Ronald said. "The one you did yesterday. They think it's a great way of introducing their movie-addicted kids to classic books. I agree. Bertie, weren't you going to give a talk one afternoon about Jane's life? I'm sure there's interest in that."

Bertie sighed. "This couldn't have come at a worse time. I said I'd give the talk on the spur of the moment, but I have too much to think about these days to find time to prepare. My Austen knowledge is rather rusty. Sorry."

"We've been answering the same questions all day," I said, knowing that the murder of Jonathan Uppiton had to be prominent in Bertie's mind. " 'When and where was Miss Austen born?' 'How did she come to write?' "

" 'Where did she get her ideas?' " Charlene said, with a laugh. " 'How did she find a publisher?' "

"Why don't we offer a lecture series? The life and times of Jane Austen." I glanced around the circle at three doubtful faces. "I'll do it," I said, wondering what I was getting myself into.

"Great idea!" Ronald and Charlene chorused.

Bertie smiled. "Thank you, Lucy. Let's give it a try and see how much interest we get."

We settled on two times a day. Once in the morning, and another in the late afternoon. If no one came, then no bother.

We stayed late Tuesday night to update the library's Web page and run off posters (more work for Ronald and Charlene, assigned to hang them all over the Outer Banks) advertising the lecture.

Wednesday morning, I came down early with Charles at my heels, both of us yawning and stretching, him because that's what cats do, and me because

I'd been up most of the night. I didn't know much more about Jane Austen than any book lover, so I'd spent the night on the Internet, doing research as well as poring over a biography I'd managed to save from being lent out only because I was faster than Mrs. Fitzgerald.

Bertie had already arrived, and we pushed shelves aside, took down pictures, and set up two rows of folding chairs by the alcove, facing a blank wall on which to show slides off my laptop.

We'd just finished and had stepped back to admire our handiwork when Ronald walked through the door with a mischievous grin. He wore striped black-and-gray trousers, a top hat, and a red satin waistcoat with a pocket watch secured across the chest by a gold chain.

Bertie clapped her hands. "You look wonderful. Where on earth did you get those clothes?"

"A little something in the back of my closet from my acting days." A large, sturdy round box, decorated with a pattern of pink roses and secured by a length of gold rope, swung in his hand.

"Dare I ask," I said, "what's in there?"

"You may. If we're going to be all Austen all the time, we might as well dress the part." He put the box on the desk, untied the rope, and opened it. Bertie and I leaned closer. Ronald pushed tissue paper aside, and we gasped.

It was a hat. And what a hat. A dusty rose Victorian delight of feathers, lace, and ribbons.

Ronald lifted the hat out of the box. He held it out to Bertie. "Try it on."

"Oh no! I can't wear hats. Besides I'm . . . well . . .

I'm not always here these days. You wear it, Lucy. You have the face for big hats."

"I can't," I protested feebly.

"Sure you can," Bertie said. "It'll be perfect for your lectures."

"It's not historically appropriate. Hats of that size only came into fashion in the Victorian era. Jane Austen would have worn a simple bonnet tied under her chin."

"If anyone challenges you as to the accuracy of your haberdashery," Ronald said, "you can say you're blending time frames."

"Do wear it, Lucy," Bertie said. "It's perfect."

I practically snatched the hat out of Ronald's hands. I put it on my head, and Bertie and Ronald exclaimed how fabulous it was. I went to the restroom to admire myself. I thought I looked rather foolish with the gigantic hat above a scooped-neck T-shirt with gold glitter, topped by a black linen jacket, but I still loved it.

So did my audience.

As with yesterday's talk to teens, my first lecture was standing room only. We soon ran out of even that, and ended up putting Charlene at the door to tell new arrivals the library was temporarily closed. When we reopened, a couple of elderly ladies almost trampled Charlene in their eagerness to get in. They asked me if they could reserve a spot for the next talk.

I opened a fresh notebook and began taking reservations.

More work!

Ronald had the idea of making one lecture a day

appealing to children. Wednesday, I was up late most of the night, doing research into Miss Austen's childhood writings, her juvenilia, while Charles dozed on my bed after an exhausting day of accepting tummy rubs, behind-the-ears scratches, and admiring comments.

That's when I happened across my name on the Internet. Apparently, I was now being called "a foremost Austen scholar and lecturer." I wondered whether I'd soon begin receiving notices from real Austen experts to cease and desist.

On the other hand, maybe I could start a second career, touring and charging for my lectures. I sent the link to my mom, knowing she'd be proud, and to some of my friends back in Boston, knowing they'd have a good laugh.

But it wasn't, in Ronald's words, all Austen all the time. Bertie and Uncle Amos had been called down to the police station several times over the last couple of days. She came back with a set to her face and a shadow in her eyes, and threw herself even more into her work. She began taking shifts behind the circulation desk or answering questions if Ronald, Charlene, and I were exceptionally busy.

A few people were starting to whisper that Bertie would soon be arrested. I didn't know if they had inside information or were simply enjoying spreading malicious gossip. Ronald went so far as to ask a couple of local busybodies to leave the library when he overheard them whispering loudly behind the magazine rack, speculating as to whether Bertie would find prison as comfortable as (apparently) Martha Stewart had.

Thursday, we shooed the last patron out the doors, and I collapsed into a chair in an exhausted heap. Bertie dropped to the floor into a Downward Dog. Charlene brought out the CD player that was kept behind the desk and plugged it in. She began hunting through the drawers. "Anyone seen my CDs? They don't seem to be here."

"Must have been misplaced when we put out that new shipment of books." Ronald opened his watch. He would regularly and ostentatiously flick open the watch cover to check the time, which always elicited fits of giggles from the youngest of our patrons. Earlier today, he'd taken advantage of the chaos when three busloads of book clubs arrived at the same time to slip Charlene's musical selections underneath a stack of cooking magazines.

"Not to worry," Charlene said, "I'll bring more from home tomorrow."

"How nice," Bertie, still upside down, said.

"I think those kids from North Dakota particularly enjoyed your talk," Ronald said to me. "When they left, I heard them asking their mom to take them to the store *right away* so they could buy journals."

I preened, pleased. We'd decided that the four o'clock lecture would be the one aimed at a younger audience. I talked about the juvenile writings of not only Jane Austen, but also the Brontë sisters, and finished by suggesting the kids take advantage of their time at the coast to jot down observations and ideas and make sketches.

Bertie glided easily into Cobra position. "You people are doing a great job. I'll be mentioning it to the library board." We smiled at each other. "Let's clean up and go home. Do you think you can fit in another lecture tomorrow, Lucy? The waiting list now has a waiting list."

"If you want, but I won't be able to do much else to help out. I could schedule it for right after lunch."

"Those English guys left for a week," Charlene said. "They said they'd come back when I have time to do my job and help them with their research. I can take on some of your work, Lucy."

"Thanks."

Bertie stood up slowly, unwinding each vertebra. "I'll be in my office for a while still." She headed for the hallway. She stopped in front of the alcove.

"Lucy?"

We looked over at the sharp tone in her voice. "Is something the matter?"

"Where's *Sense and Sensibility*?"

Chapter 11

The four employees of the Bodie Island Lighthouse Library stared into the cabinet. I counted books. Five. Plus Jane Austen's notebook.

That couldn't be right. We had six books: *Sense and Sensibility*, published in 1811; *Pride and Prejudice*, 1813; *Mansfield Park*, 1814; *Emma*, 1816; *Northanger Abbey*, published in 1818, after Miss Austen's death; and *Persuasion*, also 1818.

Bertie opened the cabinet. As an indication of how upset she was, she didn't even put on the white gloves before she lifted each of the five books, as if *Sense and Sensibility* had somehow fallen into a gap beneath.

"It's gone," Charlene said redundantly.

"It can't be," Ronald said.

"When was the last time you saw it?" Bertie asked.

We glanced at one another, empty faced. "I've no idea," I said.

"A lady came in who's the head of the Virginia chapter of the Emma Thompson Fan Club. She wanted to read a paragraph Thompson said in the movie version," Charlene said. "I took the book out and showed her. You said we could, as long as the patrons don't hold the books themselves."

"When was that?" Bertie asked.

"This morning. I think. Or it might have been yesterday afternoon. We've been so busy, I can't keep anything straight."

"It was there last night," Bertie said. "I always check when I leave."

"And this morning," I added. "I like to take a quiet moment to admire them. I would have noticed if one had been missing."

"Let's search. I want every nook and cranny in this room turned over. It's entirely possible someone took the book out when we were too busy to show it to him and then stuck it on the shelves."

We divided the main room of the library into quadrants, each of us searching one. I pulled out every fiction title from Roberts to Zelazny, checking the space behind, and then did the same for North Carolina history.

"Here they are," Charlene said.

"Thank heavens," Bertie said.

"Sorry. I meant here are my CDs. I wonder how they got in there. I'll put some music on in the background for while we search."

"No." Such was Bertie's tone, Charlene didn't argue.

I went upstairs to search the mystery section, while Ronald tackled his children's library, Charlene her reference books, and Bertie the rare-books room.

It was long after dark before we met back downstairs. Charles had been trying for some time to remind me that it was past dinnertime. I'd even looked in the bag of cat food to see if *Sense and Sensibility* had somehow found its way there.

Nothing.

Bertie slumped into an armchair.

Ronald leaned against the wall and crossed his arms. "We have to call the police."

"I know," Bertie sighed. She looked, quite simply, dreadful, as if she'd aged ten years in the past couple of hours. She didn't need this—the library didn't need this—on top of a murder investigation. "They'll blame me."

Ronald, Charlene, and I spoke at once:

"Nonsense."

"Not your fault."

"No one could have . . ."

She held up her hand. "It was my decision not to lock the cabinet. I wanted to be able to show the books without rushing about trying to find keys. I trusted people."

I took the desk phone off the hook. "Do you want me to call?"

"I'll do it."

Detective Watson, accompanied by Butch Green-blatt, arrived even faster than they had to the report of a dead body.

Butch started to make a list of everyone who'd been in the library today. He soon stopped. It would be a shorter list of everyone who hadn't.

Between us, Bertie, Ronald, Charlene, and I had seen everyone on the library board at least once, most of them strutting with pride at the success of the Austen exhibit. Mrs. Fitzgerald had stood at the door, greeting guests as if at a house party; Louise Jane (and Andrew, of course) had come, too. Louise Jane surveyed the barely controlled chaos, sneered at my hat (which had come askew when I'd tried to let some air underneath), and told everyone who would listen, and many who did not want to, that the library was clearly overwhelmed. A weepy Diane Uppiton had suggested to Bertie that the last lecture of the day be dedicated to Jonathan Uppiton, "whose inspiration and vision for this library and the Austen collection was tragically cut short." Bertie agreed, just to keep the peace, and delivered the words through gritted teeth. Diane had been accompanied by the man she'd been talking to at the party, the one she'd had dinner with the other night. Curtis Gardner, Bertie whispered to me, had joined the board only last month, despite knowing nothing whatsoever about libraries, and caring even less. Perhaps, she added, as Curtis comforted Diane, he had other interests.

Connor had been there, standing at the back while I stumbled my way (nervous that one time only) through my lecture. Mrs. Peterson had brought all five of her daughters to the children's talk, to which two paid rapt attention while two snapped gum and openly checked their smartphones, and the oldest attempted to attract the attention of a young man who'd brought his younger sister. The young man seemed to suddenly decide the children's group was worth paying attention to.

Aunt Ellen and Uncle Amos had sat through one of the lectures, while Aunt Ellen snapped pictures to send to my mother. We'd been too busy for lunch breaks, so, at Bertie's suggestion, I'd called Josie and ordered drinks and sandwiches from the bakery. She'd delivered them herself.

Who else? I thought.

"Theodore Kowalski," Bertie said to Detective Watson. "He was here, drooling all over the collection."

"You let him do that?"

"I meant figuratively speaking," Bertie said, with a barely controlled sniff. "He fancies himself a rare-book collector. Wouldn't he just love to add a first-edition Austen to his collection?"

"Did you see him take the book out of the cabinet?"

"Well, no."

"Any of you?"

We shook our heads. I'd noticed Theodore. Either he'd been in the library several times throughout the day or he hadn't left. Standing in the alcove most of the time, not quite drooling but certainly admiring the books.

"That reminds me," I said. "He was poking around on Sunday."

"Aren't you closed Sundays?" Watson asked.

"That's the point. He was poking around *outside*. He said he was bird-watching in the marsh."

"Lots of folks do that."

"Yes, but Theodore didn't have binoculars or any other birding equipment. He'd come across the water in a boat less seaworthy than something found in a child's bathtub. I thought maybe he was going to try the door. See if we'd left it unlocked."

Bertie snorted. "As if. He's a menace, that one."

"I appeared and surprised him." I didn't mention that he'd almost given me heart failure in return. "I walked him back to his boat and waited until he rowed away."

Watson shrugged. "Nothing like a crime scene to attract snoops."

I bristled. "He was up to no good."

"And you know that how, Miss Richardson? Because he wasn't carrying binoculars? You said he came by Sunday morning. In daylight, I assume?"

"Well, yes."

"Not a lot of breaking and entering happens in broad daylight in public places."

I was going to retort, but instead I bit my tongue. Nothing I said seemed to have much effect on Detective Watson.

"Bertie," Butch said, neatly changing the subject. "I can't understand why you didn't lock the cabinet. If those books are as valuable as you claim."

Bertie's color rose in her cheeks. "This is a library. Not a bank. And those books *are* extremely valuable." Her shoulders slumped and she deflated. "Perhaps I should have, but we . . . I mean I . . . wanted people to be able to get close to them, and for my staff to be able to handle them as they saw fit."

"How much would you say that book's worth?" Watson asked.

"Not as much on its own as part of the full set," Bertie said, naming a sum.

Watson and Butch whistled simultaneously.

"For a book?"

"Yes, for a book," Charlene snapped. "Even more than your baseball-card collection, Butch."

"Hey, I've spent a lot of money on those cards," Butch said.

"One of my brothers collects cards," I offered.

"Do you know if he has . . ."

"Enough," Watson said. "You can trade cards later." He walked over to the cabinet. "I don't think there's any point in taking prints. Everyone and their dog has been through here the past couple days. I don't suppose y'all have security on the door?"

"I do some crowd control," Charlene said.

"Stopping little old ladies from stepping on each other's sensible shoes. I meant like a bar-code detector. Alarm. Things like that."

"This is a library. Not a jewelry store. And we're in the Bodie Island Lighthouse, not the Bronx. No, we do not have alarms."

"Perhaps you should get one," Watson suggested.

"Wouldn't that be like closing the barn door after the horses have escaped?" Charlene said.

"I assume you searched for this book?"

"We looked everywhere," Ronald said. "Absolutely everywhere."

"Butch, take a statement from these folks and get a description of the stolen goods. I'm going back to the office. I do," he looked at Bertie, "have a murder to investigate. Funny how trouble seems to be following you, Ms. James."

He left.

"I'll be in my office," Bertie said. "You don't need all of us. Let Ronald and Charlene go home."

"That should be okay," Butch said. "Lucy, will you give me a statement?"

"Sure."

Ronald and Charlene gathered their things, said good-bye, and went into the night, letting in air full of salt and sea spray.

Butch pulled a notebook out of the pocket of his leather jacket. "Talk to me, Lucy." Charles wrapped himself around his ankles.

"Butch, I am absolutely beat. I've been up all night researching nineteenth-century English literature, worried to death about Bertie, and now this."

"Why are you worried about Bertie?"

"Because she's suspected of a murder she didn't commit. Why do you think?"

He held up one hand and gave me a warm smile. "I'm on your side, Lucy. I have some idea what it's been like here the past couple of days. My mom wants to attend one of your talks and she couldn't get a reservation until next week. She's a local woman whose family's lived in Nags Head forever. She went to New York City on a bus tour once and didn't like it. Let's say she wasn't happy at being told she had to wait her turn in her own library."

"Mrs. Greenblatt. Sorry, I didn't make the connection. I spoke to her. She was"—I didn't say "rude and insulting"—"annoyed."

"Pay her no mind. She's having no trouble taking the money all these book tours are dropping at the artists' co-op. She's already sold most of the seashell art she makes for Christmas craft fairs."

I felt some of the tension melting out of my shoulders. "Like I said, I'm beat. Do you mind if I give my statement over a glass of wine upstairs?"

He gave me that gorgeous hazel-eyed smile. "Not a problem."

We made our way upstairs, Butch almost tripping several times over the adoring Charles.

I unlocked the door and waved in my guest. "Welcome."

Butch took a seat. Charles leapt onto his lap while I busied myself in my small kitchen—a glass of wine for me, a sweet tea for him.

I perched on the edge of a chair, sipped wine, took a deep breath, and tried to remember how the day had unfolded. I told Butch I'd seen *Sense and Sensibility* this morning before we opened; I was positive of that. I couldn't remember seeing it again, which didn't mean it wasn't there. Or maybe it was. I hadn't opened the cabinet myself, as I was usually busy giving my lecture. I named all the people I recognized who'd come into the library, but there were so many visitors.

"Anyone could have taken it," I said, "Poor Bertie. She'll be beside herself."

"Why do you say that?"

"Because the library's her responsibility, of course. We had no idea how popular the collection would turn out to be."

"She's not married, is she?"

"Bertie? No. I don't know if she's ever been, but Aunt Ellen didn't mention it. She doesn't have any children; she's kept busy with the library and her yoga studio."

"She has two jobs?"

"She's a yoga instructor also. Partner in the Asante Studio, Aunt Ellen told me."

"That's a nice place, out by the beach. Newly renovated. Rent must be high. I didn't know Bertie was involved. My mom takes classes there. She says she thinks the new owners have overextended themselves." His voice drifted off, and I tried to guess at his thoughts.

"They're investing in the future. That's what businesspeople do."

I sipped wine. It was cold and crisp and delightful. I wanted to take my shoes off and tuck my feet beneath me, but I didn't want to look as though I was giving Butch any hints. This was a police interrogation, after all. If I did decide to give Butch hints, it would be at a more opportune time.

Butch. Connor. Like that song in the movie version of *Bridget Jones's Diary*. It was raining men!

"Bertie ever seem to be short of money?"

I sat up straighter. "You can't be suggesting Bertie stole the book! That's out of the question."

"No one's out of the question, Lucy. Even you."

"Me?"

"Well, maybe not you. I'd better be going." He tucked his notebook away, finished his tea, and tried to nudge Charles off his lap. When gentle nudging didn't work, Butch had to resort to pushing, and then lifting and dropping. Charles glared at him and stalked off to the kitchen, as if that was his intention all along. Butch got to his feet. He loomed over me, all six foot five of him. I leapt up also. Only minimally better. And now I was so close I could smell the waves of male hormones coming off him, along with a spicy aftershave. I took a step backward, crashed into my chair, and almost fell into it. I dodged to my right, all the while blushing and grinning like an Austen spinster who's been asked for a dance by the handsomest young sublieutenant at the ball.

"Look, Lucy, I've been wanting to . . . spend some time getting to know you better. But with this case and everything, Watson's got me working day and night. Can I take a rain check?"

"Sure," I squeaked. "I mean, yes, that would be nice."

He headed for the door.

I remembered why he was here. "Theodore Kowalski has to be your number-one suspect. A book collector. Without suitable funds to sustain his passion. Found snooping around when the library was closed. Bertie warned me when I first arrived that we had to keep an eye on him."

"Bertie again. I'll mention it to Watson, although you'd be surprised at how many collectors who have plenty of money still get light-fingered."

"Speaking of Theodore, I told you he'd snuck up the back stairs during the party on Thursday. Shortly before Mr. Uppiton was found dead. What did he have to say for himself? I assume you questioned him."

"We did."

"And . . ."

Butch gave me a long look. He did have lovely brown eyes. "I suppose it can't hurt to tell you. He says he figured Bertie and Jonathan Uppiton had kept a piece of the collection behind to bring out in a big flourish, and he wanted to have a peek before everyone else."

"The notebook. He intended to steal it, the rat."

"Maybe. Anyway, he'd only been in the room a

minute when Uppiton came in and ordered him downstairs. And he left."

"I don't believe that. I saw him go up the stairs. I did not see him come down again."

"Lucy, I have to point out that that's not evidence. You didn't see Uppiton go up, nor Bertie."

"I was otherwise occupied."

"Right."

"Still, Theodore's in the frame. Isn't that what you policemen say? More than Bertie, I mean."

"Lucy, we are, as Detective Watson says, considering all avenues of inquiry."

"What about the rest of Jonathan's Uppiton's life? Apart from the library, I mean. Have you looked into his past? Maybe he has . . . had . . . enemies."

"You're relentless, you know that?"

"Yes."

"It's a good question. And, yes, we have considered that. He was involved in a nasty situation a number of years ago."

"What happened?"

"Uppiton was cutting down some branches on his property. He foolishly left one half-chopped when he went inside for lunch. Unfortunately, a neighborhood kid happened to be underneath when the branch broke. He, the kid, suffered a severe brain injury."

"How awful."

"It got very nasty. The parents sued, saying Uppiton shouldn't have left the branch unattended. It was a big tree, and an awfully large, thick branch."

"Fair enough."

"Uppiton sued back, saying the child was illegally

on his property and not being properly supervised by his parents."

"How old was this child?"

"Ten."

"Not really old enough to know better."

"Old enough to read. Uppiton did have an old Beware of Dog sign on his mailbox. Although he didn't have a dog. He claimed that was equivalent to a No Trespassing sign. Anyway, it was a nasty business all around. I remember my mom talking about it. She warned me and Jake not to go uninvited onto anyone else's property."

"What did the court decide?"

"That the kid and his parents were at fault. No settlement. Tension in town was running pretty high. Some people said the parents were railroaded because they were newcomers and couldn't afford a good lawyer. My dad said that Uppiton got lucky and the judge sided with him. He's never been a very popular guy around here."

"What happened to the family? Do they still live next to Jonathan?"

"No. They moved soon after. Can't blame them. They live in Nags Head now."

"If you were still a child, this must have been a long time ago. Why do you suspect the parents would seek revenge after all these years?"

"The kid died last month. He never recovered, and had spent fifteen years in an institution."

"How sad."

"Yeah. If Uppiton had been offed in his own house, or even in a dark alley, we might look at the kid's dad. But the guy was killed at a private function, in a building that's about as secure as it can be. No back door, no easily accessible windows. A crowded party, one where everyone knows everyone, and anyone who didn't belong would have stuck out like me at a garden party. We gave some thought to trying to figure out how an outsider would've been able to sneak in. And, don't forget, get out again. No way could we see it happening."

"What was the boy's name?"

"Fred. Fred Wozencranz."

"You said Mr. Uppiton wasn't well liked. What's that about?"

"He inherited a fair amount of money; whittled most of it away over the years, though. The Uppitons didn't exactly make their fortune by being nice to their workers. Old man Uppiton—again, so my dad tells me—and his own father were a couple of sons of bitches. Never lost a chance to cheat fishermen out of a fair price for their catch or plant workers out of their wages."

"What a couple of slimeballs."

"All that might not have mattered once they were gone if Jonathan had attempted to be a nice guy. But I guess niceness just isn't in the Uppiton blood. You met him, Lucy. The way he spoke to you that night was pretty typical."

"So, lots of people had reasons to want him dead."

"I didn't say that. I said he wasn't well liked. His father and grandfather were downright hated, and they died in their beds. Although, to hear the rumors, his father wasn't quite in his own bed, if you get my meaning.

"Watson'll be wondering where I am. I'd better be

off. Look after yourself, Lucy. You lock that door at night, I hope."

"Yes, I do."

"Good night."

"Good night, Butch."

I shut the door behind him and leaned up against it. My heart was racing, but I didn't know if it was from the proximity to Butch Greenblatt, the theft of *Sense and Sensibility*, or the ongoing question of who was responsible for the death of Jonathan Uppiton.

Butch had dismissed Fred Wozencranz's parents as suspects. But I wasn't so sure. Clearly Butch remembered the case very well. Did he have a soft spot for the parents, after what they went through? Did he not want to believe they might have sought revenge on Jonathan when their son died? The party was crowded. Plenty of people in a small space. It was supposed to be only for friends of the library, but I bet even Bertie didn't know everyone who had showed up. Easy enough for someone to slip in, spot the object of their hatred basking in the adoration of his colleagues, steal up the stairs, kill him, and get out again.

I decided to see if I could track down the Wozencranz family.

Chapter 12

When I came down the following morning, the air was full of the scent of brewing coffee, and I knew Bertie had arrived before me. Her office door was open, so after pouring myself a cup, I popped my head in to say good morning. She was on the phone and the look on her face caused me to swallow my words.

"Very well," she said into the receiver. "If you must. Nine o'clock."

She slammed the instrument back into its cradle. "That," she said, biting off the words, "was Mrs. Fitzgerald. I knew word of the theft of the book would travel quickly, but I dared hope it wouldn't be quite so fast. She has called an emergency meeting of the board. This morning. They'll be here in one hour."

"I'll put on the big pot of coffee, then. Do you want me to pop over to Josie's and get some muffins and things?"

"Let them starve. The hungrier they are, the sooner they'll leave. And no coffee, either. Don't even bring in extra chairs. I don't want them making themselves comfortable. The board usually meets at a hotel at lunchtime, giving themselves nice seats, coffee, sandwiches, and pastries. They'll be baying for blood, Lucy. Stay out of their way, and tell Ronald and Charlene to send them back here when they arrive and to go about business as usual."

"Can I bring you a coffee?"

She gave me a tight smile. "I'd like that, thanks, but wait half an hour. I need to do some stretches and meditation to get my head into a place where I can confront the board without going berserk. I've been so busy with everything that's going on, I've been neglecting my practice. I had to cancel some of my classes, and I don't like doing that. People could find a new instructor and they might not come back."

At nine o'clock, right on the dot, I unlocked the front door. Charles, who normally arrived at opening to accept the cries of adulation he took as his due, let out a piercing howl and fled for the break room, as Mrs. Fitzgerald, followed by the remaining members of the library board, marched in. I offered to show them to Bertie's office, but Mrs. Fitzgerald, who'd always been as polite as her old-family Southern roots would suggest, snapped, "We know the way."

The rest of the board, including Curtis Gardner, whom I recognized as Mrs. Uppiton's companion of the other night, passed me shaking their heads and muttering darkly to one another. Diane Uppiton brought up the rear. Her usual mutton-dressed-as-lamb attire was missing today, and she wore a very nice, and probably quite expensive, outfit of oatmeal slacks with a matching three-quarter-sleeved jacket over a baby-blue blouse. Diamond studs were in her ears.

"I think the meeting's for board members only," I said. "But I can pop in and ask if it's open to the general public."

Diane gave me a sly smirk. "Naturally, I will be taking my late husband's place on the library board."

"Note how Jonathan has been upgraded to late husband from late ex-husband," Ronald muttered, after the parade had disappeared down the hallway.

"Upgraded from two-timing son of a bitch," Charlene added. "Do you know if they were legally divorced, or just separated?"

"I wasn't interested enough to find out," Ronald said.

"It will certainly make a difference in the distribution of his estate. That outfit looks new to me. Did you catch the earrings?"

Members of the board were soon back, calling for chairs, ordering Charlene to put on coffee, asking where the cookies were kept.

I was in the break room, arranging my hat and getting a glass of water to sip during my lecture, when the door to Bertie's office flew open. The library board sailed past, heads high, faces set into hard lines. Diane Uppiton brought up the rear. She glanced into the staff room and saw me watching. "There will be some changes around here. Very soon." She marched away, heels tapping on the black-and-white marble floor of the hallway.

They hadn't bothered to shut the door to Bertie's

office after them. I knocked lightly and peeked in. "Would you like a glass of water? Tea?"

"Thanks, Lucy, but I'm fine."

"How'd the meeting go?"

"Better than I expected."

"Diane Uppiton seemed pleased with herself."

"She shouldn't be. Not yet. She and Curtis Gardner have it in for me, but Eunice Fitzgerald, Elaine Rivers, and Graham Luffe aren't so hasty."

"Is Diane really allowed to be on the board in her late husband's place?"

"So it seems. Although she, fortunately, is not the chair. Mrs. Fitzgerald will take that on until a new chair can be voted in."

"Do you think Diane cares about the library?"

"If anything, the opposite. This library was Jonathan's passion. He was difficult to work with— interfering, demanding, stubborn as a mule."

"I noticed."

"Yes, but he was also dedicated to the Lighthouse Library, although perhaps he wanted to see too much of his own glory reflected in it. But Diane . . . Jonathan loved the library, and Diane believes it came between them. Now, rather than maintaining his legacy, she intends to destroy it."

"You're exaggerating."

"I wish I were. Diane seems to have gotten close to Curtis Gardner all of a sudden. Until the reception the other night, she wouldn't have given him the time of day. Another library board member. She was flirting with him at the party, probably in an attempt to make Jonathan jealous."

"I saw them having dinner together at Jake's on Saturday night."

"Plotting my downfall."

"Maybe they were just eating good seafood?"

Bertie smiled. "I'm sure they can do two things at once. I've never liked Curtis. I doubted he joined our board because he had the interest of the library at heart. He never took a position, never made a decision; just followed Jonathan's lead. Now he's doing the same with Diane."

"But the others are behind you? Behind us?"

"For now they are being cautious. Obviously the theft of *Sense and Sensibility* is a huge blow to this library's reputation. Fortunately, we took out a generous insurance policy on the collection, so we won't be out of pocket. But I'm afraid we'll have trouble ever getting anything like it again."

"So, we have to find the book?"

"Yes. We do."

"Lucy, your fans are waiting," Charlene called from the end of the hall. I adjusted my hat and went to talk about Jane Austen.

Bertie had allowed us to close the doors for a half-hour lunch break. Normally we took lunch in shifts, but with being so busy, anyone left on the desk was overwhelmed. Charlene had been shutting the door, but she wasn't fast enough, and Louise Jane and Poor Andrew squeezed themselves through. "Library business," Louise Jane said airily.

I'd just put up my aching feet and my hand was hovering over the sandwich tray delivered from Josie's Cozy Bakery, when Louise Jane and Andrew breezed in. A shamefaced Charlene threw a *sorry* glance at Bertie. Charles retreated to a corner, where he watched us with narrowed blue eyes.

"I have a wonderful idea for a special exhibit." Louise Jane McKaughnan dropped into a chair in the break room.

"Wait until you hear." Andrew hovered at her shoulder. "It's a wonderful idea."

"Didn't I just say that, Andrew?"

"Sorry."

"We've got enough on our plate at the moment," Bertie said.

"I happened to run into Curtis Gardner and Diane Uppiton at the market," Louise Jane said, selecting a ham and cheese sandwich on rye. I bit into my crab salad on a fresh baguette. Josie's baguettes were the best I'd ever had, and this one was still warm from the oven. Andrew bypassed the sandwich tray and went straight for a pecan tart. He looked like a tourist in his blue-and-red-striped Bermuda shorts and Hawaiian shirt patterned with orange and purple flowers.

"They're giving you another chance, Bertie, to keep this library from falling into disaster," Louise Jane said.

"How kind of them."

"I thought so, too. Anyway, I told them my idea. . . ."

"It's a wonderful idea," Andrew said, pastry crumbs dripping down his chin.

"I can't wait to hear," Ronald mumbled. He glugged half his bottle of Arizona Iced Tea in one long gulp.

"And they loved it. Hauntings of the lighthouse! It will run from the end of the summer until Halloween."

No one exclaimed in delight, and Louise Jane deflated. But only for a moment. She turned to me. "There are so many fascinating stories about this lighthouse. Do you know that two men died during the construction? Crushed beneath the weight of the stones. It was late at night, a terrible storm building, and no one knows why they would have been working in those conditions. It's said you can hear the stones falling and the men crying out in terror on nights when a storm comes up from the south. And then there's the lighthouse keeper's little son—such a tragic story. The boy was playing on the top of the stairs, by the light, where he wasn't allowed. He fell. All the way to the bottom. He would have gone right past your door, Lucy, screaming in terror all the way. My grandmother says the thud when he hit the bottom could be heard all the way in Nags Head. You know that story, Ronald. Island children who visit the library sometimes see a little boy, wearing short pants and a cap, who asks them if they want to play with him. Remember when Roseanne Peterson went missing from story time, and how frightened we all were? She said she saw him, the little boy, beckoning to her to join him on the stairs."

"Roseanne Peterson wet her pants and was afraid she'd get a spanking when her mother found out. She hid behind the toy box and repeated a story her mother had told her. Mrs. Peterson has an overactive imagination. Like some people I could mention."

"Oh, you can mock me, Mr. New York, but I can

tell you stories that would make your hair stand on end. This whole area is full of ghosts. You do know why it's called Bodie Island, don't you, Lucy?"

"No. I don't," I said, once again stepping into her trap. Despite myself, I found the hair on my arms standing up at the thought of the ghostly little boy, never growing up, always searching for someone to play with him, through all eternity. My sandwich, delicious as it was, lay abandoned on the plate.

"Bodie, pronounced 'body.' Because of the number of bodies that washed up here over the years. Shipwrecks, pirates, ships lost at sea and never seen again. The Graveyard of the Atlantic."

"Louise Jane, you know as well as I do," Bertie said, "the island was named for the Body— B-O-D-Y—family."

A plaque by the front door announced that this was Body's Island Light House, erected 1872, and gave the latitude and longitude. I'd thought that nothing but a quaint spelling mistake.

"Was it, really?" Louise Jane said. "Or is that a pretty story made up so as not to frighten tourists?"

"This is a library, not a haunted house. As a library we deal in facts, not wild flights of imagination."

"There's no shortage of books, scholarly books as well as popular, dealing with the paranormal history of the Outer Banks."

"For once I have to admit that Louise Jane is right," Charlene said. "And they're very popular."

"See," Louise Jane gloated. "Anyway, Diane and Curtis just loved the idea."

"So there," Andrew added.

Bertie stood up. Her roasted vegetable and hummus sandwich remained uneaten. "Thank you for your suggestion, Louise Jane. Diane and Curtis do not run this library. I do. It's time to get back to work. Ronald, I need to talk to you about the schedule of children's activities. I got a phone call from . . ."

Charlene grabbed a chocolate-chip cookie and followed Bertie and Ronald out. I returned my attention to my baguette.

"I have plenty of books and other material," Louise Jane said. "My great-grandmother collected word-of-mouth stories and passed them to my grandmother, who wrote them down. They'll be a great addition to the exhibit. I'd be awful happy to lend them to you, Lucy."

"Thanks. Although I don't have much time to read for pleasure as long as the Austen exhibit's here."

"Oh, Lucy, honey, I didn't mean for you to read for *pleasure*. No, if you're going to live here, in the lighthouse itself, you need to understand what forces move in the dark. Not that anything's likely to happen, of course."

"Forewarned is forearmed," Andrew added.

Charles dug his claws into Poor Andrew's ankle.

That evening Theodore Kowalski dropped into the library as the last of the bus tours drove away, directed by Charlene to the craft co-op. Which not only had adjusted its hours so as to remain open after the library's Friday closing, but was suddenly selling barely dry paintings of long-dressed women in bonnets staring out to sea, Victorian tea sets, knitted book covers, and anything and everything that could be passed off as "olde" English.

"What's this I hear?" he boomed from the doorway.

"Go away, Teddy," Bertie said.

"I'll remind you, Albertina, that my name is Theodore." He walked into the library in a wave of cigar smoke and damp wool. "I spent the day in Raleigh, deep in research at the Duke library, and as soon as I turned on my phone, to my horror, I had a screen full of messages telling me you managed to lose *Sense and Sensibility*!"

"I didn't lose anything," Bertie said. "It was stolen."

"How could you be so careless?" Somehow, in Theodore's fake British accent, the sentence sounded even more accusing.

"Lucy, Charlene, did you see Teddy here yesterday?"

"Yup," Charlene said. "You spent a lot of time in the alcove . . . Theodore."

"A lot of time," I repeated.

"I resent your insinuations," he said, nose pointing to the ceiling.

"Okay," Bertie said, "No more insinuations. You stole it, Teddy. Give it back."

"I won't dignify that accusation with a reply."

"You must know the book is comparatively worthless without the rest of the collection."

"Great books are beyond monetary value."

"Great books are to be enjoyed by the public. Not by some foolish man gloating over them in the dark."

"Careful, Bertie," Charlene warned. A few patrons still lingered in the library. They'd stopped what they were doing and their ears were flapping.

"I'll forgive that slanderous statement in light of your obvious agitation, Bertie. Pay me no further mind. I'm going to have another peek at the remaining books."

"Lucy," Bertie ordered. "Check that the cabinet is locked. And don't take your eyes off him." As I'd told Butch, it was like shutting the barn door after the horses escaped, but after *Sense and Sensibility* disappeared, Bertie agreed to keep the rest of the books locked up.

Footsteps thundered down the main staircase. Ronald's regular Friday evening program for preteens had finished. Parents, who'd been eagerly listening to Bertie and Theodore squabble, gathered their children and left. Except for the staff and Theodore, the library was empty.

"It's five to eight," Bertie said. "Turn the sign to Closed, Charlene. "

"Do you have the cabinet key?" Theodore asked me.

"No."

"Run and get it, will you? There's a good lass."

"No." I couldn't resist adding, "Seen any interesting birds lately?"

"Birds? Oh, birds. Uh, yes. A yellow-breasted . . . something or other. Pay Bertie no mind, young lady. She and I have had our . . . disagreements in the past, but I like to think that our love of great books binds us together in respect and friendship."

I saw my opening. This might be the only chance

I'd get to speak to Theodore privately. Unless he came poking around under the pretense of bird-watching yet again.

I tilted my head to one side and smiled up at him. "That's great to hear. I love men who appreciate books."

He stretched to his full height and sucked in a nonexistent stomach. He carried with him an aura of cigar smoke, but his fingers showed no yellow nicotine stains and I had never seen him smoking. I wondered if he hung his tweed jackets in a smokehouse to get the effect. "Only natural, my dear. Great minds seek out similar." He gave me a wink that was probably intended to be flirtatious but rather looked as if he were attempting to clear a dust mote from his eye.

"At the reception the other night, I saw you go up the back stairs. Were you looking for something in particular? Something I might be able to . . . help you find?"

"How kind of you to offer. Bertie allows me complete freedom and the run of the library . . ."

I swallowed a laugh.

". . . and I wanted a private viewing of her big surprise before it was unveiled."

"Did you see the notebook?"

"Regretfully, no. Jonathan interrupted me and rudely ordered me downstairs, as though I were one of the hoi polloi." Theodore sniffed. He really was quite good at that. "Naturally, I complied. I didn't want to make a scene."

"What do you think Jonathan was doing upstairs?"

Theodore shrugged. "I've no idea. I know one

isn't to speak ill of the dead, but I've always believed in total honestly. Jonathan was, truth be told, somewhat of a philistine when it came to books."

"Honesty is always admirable," I said.

"Teddy," Bertie shouted. "We're closed."

He checked his watch. "It is two minutes before eight o'clock."

"Today I'm closing two minutes early. Get lost."

Theodore turned to me. His smile was strained. "That Bertie. Such a delightful tease. I am, of course, free to come and go as I like, but I don't usually care to take advantage. Some of the other, less educated patrons don't understand. Still, I try to keep Bertie happy when I can. Perhaps I'll see you tomorrow, my dear."

"I'll be here." I wiggled my fingers in farewell.

Theodore sailed out of the library.

I wasn't much of a detective. I'd been hoping he'd tell me a different story from the one he'd given the police, perhaps be more forthcoming if he wanted to impress me. I'd learned nothing, and all I'd achieved was making him think I liked him.

Chapter 13

Just when I thought the situation at the Bodie Island Lighthouse Library couldn't get any worse, it did.

We lost *Pride and Prejudice*.

Saturday morning, I noticed the volume was gone. I'd finished my first lecture of the day and was taking questions. As usual, the audience was mostly interested in learning more about Miss Austen's best-known book, and I had, over the past few nights, become something of an informal *Pride and Prejudice* scholar. A teenage girl asked why anyone would bother reading the book, now that so many movies had been made of it. Wasn't that good enough?

I was explaining that movies could capture the essence of the story itself, but to really understand Miss Austen and the customs and people of her times, her own words were invaluable. I swept my arm toward the cabinet containing the collection to illustrate my point.

My heart missed a beat and then it sped up. Only

four books, plus the notebook. I took a quick look around the room. Charlene sat at the circulation desk. A burst of childish laughter came from upstairs, where Ronald was leading story time. (He'd managed to beg and borrow all the long dresses, big hats, and woolen jackets and trousers in existence over this half of the state, so his young charges could play dress-up in Jane Austen's world.) Bertie, I remembered, was in her office, going over the budget, trying to find some funds, someplace, to pay us for all the overtime we were putting in.

"Thank you for coming," I said to my audience. I whipped off the heavy hat and bolted for the hall-way. I charged into Bertie's office without knocking. "*Pride and Prejudice*—did you take it?"

She looked up, her glasses perched on her nose, her mouth open in surprise. "Don't tell me. . . ."

"It's not there."

Bertie got to her feet in one swift movement. "I didn't authorize anyone to take it. Run upstairs and ask Ronald. I'll speak to Charlene. And, Lucy, please be discreet. We don't want word to get out."

I dashed up the spiral staircase to the children's library. The room was a riot of color, brightly painted walls, beanbag chairs, cushions, quilted wall hangings, soft toys for the younger children. Ronald, wearing his costume, sat on a stool in the center of the room, his young listeners spread out on the floor all around him. The kids looked absolutely delightful in their mishmash ensemble of historical garb. Some of them had brought clothes from home, and one cute little guy was highly era-inappropriate in a plumed helmet and breastplate. Charles dozed in a girl's lap, a big blue bow fastened to his head by a hair band. They all looked so adorable, I almost forgot why I was here.

Ronald saw me and raised one eyebrow.

"I'm sorry to interrupt, but I need to talk to you for a minute."

"Be right back, kids," he said. He lowered his voice when he reached me. "What's the matter?"

"Do you have *Pride and Prejudice*?" I whispered.

"No."

"Gone."

He opened his mouth to let out an obscenity and then remembered the little ears surrounding us. "Oh, dear."

I dashed downstairs. Bertie and Charlene were also conferring in low voices. I shook my head.

A patron asked Bertie if we had the latest Jamie Oliver cookbook. Our head librarian smiled and chatted as if she didn't have a care in the world.

At noon, she couldn't slam the door fast enough when she flipped the sign to CLOSED.

"Think, everyone," she shouted. "When did you see it last?"

We exchanged blank looks.

"We have a half hour to find that book. I don't dare hope it's been mislaid, so we have to search. The cabinet was locked when we closed up last night; I checked."

I rattled the handle. It was locked now.

But the book was not there.

"Who has access to the key?" Ronald asked.

"Anyone who knows where I keep it," Bertie said. The key hung on a hook on the back of Bertie's office door, where any one of us could grab it if we had reason to take out the books. Bertie's office was never locked. Why should it be? Staff records and budget papers were the only things that needed privacy, and they were kept in a secure cabinet.

"Where's the key now?" Ronald asked.

Bertie dug into her pocket and held up the tiny bronze key. "When Lucy told me we'd had another theft, I grabbed it. It was hanging in its usual place."

"How many keys to the cabinet are there?"

"One. Just this one. The cabinet was custom-made to hold this exhibit, and we asked for only one key to keep things simple."

With a strong feeling of déjà vu, we searched the library. "Whoever took it," Charlene said, "has to be pretty quick of hand. This room was full from the moment we opened the doors at nine."

"Did anyone see Teddy?" Bertie asked.

"He was in earlier," Ronald said. "He brought a deerstalker hat for the children's costumes. I thought it was nice of him to do that."

Bertie harrumphed. "Diane and Curtis came to my office, wanting to talk about next year's budget. I told them to make an appointment when all this is over."

"I saw them," I said. "Diane didn't look at all happy. I don't think they stayed after leaving your office, but I can't remember actually seeing them go out the door."

"Louise Jane was here," Charlene said. "She checked out some local history books, research for the haunted-island exhibit. Lucy was getting ready for her talk, and I was on the desk, so she and Poor

Andrew were in the reference room on their own. I can't say for how long though."

"Keep searching," Bertie said. "I'll be right back."

She came out of her office a few minutes later, carrying a book, a new Elizabeth George hardcover that had been waiting to be shelved, as well as a single piece of paper. Printed on the paper was an image of a book jacket that matched the covers of the Austen collection. She wrapped the paper around the spine of the George. "Won't fool anyone on close inspection. So let's make sure there is no close inspection." She unlocked the cabinet and arranged the book underneath *Persuasion*, so only the spine was showing. She then locked the cabinet and put the key in her skirt pocket. "From now on, this key remains with me at all times. If the library catches fire in the night, Lucy, you have my permission break the glass. Otherwise the books are not to be taken out for any reason."

Ronald, Charlene, and I exchanged nervous glances. "You can't keep this a secret, Bertie."

"Not for long, no, but I intend to delay informing the board for as long as possible. I hope not to have to tell either the general public or the books' owners that we have, shall we say, misplaced another volume. In the meantime, if I have to beat a confession out of Teddy, I will."

"You think Theodore's the thief?"

"Who else?"

Plenty of people, I didn't say.

"You have to report this to the police," Ronald said.

"I know, I know. Lucy, you seem to have estab-

lished a relationship with handsome Officer Greenblatt. Give him a call and explain what's happened."

I sputtered. "I haven't . . ."

"Whatever. They're already keen on charging me
with the murder of Jonathan and not inclined to listen to anything I have to say." She rubbed her forehead. "This is such a mess."

We turned at a knock on the door. The big clock
over the desk said 12:32.

Showtime.

"Not again," Butch groaned over the phone.

"Please," I said. "We want to keep this quiet.
We're hoping the thief will have a . . . uh . . . change
of heart and bring the books back."

"Right. Like they do that all the time."

"Please."

"I'll speak to Detective Watson, but I agree with
you, Lucy. There's no point in putting it in the papers. A book like that isn't going to turn up at a
pawnshop or be left on a park bench."

"Whoever took it knows it's valuable. If he tries to
sell it for what it's worth, a rare-book dealer would
ask for proof of providence, so he must want it for
his own collection."

"You say 'he.' You think it's a man?"

"Figure of speech." After talking about it with
Bertie, I was convinced that the thief was Theodore.
Who else was constantly in and out of the library,
knew his way around, and had a reputation for
taking what didn't belong to him? And was a book
collector short of funds to boot? "How's the investigation into the murder going? You can't possibly

believe Theodore's story, can you? He says he left when Jonathan told him to. We have no reason to believe that. He's not exactly the sort to meekly do what he's told. He seems to think the library is his personal domain."

I heard Butch chuckle down the line. "'We,' is it now?"

"Figure of speech."

"*We* are, as Detective Watson will tell you, keeping our options open. Do you like live music?"

"What?"

He cleared his throat. "There's a local band playing at a bar in Nags Head tonight. They play good old traditional bluegrass, and give it a local flavor. I thought it might be a nice introduction to the place for you."

I might not be a longtime resident, but I wasn't a complete newcomer, either. Still, it was nice of Butch of suggest it. "I'd like that."

"I'll pick you up at nine?"

"See you then."

I tucked my phone into my pocket with a smile. Call the police to report a theft, get a date. The Outer Banks was turning out to be an interesting place to live.

My smile faded as I remembered precisely how interesting it was these days.

Bertie's deception lasted until the end of the day.

A few minutes before closing, I was telling a middle-aged woman who'd gotten too much sun at the beach the dates of publication of Jane Austen's books when Diane Uppiton slid up to me. I'd noticed her earlier, peering into the cabinet, but other than wonder what had brought her back again, I paid her no further mind. From a distance, Bertie's fake *Pride and Prejudice* spine was a match to the others. "Miss Richardson," she interrupted. "If I may have a word."

"I'm busy at the moment. Give me a few minutes."

"Now, Miss Richardson."

The sunburned lady said, "Not a problem. I'm done. Thanks."

Ronald announced that the library was now closed and would reopen on Monday at nine. People began to file out.

"I need," Diane declared, "access to the cabinet."

"It's locked."

"So I noticed. Unlock it."

"I don't have the key."

Her eyes shone with spite, and I knew something was up. "It isn't in its proper place in Bertie's office, either."

"How do you know where the key's kept?"

"I was married to the chair of the board of this library, and I am now a board member myself. It will suit you, Miss Richardson, to remember that means I'm your employer. Open the cabinet."

"I don't have a key." And that was the truth. The key was in Bertie's pocket. Where Bertie was, I didn't know. Hiding in the closet, quite possibly.

"Is there a problem, Diane?" Ronald said. "We're closed now."

"I can see that, you fool. I want that cabinet opened. Immediately."

Ronald shrugged. "It's locked."

"So I see. No doubt it's locked so no one can see that one of the books—two of the books, in fact—are missing."

Three guilty faces stared at her. "What?" Charlene said.

Diane swept her arm in a theatrical gesture, pointing to the cabinet. She was quite clearly enjoying this. Ronald, Charlene, and I were not. "What," she demanded, "do you mean by that?"

Almost against our will, we leaned closer. I saw it first and sucked in a breath. "Oh."

One of the classic volumes was now titled *Pride and Prejudise*.

Not only had poor Bertie been so upset at the theft of the second book as to make a typo on her fake cover, but Ronald, Charlene, and I hadn't noticed.

Diane beamed as recognition crossed our faces. "Bertie has some explaining to do."

"As do you, Diane," said Bertie.

She had come into the room unnoticed and swooped immediately into the attack. Aunt Ellen had told me Bertie was a huge football fan. What did they say in football—the best defense was a good offense? "I've never before known you to have an interest in literature, or to spend any time in the library. And here you are, twice in one day. Any particular reason you are, uncharacteristically, wanting to get close to the Austen books?"

"As the newest member of the library board, it's my duty to know what's going on."

"Very commendable of you. I would have thought, however, you'd begin with the budget, or perhaps the staffing requirements. Not one particular item."

Diane harrumphed. "Earlier today you reminded me yourself, Bertie, that it wasn't a suitable time for budget talk. I'm wondering where else I can be of assistance." She waved a hand in the air. Her nails were long and painted a bright red that matched her lipstick. Today she wore a pink wool suit that looked far too warm for the day and too formal for a summer's Saturday afternoon in the Outer Banks. "Isn't literature the business of this library?"

"Not as far as the board's concerned. Your business is finances and the employees. We can discuss that another time, in the presence of the full board. It's been a long week, and my staff and I are very tired." Bertie walked to the door. "I'll let you out."

Diane began to follow. Then she stopped so abruptly, Charlene crashed into her. "Hey. You're changing the subject. I might not have a fancy-dancy university degree, but I can spell, you know. That book's fake."

"Yes," Bertie said. "I'll take you into my confidence, Diane. *Pride and Prejudice* is, like *Sense and Sensibility*, missing."

"You mean it was stolen."

"For now, let's say 'missing.' I don't want word to get out. We have to maintain the reputation of the library."

"Maintain your reputation you mean, Bertie."

"You wouldn't know anything about this, would you, Diane?"

Diane sputtered. "Are you accusing me?"

"Just asking."

"Well, I never. I couldn't have stolen the book if I'd wanted to. The cabinet is, I'll point out, locked."

"Good. Then you'll understand why I don't want this to become public knowledge. We need to find out what's going on. Can I count on your discretion, Diane?"

I watched, fascinated, as a battle raged across Diane Uppiton's excessively made-up face. The battle between knowing what was the right thing to do verses the desire to be purely malicious.

In the end it wasn't much of a contest. "I have to inform the rest of the board immediately. I don't know how you could be so careless, Bertie." She sailed toward the door, her head held high. So high she didn't see Charles slip between her feet. With a shriek Diane tumbled forward, arms windmilling to keep her balance. She crashed headfirst into the door.

As I took a step toward her to offer assistance, she whirled around, face red, helmet of hair mussed. "You stay away from me." She jabbed her index finger at me. "You're in it with her. I know you are." She wrenched open the door and disappeared into the salty air.

Chapter 14

The bar where Butch took me that night was packed. When we walked in, all conversation died as every head in the place swiveled in our direction. Butch looked over heads and spotted Josie, who was waving to us from the front of the room by the stage. Josie made gestures to indicate we should join her and Aunt Ellen.

"Jonathan Uppiton would have put a stop to it," I heard one woman say as I followed Butch through the room.

"Albertina James," her companion said, "never did have a lick of common sense."

"All that yoga nonsense has addled her brain," a man commented.

Josie and Aunt Ellen had snagged seats on a comfortable although battered couch at the foot of the stage. Josie wrapped me in a big hug. "I heard the news. First *Sense and Sensibility* and now *Pride and Prejudice*. You must have some idea of who's doing this, Butch."

Butch glanced at the crowd of onlookers not bothering to pretend they weren't paying rapt attention to us. "Can I get you a drink, Lucy?"

"White wine, please."

"Come on," Josie said, "you two can squeeze in beside us. The band's about to come on."

I took a seat. The couch was badly sprung and I slid lower than I might have liked. The bar was done up like a sixties-era coffee shop. The furniture was mismatched and ragged, the low stage little more than a platform along one wall. Guitars leaned against the walls and a spaghetti-like tangle of black cords ran from electrical outlets into microphones and amplification equipment. Photos of smiling people playing music or lifting beer glasses covered the walls, along with posters advertising concerts as far back as 1959.

"Does the entire town know what happened?" I said, struggling to get upright once again. Fortunately, I'd dressed appropriately for the venue in capri-length jeans and a summer T-shirt.

"It's pushed the murder from the forefront of everyone's mind, I can say that," Aunt Ellen said.

"Is everyone against Bertie?"

I accepted my glass of wine from Butch, and wiggled closer to Aunt Ellen to give him room on the couch.

"Not everyone. But there are whispers that this wouldn't have happened if Jonathan Uppiton was still around."

"That's ridiculous. Mr. Uppiton was the chair of the library, not the head librarian. The day-to-day running of the library is the staff's responsibility, not the board's." I realized what I was saying and snapped my mouth shut. I might as well have come right out and accused Bertie, as well as the rest of us, of being careless, if not outright thieves. "Bertie's confident the books will soon be recovered."

Aunt Ellen patted my knee. "I'm sure they will be, honey."

The band trotted on stage, and conversation ended.

Despite our troubles, I had a wonderful evening. The music was great, the company even better. Aunt Ellen and Josie left after the first set and Butch and I had the couch to ourselves. During the breaks, we chatted comfortably about my life in Boston (of which I left out a considerable amount) and his life growing up on the Outer Banks. Various people came over to chat with us, but (thankfully) no one asked about the police investigation into Jonathan Uppiton's murder or the rapidly dwindling Austen collection. Butch got more than a few winks and nods from his friends, and I blushed to realize they thought we were dating.

Are we?

"Ready to go?" he said as the band packed up their equipment after the last set.

"Yes. It's been a long day. I enjoyed that very much. Thank you for bringing me. What fun music."

"Glad you liked it." He got to his feet and held out his hand. I took it in mine, and he pulled me up. We stood together for what felt like a long time, close but not touching. His bulk loomed over me and I had to crane my neck to look up at him. His eyes were warm and soft, his lips full and pink.

"Lucy, I . . ."

"Having a nice evening?" Louise Jane McKaughnan trilled.

Butch stepped back. "Very nice."

"I'm awful proud of you, Lucy," Louise Jane said.

As was becoming my habit, I stepped into her trap. "What do you mean?"

"Keeping up such a strong front. After all that's happened. Still living at the lighthouse." She shuddered in delight. "You're so much braver than me. I don't think I could bear to be alone in that place, not with the *permanent resident* on the move."

"You're brave, Louise Jane," Poor Andrew said.

"I'm making a point, Andrew."

"Permanent resident?" I asked.

"Strange things have always been happening in that place. Books rearranged in the night, furniture overturned. It's the little boy, they say, the lighthouse keeper's small son, up to mischief when no one's around. Tell her, Butch."

Butch shrugged his big shoulders. "Stories—just stories."

"You saw it."

"I was a kid. I don't know what I saw."

"Butch and I grew up together. Did you know that, Lucy? We've always been such *great* pals. We were—what—fifteen, sixteen that night?"

"Just kids." Butch was looking highly uncomfortable. He would have walked away, had Louise Jane not put her hand on his arm. Her grasp looked more like an iron grip than a friendly touch.

Louise Jane lowered her voice. Almost against my will, I leaned in closer to hear. Andrew was staring at the spot where Louise Jane's hand touched Butch's heavily muscled arm. Poor Andrew did not look any more pleased than Butch was, but he, characteristically, said nothing. "A bunch of us had rowed over to the marsh after dark. We were going to have a late-night picnic. Celebrate winning the state championship. Some of the guys brought beer, although we were underage. Butch and Lorraine MacIntyre went farther down the boardwalk to do some celebrating together. Private celebrating."

Butch shifted uncomfortably.

Louise Jane turned to me, her smile as sweet as that of a circling shark. "That was before the lighthouse was turned into the library. The last lighthouse keeper had moved out many years before, when the light had been automated. The building was empty for years, falling into disrepair. It was winter, so the area was pretty much deserted—just us, a group of high school friends, the blazing fire, the stars overhead. To this day I can still hear that scream." Louise Jane shivered.

"Scream?" I squeaked. "I mean, did someone scream?"

Lorraine came down that path so fast, it was as if something was chasing her. Of course the boys laughed at first, thinking you'd been trying something you shouldn't, Butch. But I knew right away that wasn't it. Your face was as a white as a sheet."

"What happened?" I asked him.

"It was nothing. A scare—that's all. Lorraine had an active imagination. She's working in Hollywood now, writing screenplays. Doing very well, from what I hear. Come on, Lucy. Let's go."

"That's not what you said at the time, Butch."

Louise Jane turned to me. "What they told us, when they were calm and breathing normally once again, is that when Lorraine and Butch reached the end of the boardwalk, they saw a light in the window. The very window where your room is now, Lucy. Remember, the lighthouse was abandoned back then. No one should be *inside*. They saw a light where one shouldn't be, but more than that. A face was staring out at them. A round white face, framed in long, dark hair, its mouth open in a scream of unending terror."

"I thought you said the ghost was a mischievous little boy."

"The boy wanders the library. I told you he died falling from the top when playing. But the specter Butch and Lorraine saw was the Lady. Frances, the young bride, locked in that room by her old husband. She never leaves that room. She *cannot* leave that room."

"You should lead the haunted walking tour, Louise Jane," Butch said. "You'd do a good job, the way you can embellish old stories and make them sound almost real." He pulled his arm out of her grip. "Let's go, Lucy."

Butch didn't know about Louise Jane's plan for a special Halloween exhibit. Rather than taking offense at his words, she beamed. "What an excellent idea. And that's only the specters *inside* the lighthouse, Lucy. I haven't mentioned the Civil War soldiers patrolling outside. They say on some nights . . ."

"They say the moon is made of green cheese," Butch said. "And I'm going to turn into a pumpkin at midnight if we don't get out of here."

He took my hand and led the way across the room.

Louise Jane called out to me one last time. "It shouldn't be a problem leading the haunted lighthouse tour into *the Lady's* room, Lucy. You'll be gone by Halloween, isn't that right?"

Chapter 15

"I hope you had a nice evening, despite how it ended," Butch said as we walked to his car.

"I did. Thank you for bringing me."

"Don't pay any attention to Louise Jane. She loves nothing more than to stir the pot. Even back in school, she'd leave some poor guy holding the ball that broke the principal's window while she smiled, all sweet and innocent."

Judging by the set of his jaw, I suspected that story wasn't rhetorical. "She had a way, even then, of attracting lapdogs like Andrew. Guy needs to grow a spine." Butch hadn't released my hand, and I was enjoying its solid warmth. "That story she told you. It didn't really happen like that. I'll admit that I was thinking of trying to touch Lorraine's . . . uh . . . breast." We passed under a streetlamp, and I noticed a blush cross Butch's face. "She started screaming, practically scared the life out of me. When I realized she hadn't even noticed my feeble attempts to get fresh, I turned around to see what had scared her. A light was shining from a window in the lighthouse, but I didn't see anyone there. It wasn't all that late, either, and although the lighthouse didn't have a keeper, it wasn't unusual for people to go in to do maintenance and other chores. But Lorraine insisted she'd seen a ghost, and I, well, what can I say? I was at the age when I thought it would be fun to scare a girl so I could act the big strong man, and I went along with it."

"Thanks for telling me that," I said. "I know the lighthouse is old and it has a lot of history, but I've never felt anything but comfortable there. Nor has Charles. Animals are sensitive to the paranormal, isn't that what they say?"

"The paranormal is the least of your worries right now. I don't like these books disappearing."

I tried to laugh. "Neither do we. A librarian's worst nightmare."

"Think about it, Lucy. Why one book at a time? Why not take all of them at once?"

"Easier to get one book out of the library under a coat or in a small bag or purse?"

"Might be. It might also be that this is more than a simple theft."

"What do you mean?"

"What are we talking about right now, Lucy? What was everyone in the bar talking about? A man was killed in that library, not more than a week ago, but the total focus of this town has shifted onto two books."

"You think the books are being stolen to take attention away from Mr. Uppiton's murder? That's ridiculous. Wouldn't the killer, whoever he is, not want to do anything to draw attention to himself? Suppose he or she gets caught taking the books?"

We reached Butch's car. I might have expected a guy like Butch to drive something manly. An SUV or a truck with big tires, maybe a Mustang, bright red. Instead, he drove a practical Ford Focus. His legs were so long, the driver's seat was pushed almost up against the back passengers' seats. He'd parked under a streetlamp, and the light threw deep shadows onto his handsome face. The night was warm and soft, full of the scent of the sea.

"Look, Lucy. It's been a really nice evening and I hate to end it on a downer. Any more of a downer than Louise Jane, that is. But haven't you considered that the person best positioned to steal the books would work in the library itself?"

"Librarians handle books all the time, some of them very rare and valuable. We don't *steal* them, Butch."

"Not normally, no." His voice trailed off.

"What are you saying?"

"I'm saying that Bertie has reason to create chaos and confusion. Distract the police, shift attention, mess up the investigation into the killing."

"That's ridiculous. Bertie told us to keep the theft of *Pride and Prejudice* quiet. The last thing she wanted was for word to get around."

"So she said. How well did that work out?"

"What do you mean?"

"Lucy, consider that fake book jacket. She spelled 'prejudice' wrong. How could an educated woman, and a librarian to boot, make a mistake like that?"

"You might as well ask how I, also a qualified librarian, didn't notice the mistake. No, Bertie's too smart to make a deliberate error of that nature in front of us. But people make crazy mistakes when they get flustered. And other people don't notice things right in front of their eyes."

"I'll have to give you that one," he said. "But that's the way Detective Watson's thinking. I thought you deserved to know, that's all."

"I'd like to go home now."

"Sure," Butch said.

I've never believed in ghosts. My practical New England upbringing and no-nonsense parents guaranteed that the paranormal had no place in our lives. I never, ever go to horror movies, but in my reading life, I enjoy a good ghost story now and again, as long as it's not too scary. Nothing modern, but I've enjoyed classics such as "The Legend of Sleepy Hollow," "The Tell-Tale Heart," and *The Haunting of Hill House.*

I didn't sleep well that night. My dreams began with handsome police officers driving fast cars, but soon turned into terrifying creatures dripping blood onto leather-bound books. I tossed and turned so much, Charles finally moved to the window seat to get a good night's rest.

I woke early, when the sun was an orange ball touching the ocean.

Here I was, living in the place I loved most in the world, and I'd barely stepped foot out of the library. It was a beautiful day, and I was determined to enjoy it. I showered and dressed quickly and pulled shorts and a T-shirt over my bathing suit. I stuffed my unruly hair into a Boston Red Sox baseball cap, and threw a towel, sunscreen, a bottle of water, and *The Moonstone* into my beach bag.

First, I had to remove Charles from the bag. The beach was not a place for library cats.

I began my day at Josie's Cozy Bakery. The place was quiet at seven a.m., so Josie came out to say hi while I sipped my latte and gobbled down a muffin, heavy with juicy, plump blueberries, and warm from the oven. The café smelled of yeast, cinnamon, pastry, and good strong coffee. "I've got a tray of scones almost ready," my cousin said, "so I have only a minute. Nice to see you with Butch last night." She wiggled her eyebrows. "He's nice, isn't he?"

"Yes."

"Good-looking, too."

"Is he? I hadn't noticed."

She laughed. "And, dare I mention, single. He dated a cop from Raleigh for a long time, but they broke up a couple months ago. She, or so I heard, dumped him for another guy."

"He's on the rebound, then. That's never good."

"He wasn't all that upset about it, Jake says. Butch knew the relationship wasn't going anywhere. Then again," Josie teased, "there's Connor McNeil. Dr. McNeil, that is."

"He's also nice," I said.

"And also single."

"Josie, I've just arrived here. I'm in the midst of changing my life. I'm meeting people and enjoying making new friends. That's all."

"I'm pleased that you are," she said.

We jumped at a loud crash from the kitchen, followed by a string of curses. "A new assistant," Josie said. "She's not working out too well. Catch you later, Lucy." She hurried away to attend to the disaster. I hoped it wasn't the scones hitting the floor.

I sipped coffee and nibbled on my muffin while I watched the bakery get ready for the day. First through the doors were ruddy-faced men and women, the sort of hearty tourists who got up early to see the sun rise over the ocean, then early-morning joggers, some with kids in those strollers specially built for running. The next wave consisted of older couples or young families, faces scrubbed, carefully dressed, heading off to or returning from church. After them the tourists began to dribble in, and the seating area rapidly filled with good-natured conversation and much laughter. I didn't see my cousin again, just a steady stream of wonderful things coming out from the back, to be arranged on the shelves and the counter. Where they didn't remain for long.

It was nice to see Josie's business doing so well. I hoped she'd be able to last through the winter, when most of the tourist traffic dried up. On my way out, I stopped at the door to let four businessmen in. Two of them snagged a table and spread out binders and papers in front of them, while their friends went to the corner to order. Locals. A good sign.

It was still early, and I had the day free. I was so looking forward to having some time to myself, but I might not have another chance to speak to the parents of Fred Wozencranz, the boy who'd been critically injured while playing in Jonathan's yard. It was Sunday, the best time for finding people at home.

I didn't expect them to break down and confess to me, a total stranger, that they'd killed Jonathan Uppiton. But I might be able to see if I recognized one of them, if either had been at the party. Then I could tell the police. I've got a pretty good memory for faces (that goes with my perfectly dreadful memory for names) and, unlike everyone else at the reception, I'd been on high alert. I was meeting a roomful of people for the first time and desperate to make a good impression. I didn't have anything to drink all evening, and I'd paid close attention to all the people there. (Except for when I was being charmed by Butch and Connor, but the rest of the time I'd been paying close attention.)

Wozencranz wasn't a common name, and I found them easily enough just by checking the online phone book. Ron Wozencranz. Nags Head. Not far from Josie's.

I found the house with no difficulty. It was small, tucked into a side street. Some of the neighboring houses, cheap summer rentals, were in poor repair. But the one I was interested in had a fresh coat of beige paint on the siding and shutters. Two plastic flowerpots full of red and white geraniums stood beside the front door. I drove past and parked my car on the next block. Then I walked down the street, trying to march purposefully, as though I had reason to be here.

I walked up the recently swept path. A ramp had been installed leading to the front door. I knocked briskly.

The door opened and a woman's head popped out. She wore a flowered red dress with all the shape of a tent. That would be because she weighed about three hundred pounds. No way she had dashed up the lighthouse steps and slipped quietly out again.

"Good morning," I said cheerfully. "Isn't it a lovely day?"

She gave me a warm smile. "That it is, hon. Can I help you?"

"Are you Mrs. Wozencranz?"

She laughed. "Heck, no, hon. I'm May-Belle Nicholson. Mrs. Wozencranz passed some five years ago."

"I'm sorry to hear that. Is Mr. Wozencranz at home, then?"

"He sure is, hon. I've just dropped in to help him get ready for church. I'll call him for you."

A man's voice came from behind her. "Who's that, May-Belle? Are they selling something? Send them away."

May-Belle half turned, and I was able to peer around her bulk. A man was coming down the corridor. He was about the right age, in his late forties. His thin brown hair was neatly combed, and he was dressed in a lightweight suit and a tie.

"Lady lookin' for you, Ron." May-Belle said.

He hadn't climbed the lighthouse stairs, either. He was in a wheelchair. A blanket was tossed over his knees, but I could tell that his legs were little more than sticks.

"Hi. I'm Ruth," I said, coming up with the name on the spot. "I'm from the United Pentecostal Church of Our Lord. I was hoping to invite you to join our congregation, Mr. Wozencranz. You, too, May-Belle."

He waved his hands at me. "Get away. I've my own church."

"You'll like our church better." *What a thing to say!* I didn't even know where my ridiculous ideas were coming from.

"Finish your breakfast, Ron," May-Belle said. "It's almost time to go." She stepped onto the porch and half closed the door behind her.

"I'm sorry," I said. "I must be thinking of another Mr. Wozencranz."

She laughed again. I liked May-Belle very much. I almost invited her to come to the library. Then I remembered my name wasn't really Ruth.

"No other folk by that name around here," she said.

"A brother or son, maybe?"

The smile faded from her face. "Poor Ron, he doesn't have anyone. Anyone, that is, except the good folks from our church. You see, his only child died not long ago."

"I'm sorry to hear that."

"I can't say it was a blessing, but the poor boy wasn't right in the head. Some terrible accident when he was little. Ron's had a hard row to hoe. His wife died in the accident that left him unable to use his legs. But he's a good man, a real good man. His church family does what we can."

"That is so nice of you," I said.

"What's that church you say you're with?"

"United Evangelical Church of Christ. I think. I mean, yes, that's it."

"Never heard of it. You get tired o' goin' there, hon, you'd be welcome with us."

"Thanks. Gotta run. Uh, have a nice day."

I dashed down the street, feeling like a total and complete fool.

I drove out of Nags Head on Highway 12, toward the lighthouse. Instead of turning right, back to my aerie, I turned left, into the Cape Hatteras National Seashore, and parked at Coquina Beach. I left my beach things in the car and slipped off my sandals. I walked for miles and for hours, through the surf and the soft sand, watching the rhythmic movement of the waters of the blue ocean, thinking about everything and nothing. Gulls swooped overhead, and sandpipers darted through the waves on their long, fast legs. The surf was high and waves pounded the shore.

Unlike farther north, in the towns of Nags Head, Kill Devils Hills, and Kitty Hawk, there was no development here. No beach homes or holiday rentals. Just the dunes, the beach, the sea. And not many people, either. Fishermen and -women were out, sitting at the water's edge, watching their long poles arcing into the surf. I wondered, not for the first time, at the attraction of the sport. Looked mighty boring to me. These people didn't even cast, just sat and stared at their poles and waited. Perhaps they enjoyed the peace and time for contemplation. A young family, with three squealing toddlers in colorful bathing suits and matching ribbons in their hair, were clamming. Or attempting to clam. They had a proper rake, but nothing that I could see to take their catch home in. The children laughed and splashed in the waves, and I guessed that was the point in itself.

When I finally tired of walking, I retraced my steps. The fishing people didn't look as though they'd so much as twitched in all the time I'd been away. I collected my beach paraphernalia from the car. The ocean was rough today, as it ⟨...⟩ the coast, so rather than ⟨...⟩ up to my knees and let the ⟨...⟩ Then I got my book and sat at ⟨...⟩ sand, with my legs stretched ou⟨...⟩ pounding surf. I was content to sit ⟨...⟩ time.

People tell me that e-book readers a⟨...⟩ic for carrying piles of books, light and easy to r⟨...⟩. But I'm not converted yet. The tide was coming in; a rogue wave roared ashore, splashing me and my book with salt water. I certainly wouldn't be able to sit here with an electronic device in my hands.

When my back started to ache and the water was rising higher and higher, I struggled to my feet, unfolded my beach chair and umbrella, got snacks and a soda out of my small cooler, and read on. Yes, *The Moonstone* would do perfectly as an introduction to classic novels for my group. We would talk about the origins of the mystery genre as an illustration of how much influence the classic novels still have on our entertainment habits today.

If my group ever got started, that is. I put down the book and stared out over the blue sea sparkling in the sun.

I felt as though a dark cloud had suddenly appeared overhead. A single, dark cloud, intended only for me. If the reading group didn't start? If the library had to close under the scandal and the theft? What on earth would I do then?

There were other libraries, of course. Lots of them. One in Kill Devil Hills, one in Manteo, more libraries all over the state. But in the short time I'd been here,

Lighthouse Library had planted it-
in my heart. That crazy library, with the
whitewashed walls, the spiral stairs, curling
upward in imitation of a nautilus shell, the too-small
rooms crammed with too many books. And my
lovely, cheerful, welcoming lighthouse aerie.

Ronald, Charlene, Bertie. My coworkers, people
I'd already grown to love.

Bertie.

The sun was behind me now, and my umbrella
cast a long shadow. Time to finish my book, then
pack up and go home. Right now, the best I could do
for Bertie and the library was the very best job I
could do.

Chapter 16

Monday morning, Bertie came in carrying a big cardboard box with Josie's logo. My nose twitched at the scent of warm, fresh baking. "For us?" Charlene asked hopefully.

"No. I have a very special meeting this morning and want it to go well. Put the coffee on, will you, Lucy? I bought fresh cream."

"Are you expecting the library board?" I asked.

"As if I'd cross the street to feed that lot." She put the box on the circulation desk. It was quarter to nine, and we were still closed. "Is Ronald here yet?"

"Arriving now," Charlene said as our children's librarian's 1996 Honda Civic swept into the parking lot.

"You three," Bertie said, when Ronald had joined us, "have been magnificent through all this."

"Just doing our jobs," Ronald said.

"You've been doing far more than that. Not a word of complaint about the extra hours you're putting in. Lucy up all night, studying up on Jane Austen; Ronald with your costumes and extra programs;

Charlene giving up your precious research work to answer yet another question on where in North Carolina Miss Austen lived."

We all smiled. Yes, that was a question we got a lot.

"And the murder of Jonathan and the theft of the books on top of it. The Austen collection has proved to be popular beyond my wildest dreams. I was informed yesterday that the number of visitors to town last week was up more than ten percent from last year. The people who supply the craft shops and the art galleries are working around the clock to produce more stock, the demand for holiday rentals is up, some of the B&Bs and hotels are turning away customers, and the restaurants are bursting at the seams. Josie told me this morning she's had to hire more help. I had a call yesterday from a friend who works in the shop at the Elizabethan Gardens. She says they and the Fort Raleigh National Historic Site are, and I quote, 'delightfully overwhelmed with customers.' Some of our more patriotic readers don't want to believe that Miss Austen was a loyal subject of George the Third, and have decided she's more suited to Queen Elizabeth the First."

Charlene, Ronald, and I laughed. But Bertie did not. "Everyone's thriving and happy and making money hand over fist."

"That's good," Charlene said. "But you're not sounding happy about it, Bertie."

"You're darn right I'm not happy. Everyone, from Josie at the bakery to Mr. Miller with his handcrafted wooden lighthouses—some of which, I'll point out, he has begun adorning with Miss Austen's portrait—is doing well."

Ronald laughed. "No wonder people think she's an Outer Banks girl. Her face has started appearing on everything."

"Everyone's raking in the dough. Everyone except us. We're packed to the gills, but we don't charge admission."

"Of course not," Charlene said, shocked. "We're a library!"

"Right. We don't charge to see the books. We don't have jams or teacups to sell. Ronald entertains and educates the kids while Lucy does the same for the adults, and Charlene turns away her core patrons because she doesn't have time for them. We're all working incredible amounts of overtime without getting paid for it. I've had to dig deep into next quarter's book-purchasing budget to buy more books by Austen and her contemporaries, which means I won't be able to get many fall releases. And fall, as we all know, is the time when the biggest bestsellers are released. I don't want to be the one to explain to George O'Reilly why we aren't stocking the latest James Patterson."

"So, you are going to speak to the board, then?" Ronald said.

"Pooh. What can they do but shift money around and tell me to find efficiencies? And then take themselves out for lunch. On *my* budget." Bertie hefted the bakery box. "No, I'm going straight to the top. This library has been a boon to the town, and it's time for the town to pay up. Good, here he is now. Lucy, you may admit His Honor."

I opened the door for Connor. He stopped in the doorway and studied us. We were all watching him, probably like kids seeing Santa come down the chimney. "Sorry, have I interrupted something?"

"No."

"Nothing."

"Off to work now."

We scurried to our respective tasks while Bertie escorted the mayor to her office. It was five to nine, so I left the door open. The first tour bus of the day was pulling into the lot. I went into the back to make the coffee.

"I can't deny that would be a help, Connor," Bertie was saying as I carried in the tray. "But, really, Louise Jane?"

My ears twitched as I settled the tray on Bertie's desk beside the box of Josie's baking.

Connor gave me a smile. "Thanks, Lucy. Your first week here hasn't exactly been uneventful, has it?"

"I'm getting used to it."

"Lucy's doing a wonderful job," Bertie said. "We wouldn't have been able to manage without her."

I closed the door behind me as I left the office to once again plunge into the world of Jane Austen.

Connor was ensconced with Bertie for about an hour. I was in the lounge, arranging my attire for the lecture, when they came out. They were both smiling, so I guessed the meeting had gone well.

"You look great in that hat, Lucy," Connor said. "But Jane Austen wouldn't have worn anything so elaborate, would she?"

I lifted my fingers to my lips. "No, but don't tell anyone. It's the best we could do at short notice." I shifted the substantial weight of the ornate hat. "And," I coughed, "without money for a proper costume."

"Bertie and I have come to an arrangement. I recognize the value of this library to the town, and I've agreed to a substantial increase in the library budget for the duration of the summer."

"We do appreciate it, Connor," Bertie said.

"What the commissioners will have to say when I present the figures to them, I have no idea. But I should be able to bring them around."

"Didn't I see a No Vacancy sign hanging outside Mrs. Kimstock's B&B on Tuesday? Isn't Ed Miller, he of the popular lighthouse statues, one of the commissioners?"

"Don't worry, Bertie," Connor said, "I'll make your case for you." He gave me a smile and left.

"Sounds like that went well."

"It did. Connor's sticking his neck out, promising us an increase without speaking to the commissioners. But we need that money now, and he knows it. I want you to submit your overtime to me, Lucy. I'll tell Ronald and Charlene to do the same. Don't forget to include the time you've spent researching after hours."

"I heard mention of Louise Jane. . . ."

"We need another staffer, Lucy. Mainly to be on the circulation desk so Charlene can get back to her own job in the reference library. Checking out books doesn't require a qualified librarian, and we need someone immediately. Louise Jane is, as we know, very keen on working here. I'm going to call her now. Offer her a job, and see if she can start tomorrow. I expect she'll say yes."

Louise Jane did indeed say yes. She was on our doorstep before lunch, looking very much like the cat who had bought the whole dairy factory. She swept in, not followed, for once, by Andrew. Maybe the guy did have a life apart from Louise Jane after all.

"I've come to sign my employment papers," she said to Charlene and me. "As you're so busy, I'll tell Bertie I'm happy to start work right away. I remember how it's all done. Lucy, why don't you show me to my desk, so I can get settled in."

"You don't have a desk," Charlene said. "You're a temporary employee, remember? You can leave your purse in the staff room. It'll be safe there."

"As safe as *Sense and Sensibility* and *Pride and Prejudice*? I don't think so."

"I'll take you to Bertie's office," I said.

"That's hardly necessary. I know this library an awful lot better than you do, Lucy." She smiled at me and patted my arm. "Don't worry about a thing."

"Worry? About what?" *That trap again!*

"Why, about the job being too much for you. I suppose at your last job—somewhere in Boston, wasn't it?—you could relax at your desk, take time selecting books, help the occasional freshman who needed guidance, leave the office on time. Not like working in a real hands-on public library, is it?"

I remembered some of the teachers and grad students I'd dealt with at Harvard. One rarely became a full professor at Harvard because one was accommodating.

"Anyway, I'm here now," Louise Jane went on. "I'll take some of the pressure off you. Do you want me to give the afternoon lecture?"

"No."

"Tomorrow, maybe. Let me know when you need a break. I'm here to help." Something about her smile made me think of bottomless pits.

Charlene burst out laughing as Louise Jane disappeared down the hall. "That put you in your place. You're lucky she doesn't think you worked in the Bodleian. She told me that the English stop twice a day for afternoon tea."

"Wouldn't that then be afternoon and morning tea?"

"I have to confess that I can't stand Louise Jane, but I am happy she's here. I have e-mails from two weeks ago I haven't had time to answer yet, never mind all the rest of my work."

It would be nice to have another set of hands around the place. But now that Louise Jane's toe was firmly planted in the door, I wondered how easy it would be to get rid of her when the extra staff was no longer needed.

"Excuse me, miss," said a rotund, middle-aged woman with a deep Scottish burr. "Can ye suggest a place we could go fer lunch? Something *American*. We didn't expect to find the Outer Banks quite so much like back home."

"Many places are advertising high tea but providing afternoon tea," a man, equally rotund and Scottish, said. "I dinna think they know what high tea means."

"We dinna come ta America ta buy souvenir tea towels with images o' the Queen, ye ken."

"You might have lost the colonies back in 1776," I said, "but it looks like you're taking us over again, with Miss Austen in the vanguard. Jake's Seafood does authentic Outer Banks cooking. Try the fried green tomatoes, and ask for an extra order of hush puppies." I gave directions, and they left happy, although still shaking their heads at the fondness Americans had for the old country.

With Louise Jane's help, the afternoon settled into a more comfortable pace. She staffed the circulation desk when I was giving my lecture or helping patrons, allowing Charlene to escape into her cubicle among the old books, diaries, maps, navigational charts, and ships' logs that were her specialty.

My afternoon talk was taken over by the Houston branch of the Jane Austen Fan Club. Six women who'd driven all the way from Texas to see the books and were not happy to find only the four less-famous ones on display. The notebook, written in their idol's own small hand, went some way toward mollifying them. I knew I was in for trouble when they seated themselves in the front row and crossed arms over chests both formidable and bony, and one woman said, loudly, "Why are you wearing that ridiculous hat? Don't you know any better? You're at least fifty years before your time."

I had barely begun the lecture when I was corrected on the date of Miss Austen's birth. (Okay, so I got the digits mixed up and said December 15, 1776, rather than December 16, 1775.) From then on they seemed to delight in asking obscure questions and answering them whenever I hesitated. Finally, I suggested we turn my lecture over to a book club–like discussion led by the Houston branch of the Jane Austen Fan Club.

The ladies beamed, and began rearranging chairs.

I accepted a chair myself, hoping to learn something, and glanced toward the circulation desk. The self-satisfied smirk on Louise Jane's face as she watched me being humiliated reminded me of the gleam in Charles's eyes when he tripped Diane Uppiton.

The lecture/fan club meeting disbanded at last. One of the Texas ladies slipped me a business card. "My sister designs historic costumes. I'm sure she could do an *appropriate* early-1800s costume for you in a hurry, sugar. Just mention my name. Oh, and let us know when you have *Sensibility* and *Prejudice* back, will you? We'll be here until Wednesday."

A copy of *The Sayers Swindle* by Victoria Abbott had been left on a chair. I took it into the racks to reshelve it. The A's were disheveled, probably by patrons in search of Austen, and I took a moment to tidy them.

Ronald was upstairs, running his summer preteen program, and a few parents were gathered at the bottom of the stairs, waiting for it to end.

"I don't mind telling you, I had my doubts about bringing Justin here today," a woman said from the other side of the shelf. "Do you think it's entirely safe, Maureen?"

A long sniff that could only be Mrs. Peterson. I held my breath and leaned closer. "Needs must, my dear, needs must. Ronald does run the best children's library in the state. And my Phoebe is absolutely thriving in this program. She's an exceptional scholar, of course, but even the very best of students need extra encouragement now and again, and Ronald . . ."

"But is it safe here? That killing, and now books being stolen. I just don't know."

A long sigh. "It is a worry. Phoebe likes to stay after the program to select still more books to check out. She has such a keen desire to learn, you know, I simply can't get her nose out of books, try as I might to suggest she go out and play with the other children. She wasn't pleased when I told her that today I'd be here to pick her up as soon as Ronald finished. Don't misunderstand me, now. I'm not going to say anything against Bertie. We all know she does her best."

"I always thought it was Jonathan Uppiton who kept this place running."

"You might be right. All of this . . . nonsense never would have happened if Jonathan was still around. Bertie's always been flighty. She spends too much time on that yoga foolishness."

"I take yoga classes twice a week. It helps my back a great deal."

"I didn't mean doing yoga is foolish. Not at all. Only that Bertie has too much on her plate outside of the library to be able to step into Jonathan's shoes."

I wanted to leap over the shelf (Louisa May Alcott to Truman Capote) and throttle Mrs. Peterson. Bertie was worrying herself sick, neglecting her yoga studio, under suspicion of murder, and still managing to run a highly effective library under exceptionally difficult circumstances.

"They say Bertie was heard to threaten Jonathan only minutes before he was murdered. You were at the reception, Maureen. Did you hear her?"

"You know I dislike gossip, but in this case I have to be honest. Bertie was furious when Jonathan threatened to sack that new librarian. What's her name? Laura?"

"Lucy. She does seem to be doing a good job. I'm learning so much about English literature. Makes me wish I'd gone to college as I wanted to. But my mother said . . ."

My smile at the praise didn't last. Mrs. Peterson sniffed once again and interrupted reminisces of what Mother said. "Anyone can dress up in a big hat and recite facts. I have to say, I agreed with Jonathan that Bertie's allowing expenses at this library to get out of hand. Jonathan was always after me to join the library board. He needed, he insisted, my sensible and practical outlook, but I, what with the girls and the house and entertaining Al's business associates, simply don't have the time." She sighed mightily. "I'm sorry about that now. They could use my sharp eye on expenses. If I know one thing, it's how to rein in out-of-control spending. My Dallas, now, thinks money grows on trees. That girl has a mind to . . ."

"You think spending at the library's out of control? I don't see anything being wasted."

Mrs. Peterson coughed. "Not out of control, perhaps, not yet. But, really, losing two of those books? The security in this place is sorely lacking. Take my word: Jonathan would have put a stop to it. Did I mention that he almost pleaded with me to join the board? I now realize I should have. But what good are regrets? Bertie simply refused to accept that Jonathan was in charge here, and insisted on doing things her own way. Well, she got what she wanted. And look at the result."

"Do you think . . . Bertie . . ." the unknown woman said, sotto voce.

"Killed Jonathan?" Mrs. Peterson did not bother

to lower her own voice. I doubt she knew how. "I hate to say it, but Bertie was in the right place at the right time, and she had a motive."

I'd heard enough. I was about to reveal myself, in all my righteous indignation and ostentatious Victorian hat, when Mrs. Peterson continued. "Others, mind, had reason, as well."

"What do you mean? Everyone loved Jonathan."

"Not everyone. You might have noticed that Diane stepped into his shoes here at the library with great speed. She was seen at the Chevrolet dealer in Kitty Hawk the day after his death, checking out . . . get this . . . a new Corvette."

"No! But weren't they divorced?"

"Apparently it wasn't final. So she inherits."

"Jonathan wasn't rich, was he?"

"I'd say more like comfortable. You can be sure Diane wasn't going to settle for a paltry divorce settlement, not if she could get the whole enchilada. I heard her threaten him. On more than one occasion."

"No!"

"Not only right here, at the library the night of the reception. I live next door to them, you know. The fights I overheard over the years! She resented the amount of time and attention he gave to the library. Time and attention she thought he should have been giving to her. It all came to a head a year or so ago, when he first got the idea of getting the Austen collection on loan. He threw himself, heart and soul, into the project, and she walked out on him. It was her or the library, I heard her say. He chose the library. Of course, once she was gone, she couldn't stay away. Not her. Only a week before the fateful reception, she was banging on his door. Yelling something about dead books being suitable only for dead people."

"Goodness. Did you tell the police this?"

"I'm not a common gossip, Margaret. Besides, Diane has moved back into the matrimonial home. I have to get on with my neighbors."

"Lucy, what are you doing?" Louise Jane said.

I leapt out of my skin. "Shelving books." I realized I was still holding the Victoria Abbott and waved it in evidence.

The edges of Louise Jane's mouth turned up. It was not an attractive look. "Doesn't that book belong in the mystery collection?"

"Oh, right."

"How long does it take a *qualified* librarian to shelve one book, anyway? No wonder you people need me."

"What do you want?"

"There's a gentleman at the desk, asking if you'll speak to Rotary one night next week about Jane Austen. I offered to do it myself, of course, but he said his wife specifically suggested you. I can't possibly imagine why." She tossed her head and walked away.

Children thundered down the stairs, and Mrs. Peterson and her friend ended their conversation.

Chapter 17

I know from reading mystery novels that there's little the police enjoy more than nosy neighbors. Were they aware that Mrs. Peterson lived next to the Uppitons, and thus was party to their marital disputes? I could easily imagine her creeping through the shrubbery or hiding behind a potted plant to get closer to their squabbles. She might not go to Detective Watson on her own initiative, but if she was asked, she'd be pretty quick (I was sure) to dish the dirt.

Along with a hearty dose of malice and a reminder of what excellent students her children were.

I'd give Detective Watson a call when the library closed for the day.

No, I thought with a warm glow in my cheeks, *probably better to contact Butch.*

On Monday evenings, we closed promptly at five. We locked the door, flipped the sign, and let out a long breath. "A good day," Ronald said.

"I've contacted those guys from Oxford and told them I can devote several hours on Wednesday to helping them do their research," Charlene said. "They calmed down and said that would be okay."

Louise Jane preened. "Once I get things better organized around here, everything'll run an awful lot smoother. I'm going to start planning the Halloween exhibit as soon as I can catch my breath. You'll want to be involved in that, Ronald. The little ones love ghost stories, don't they? Of course, we won't be telling them any of the *true* stories about this place." She laughed. "We don't want to frighten anyone, do we, Lucy?"

She left, promising (threatening?) to see us all tomorrow.

Yesterday, on my way home from the beach, I'd swung back into Nags Head first and bought the fixings for a chicken salad, enough for two meals. I was planning to spend the evening simply relaxing at home. I didn't think I could stuff another molecule of Austen trivia into my brain. I'd finished *The Moonstone* at the beach, and was in the mood for something written in the twenty-first century.

I stuck my head out the door, checking the weather, thinking that a nice, long walk along the boardwalk before dinner would clear some of the cobwebs from my head. I needed to plan my classic readers' group, but without knowing who would be attending (would anyone?) it was hard to select the books. Perhaps after *The Moonstone*, we could move into darker novels of the Victorian era such as *Tess of the d'Urbervilles* or *Bleak House*.

Now that Louise Jane was here, and being helpful, I had to admit, I might be able to start the group soon.

I went back inside and down the hall to the office to say good night. Bertie's purse was on her desk and she was locking the cabinet when I came in.

"Off home?" I asked.

"My entire body is stiffening up. I want, I need, to get in a yoga class this evening."

"Having Louise Jane here today was a big help."

"I'm glad to hear it. You can't fault her for her passion."

"Doesn't she have a job? Other than here, I mean?"

"She flits about, doing a bit of this, some of that. She comes from a large, old Outer Banks family. Her uncles own several local businesses, and she fills in for them on and off. Working here, at the library, has been her dream for a long time, and I suspect she blew off whatever uncle she was working for this morning to get down here in record time."

"I overheard something interesting earlier. I think the police will want to know, but I wanted to run it by you first."

She sat back down, waving me into a chair. "Go ahead."

I told her about Mrs. Peterson's gossip.

"It's no secret that Diane and Jonathan had a difficult marriage. I don't think I could have remained married to him myself. I adore nothing more in a man than a love of books and libraries, but not if he loves them more than he loves me. Interesting that she was shopping for expensive cars so soon after being widowed."

"That's what I thought."

"Lucy, what are your thoughts about the books being taken?"

"Common theft. Plain and simple. We were lax in keeping them secured. It won't happen again. We just didn't realize anyone would be interested in taking them."

"Why? Why would anyone take valuable books that they can't sell?"

"To own them. To gloat over them in private. Are you thinking of Theodore?"

"Who else? I blame myself, Lucy. Totally. I've always known that blasted Teddy would attempt to pilfer the odd rare book now and again. Heavens, he had Jonathan around for drinks once and proudly showed him a cookbook from the Civil War era he said he'd recently acquired. Jonathan recognized the volume immediately, as having 'disappeared'"— she wiggled her fingers in the air—"while Charlene's back was turned. Jonathan snatched the book right off the shelf and brought it back. It was almost like a game of catch-me-if-you-can to Teddy. An annoying game, to be sure, but I've never seen any malice in him. He has to know this will damage the reputation of our library beyond redemption. If we can't return the full set, we'll never have a chance of getting anything else of value. Never mind that we'll never get insurance again, either. I have my enemies on the library board, Lucy. And among the commissioners. People who don't see the value of a public library and chafe at the expense."

"You don't mean they want to close us down?"

She nodded. "I mean precisely that. If not shut and padlock the doors, then to reduce our hours and collection to a mere token. This lovely historical lighthouse could be put, they say, to more income-generating uses. It's all about the money for some of them. The library's an expense, not a revenue source—therefore, what use is it?

"I was hoping, Jonathan was hoping, that the Austen collection would prove popular. We had no idea how popular, but now I fear it's going to blow up in my face. In all our faces. They've never had the votes before, but if this gets much worse and even our supporters begin wondering if the library's worth it . . ."

"Don't get discouraged," I said. "We got the extra funding. The town loves us. We'll make sure they keep loving us. Do you know if the police searched Theodore's house?"

"I suggested doing so to Detective Watson. He said he had no grounds to suspect Teddy other than my obvious attempt to deflect attention from myself. And I quote."

"If Watson thinks you're stealing the books, then he's a fool!"

Bertie gave me a sad smile. "I appreciate your loyalty, Lucy. But, yes, I fear that is what they suspect. That I'm attempting to create confusion and disrupt the police investigation into Jonathan's murder."

"Ridiculous."

"I agree with you. But there are those who don't. For love of the library alone, any idea that I'd kill Jonathan and steal the books to cover it up is preposterous. His family had been pillars of the business community back in the day, and people of importance in this area still respected him, despite the fact that his father's business collapsed years ago. Jonathan, for all his faults, was the best friend our library could possibly have."

"It has me. And Ronald and Charlene. And you."

"Yes, it does. But is that enough?" Bertie picked up her purse. "I'm going to the studio to practice yoga and try to forget about all this for a while. I suggest you do the same."

"First I have to tell the police what I heard from Mrs. Peterson."

I decided to drive down to the police station, rather than ask Detective Watson and Butch to come to me. I needed some air, and I needed to get my head clear.

The Nags Head Police Station is located in the center of town, in a low, four-armed building, sharing the complex with the town hall and other community offices. I found parking easily and went inside. I explained my business to the woman at the front desk, and she called Detective Watson. He did not look pleased to see me. "What do you want now?"

"I have come," I said haughtily, "to report information that may be pertinent to the investigation of a crime." Haughty I learned at my mother's knee.

"Very well. Come on in." He led the way to his office. Which wasn't much of an office, just a desk in a corner of a room crowded with other desks, computers, discarded uniform jackets, coffee cups, and piles and piles of paper. The walls were painted industrial beige and decorated with wanted posters and safety notices.

"Have a seat," Watson said. He went behind his desk and I dropped into the rock-hard visitor's chair. A framed photograph was among the debris on his desk. The picture was turned away from me, and I tried to surreptitiously twist my head so as to see it. Watson sat down and gave me such a glare, I settled back in my seat and crossed my hands neatly in my lap. I'd also learned ladylike deportment at my mother's knee. He didn't interrupt as I told him what I'd overheard earlier in the library. I refrained from mentioning that I'd been hiding in the stacks.

"Diane Uppiton had some harsh words for you at the reception, didn't she, Miss Richardson?"

"What?"

"Let me think," he said, making a steeple out of his fingers. "Dress from your mother's closet. Designs on her husband. That sound about right?"

"This isn't about me!"

"Isn't it? She also said you were not very pretty, I believe. I might disagree with her on that, but my opinion is unimportant. Are you, Lucy, trying to point fingers back at Diane Uppiton?"

Did Detective Watson just say he thinks I'm pretty?

I had no time to savor the compliment. Nor to wonder that Detective Watson could repeat that conversation so accurately without resorting to his notes. "I resent that. I have come here to tell you what I overheard. I thought you'd be interested. I guess I was wrong." I pushed my chair back and stood up.

He didn't move. "That's the second time you've reported Diane Uppiton to me. I have to ask myself why."

"Why? Because I'm a responsible citizen, that's why."

"Perhaps. Officer Greenblatt tells me that he was in conversation with you at the time of the murder. But everything was in flux that night, people coming and going, milling about, eating pastries, drinking wine and beer. Easy to lose track of time—folks think they saw things they didn't or get the time frame wrong. I also suspect that Officer Greenblatt is not entirely, shall we say, professional when it comes to you."

I sputtered. "I didn't even know Mr. Uppiton. I'd met him once before. When he came in to meet me my first day on the job. You can't possibly suspect that I would have had anything to do with his death."

"I can't? You've given up everything to come to Nags Head to take this job. Your family in Boston. A nice apartment, a good job at Harvard, where you were highly regarded and in line for promotion."

"I was?"

"You even broke off your engagement. Marriage into a prominent old-money family. All to come to work at our little Lighthouse Library. And then, only a few days after your arrival, to find that maybe the job isn't going to be yours after all. Jonathan Uppiton was about to fire you, wasn't he, Lucy? To tell you that your services wouldn't be needed. Not only would you lose your job, but the apartment that came with it."

How did Watson know about my life in Boston? My nonengagement to Ricky? "I . . . I . . ."

"People have been known to do drastic things in such circumstances, Lucy." His voice was low and soft. His kind eyes focused on my face. When I first came in, the police station was a noisy clatter of activity, but now all had fallen silent. Watson's words wrapped themselves around me. I leaned closer to hear better.

"You would have been embarrassed, wouldn't you, to go back to Boston? Beg your job to take you back, your fiancé to forgive you? Your parents to put you up while you got back on your feet. How much did the Lighthouse Library mean to you, Lucy? What would you have done to protect it? What did you do?"

I snapped out of my near trance. "Nothing. For heaven's sake, I came in to report an overheard conversation, and you're practically accusing me of murder."

"Am I?"

Is he?

"Lover of Jane Austen, are you, Lucy?"

"Of course I am. What's that got to do with anything?"

"Do you want the books for yourself, or did you take them to throw off suspicion? Are they hidden under your bed so you can pull them out at night, or resting at the bottom of the ocean?"

I stood up. "I resent your implications."

"Just thinking out loud."

"Well, you can stop thinking." To my horror, I felt tears gather behind my eyes. "I'm leaving."

"Thanks for coming in," he said. He did not get to his feet. "I'm sure we'll be talking again."

I stormed out of the police station on shaking legs. Had Watson just accused me of murder? Or was he fishing, hoping I'd break down and confess? Tears began to flow.

I was a fool. I didn't belong here. I should go back to Boston, marry Ricky, have 2.5 kids, and devote myself to a life of good works and boredom.

A car horn sounded, and I was almost jerked off my feet.

"Lucy, are you all right?"

Connor McNeil had a firm grip on my arm. I blinked and realized I'd stepped into the road without even noticing where I was going. If I'd been run down would Watson decide I'd killed myself out of remorse and pronounce the case closed?

Connor waved at the uniformed officer behind the wheel of the cruiser that had almost hit me in an "I've got this" gesture, and the cop drove away, shaking his head.

"What's the matter, Lucy?"

"Nothing." I wiped at my eyes with the back of my hand. "Everything. Oh, I don't know." I dug in my pocket and found an unused tissue. I blew my nose. "I'm sorry. Goodness, did you just save my life?"

"Saved you from getting your foot crushed, at any rate." He gave me a smile. "Want to talk about it? How about over a coffee?"

"I can't keep you. Are you going into the police station?"

"I'm popping in to see the chief, but I can tell him I've been delayed. It's just budget talk, anyway, and he'll be glad to put that off. Give him the chance to get home early for a change. How about it? Coffee? Maybe an after-work drink?"

"That would be nice. Thanks."

"Let's take my car. I can drop you back here for yours later. It should be perfectly safe outside the police station."

Connor placed a quick call to the chief, saying he'd been delayed and could they reschedule the meeting. Then he drove us to the restaurant at the Nags Head fishing pier, one of the few spots along this stretch of the coast that sits directly on the beach. This early on a Monday evening, the place was largely empty and we were able to snag two brightly painted chairs outside, and sit up at the railing overlooking the sand and the sea. I had a white wine, and Connor ordered a local beer. He didn't ask what had been bothering me, and I was glad of it. Hard to tell a man you think you've been accused of murder.

"Thank you," I said as the waitress placed our drinks on the railing, "for letting Bertie hire Louise Jane. We've been so run off our feet, we don't know if we're coming or going. Charlene was over the moon to be allowed back to her real job."

He shook his head. "I've never seen anything like it. Sure, the town gets busy, crazy busy, in tourist season, and some of the festivals attract crowds from all over. But the success of this library exhibit was totally unexpected."

"Bertie and the staff, particularly Ronald, went to a lot of trouble to promote it. In their own time, and at their own expense, too."

"You don't have to persuade me, Lucy. I know the value of Bertie and the library to this town."

"I wish Detective Watson did."

"He's doing a tough job. The chief is not happy at how long this case is taking. As the mayor, I'm not happy, either."

"It hasn't slowed down the tourist trade, though."

"Not at all. It doesn't appear to be a random killing, so people aren't afraid they're going to be murdered in their guesthouse beds. The killing didn't get much press outside the immediate area, thank heavens. Not with those shenanigans in Washington sucking up all the air."

I decided to keep mum about Mrs. Peterson and her friend wondering if the library was safe. That sort of talk would spread fast enough without me helping it along. "Do you have any ideas? About who might have done it, I mean."

"Not a clue. Jonathan could be opinionated, stubborn, full of himself. But he was like that his entire life, and I see no reason for someone to suddenly do him in because of it."

I shifted uncomfortably in my seat.

Nothing changed in Jonathan's life except a bitter divorce. And a new employee at the library.

Connor coughed, shifted in his chair, and looked out to sea. "Lucy. I've thought of you many times over the years. Since that summer."

I couldn't hide my surprise. "You have?"

"Wondering what you were up to in Boston. I'll confess that I was home one summer when I was a senior at Duke and heard you were at Ellen and Amos's. I thought of dropping by, saying hi."

I'd thought of Connor, too, sometimes when I should have been thinking about Ricky and our future. Wondering why the thought of Ricky didn't make my heart race. "Why didn't you?"

"It was no secret your family had . . . has . . . a lot of money. You seemed like a down-to-earth girl, but those brothers of yours . . ."

"Tell me about it."

"I was just a boy from an Outer Banks fishing family, struggling to get through college. I had no money for nice dinners or renting charter boats for a day on the water."

"We didn't live like that here. Which is probably why my bothers stopped coming as soon as they were old enough. I was always treated like Aunt Ellen and Uncle Amos's kid." My voice trailed off. How much I'd loved it. No county-club set, no cocktail parties with up-and-coming politicians or titans of business to impress, no social expectations.

"I guess I figured you'd have changed as you grew up." He gave me a big smile. "I'm glad you didn't."

I smiled back.

"I also heard some talk that summer about a fiancé. Maybe that was part of the reason I stayed away. That didn't work out?"

"Let's say the relationship was stronger in our mothers' minds than in ours."

Much stronger. It had been more than two weeks since that scene in the restaurant and my flight from Boston. Other than the initial text from Ricky saying he understood if I needed time, I'd heard not a thing from him. And, I now realized, only because we were talking about it, I'd scarcely spared a thought for him, either. If the library job didn't work out and I did decide to go back to Boston, not that I could see that happening, I would not be going back to Ricky.

Chapter 18

We had only one drink at the pier, and then Connor drove me back to the police station to get my car.

As I got out of the BMW, I found myself looking anxiously around, as if expecting Detective Watson to leap out from behind the bushes, waving handcuffs at me. If Connor noticed, he said nothing.

He told me he'd love to take me to dinner, but he had a meeting with the commissioners he couldn't get out of. He was going to break the news to them that he'd approved a substantial, although temporary, increase in the library budget.

He was expecting, Connor said, with a shake of his head, that the strongest objection would be from the commissioner who was also a member of the library board. Why anyone would volunteer to be on a library board who didn't think there was value in reading, Connor never understood.

Dinner another time, perhaps?

I'd agreed.

Back home in my lighthouse aerie, I prepared my chicken salad dinner and ate it with a book propped up on the sugar bowl in front of me. Charles finished his own dinner and paced the kitchen, wondering what I'd done with the rest of it.

I pulled the curtains against the light of the full white moon, and Charles and I were curled up in bed by ten.

When I woke, Charles was no longer beside me. I like to sleep in total darkness, without even the soft glow of a night-light or crack under the bathroom door. I opened my eyes, but that made no difference. I stared up into a void.

A floorboard creaked.

I rolled over. This was an old building, tall and facing out to sea. It made a great many noises in the night.

A crash.

I sat up and switched on the bedside light. Charles was at the door, his ears back, his face forward, his back arched, and the darker hair along his tail standing erect. My heart accelerated.

One of the iron steps leading up from the main floor squeaked, and I choked back a scream. I was a woman alone in an old lighthouse in the middle of the night. Charles might be large and fierce and loyal, but he was still a cat. I clutched the bedclothes tighter. My iPhone was on the bedside table, under my book. I reached for it, pushed the button to activate it. One bar. Hoping that would be enough, my finger hesitated over the Emergency Call button.

Strange, isn't it, how sometimes in the face of danger, we're more afraid of being embarrassed at unnecessarily calling for help than being murdered in our beds?

My ears strained, but I heard nothing more. The small bedside light threw dark shadows into the rounded corners of my room. Something moved, and this time I did scream.

Frances. The Lady. The woman confined in this room, trapped in a loveless marriage, from which the only escape was a desperate leap from the very window close to where I lay.

Another creak of the stairs, but this time it sounded farther away, heading down. Then all fell silent.

My eyes were gradually becoming accustomed to the dark and, with an enormous amount of relief, I saw that the shape that had moved was nothing but my jacket. I'd been too lazy to hang it in the closet when I got in, and had simply tossed it over the open door. As was my custom (as well as a childish so-there gesture to Louise Jane), I'd left the window slightly open to let in the fresh sea air. A gust must have slipped in and ruffled the jacket.

Wow! Was I imaging things, or what?

Something touched my leg and I screamed again. I dropped the phone and scrambled through the tussled bedclothes for it.

"Meow," said Charles.

I looked into his little face. He stuck his pink tongue out at me and rubbed himself against my leg, hoping for a scratch.

I obliged. Whoever—whatever—had been at my

door, a mouse, probably, was gone. If Charles wasn't frightened, I wouldn't be, either.

I straightened the blankets around me and settled back to sleep, grateful for the cat's warm bulk.

But I slipped the phone under my pillow and I didn't turn off the light.

Chapter 19

I woke when Charles sat on my chest and scratched my nose, reminding me that it was breakfast time.

It was daylight, but a storm had moved in while I slept. Wind and rain pounded the windows, but the old lighthouse stood firm against the elements. I remembered the noises in the night and what I'd thought was a floorboard creaking, right outside my door, then footsteps on the stairs. In the light of day—albeit a cold, gray light—common sense returned and I told myself it had been a mouse. A mouse would account for Charles's rapt attention. Although . . . it would have to have been a mighty big mouse. No, it was nothing but the lighthouse settling itself deeper into the rock bed against the tempest, as it had done countless times over the years.

I rolled out of bed, fed Charles (first things first), and switched the kettle on for coffee. I showered, washed my hair, and dressed for the day in a knee-length white skirt and a sheer, flowing green shirt with a matching camisole beneath. A scarf the color of sea foam completed the outfit.

I sat at the table with a bowl of muesli and yogurt, coffee, and my computer. I read the morning's news, sipped coffee, and munched on cereal. The storm raged outside, but my lovely lighthouse aerie was warm, cozy, and safe.

I convinced myself that I'd had nothing but a bad dream in the night. Most certainly no ghostly lady had been flittering about my room, intent on saving me. I glanced guiltily at the bedside lamp, still switched on, which reminded me that I'd left my phone under the pillow.

As for Detective Watson and his nasty insinuations, I hadn't killed anyone, nor had I stolen any books; thus I had absolutely nothing to worry about.

Nothing of interest had happened in the world overnight, and I switched off the computer, put my cup and bowl in the sink, rinsed the French press, and headed downstairs to work.

The first thing I saw when I reached the main level was Bertie's white face. She sat on the floor, beside the red velvet rope guarding the Austen alcove, her shoulders slumped, her legs stretched out in front of her. For one horrible moment I thought she'd had a heart attack. She lifted her head, looked at me, and blinked. "Lucy."

I ran toward her.

I stopped short.

The cabinet was locked, but another book was missing. Only three volumes remained, as well as the notebook. *Mansfield Park* wasn't there.

No need to ask Bertie if she'd taken it. Her face reflected her shock.

Sense and Sensibility first, then *Pride and Prejudice.* Now *Mansfield Park.*

The books were being stolen in the order in which they'd been written. I wondered if the thief knew that.

"Morning, all!" Ronald's cheerful voice sounded so out of place. He came in, and then Charlene and Louise Jane. Andrew followed, carrying a tray of coffees and a bulging paper bag from Josie's.

"I'm treating this morning," Louise Jane trilled. "A little something to help you welcome me here."

"It was my idea," Andrew said.

"What's wrong?" Charlene asked.

They approached us, and as one sucked in a breath.

"Not again," said Charlene.

"Again." Bertie got to her feet in a quick, fluid motion. "Ronald, go upstairs and check nothing's missing from the children's library. Charlene, you do the same in the reference room. Then meet me in my office. Lucy and Louise Jane, come with me. I'm phoning the police right away. Good-bye, Andrew, please turn the sign to Closed on your way out. We will not be opening the library this morning."

Louise Jane grabbed the bag and coffees. "Good thing I thought to bring breakfast."

"You don't sound at all concerned," I said as Ronald, Charlene, and Bertie rushed off and Poor Andrew headed for the door. The look on his face indicated he wanted to stay, but he knew better to argue with Bertie.

Louise Jane walked down the hallway beside me.

She smiled that smile. "Of course I'm concerned, Lucy honey. I don't know how you and Bertie will be able to explain this away. That's the problem with *qualified* librarians. Heads in the clouds." She sighed heavily.

I stood stock-still as a thought came to me. *Is it possible Louise Jane has stolen the books?*

The first two thefts had worked to her advantage, adding to the chaos at the library so that Bertie realized she needed extra help. But I couldn't say the same for *Mansfield Park*. Louise Jane had the job. If anything, another theft might well cause the town or the board to close the library entirely.

For the first time, I wondered where Louise Jane had been at the time of Mr. Uppiton's murder. I'd seen her downstairs, mingling with the guests, but I couldn't say exactly where she had been the moment before we all heard Bertie's scream.

Almost everyone. Bertie, I reminded myself, had gone upstairs. Alone.

We all gathered in the office, while Bertie made the call. She hung up, her face grim. "Detective Watson will be here shortly. You are all to remain here, in my office, until the police arrive. Good thing we have muffins."

Louise Jane chose one.

Ronald said, "Don't you want us to search the rest of the library?"

"What good would it do? We can't hope, this time, that it's been mislaid. No, this is nothing but a planned series of thefts. I simply don't know how I'm going to explain to the board. Or the mayor." She picked up the phone again. "Connor, it's Bertie. I'm afraid I have some very bad news."

"The book was there when we closed yesterday," I said. "Gone this morning when Bertie arrived."

"What did you do after we left, Lucy?" Charlene asked.

"I went into town. To the police station to tell them . . . something I'd overheard. And then, well, I went to the bar at the fishing pier for about an hour, and got back here around seven. I glanced at the cabinet as I passed. I would have noticed if another book was missing. I didn't go out again."

"Did you leave the door unlocked?"

"Of course not!"

"Just asking."

Had I locked the door behind me when I came home? I must have. I might be a bit forgetful sometimes, but since the books had started disappearing we were all hyperconscious of security. What limited amount of security was to be found at a small public library, that is.

"Well, someone let himself in," Bertie said. "And out again. The door was locked when I got here."

Ronald said, "The police will be able to tell us more, but I didn't see any sign of the lock being tampered with."

"What about the cabinet?" Charlene asked. "Did you check it?"

Bertie nodded. "Locked tight."

"So our thief," Charlene said, "has a set of keys."

We all looked at each other while trying not to.

"Who has keys to the building?" I asked.

Ronald and Charlene slowly put up their hands. As did Bertie and I. Louise Jane smirked. "I'm in the clear. You neglected to give me my own set yesterday, Bertie. I was going to remind you this morning."

"That's not entirely true, Louise Jane," I said. "There's a spare key hidden outside, under a rock. You let yourself in with it the other day."

Her eyes blazed. "I hope you're not accusing me of breaking in, Lucy. I used that key so you wouldn't have to come all the way downstairs. I was doing you a favor."

"I'd forgotten all about that blasted spare key," Bertie said. "For heaven's sake, with all that's going on, there's a key tucked under a rock outside! We might as well leave a sign on the door asking people to come on in.

"Do you remember Alice, Ronald?" He rolled his eyes and nodded. "She was the reference librarian before we got Charlene. The woman was a brilliant librarian but didn't have a lick of common sense. After about the tenth time I had to drive out here to let her in because she was opening but had forgotten her key, I finally had a spare made and hid it. I'll get it later."

"Was she the woman who killed herself? Back in the nineties?" I asked. "Jumping from the window in my room?"

"What? Who told you that?"

"Louise Jane."

Bertie glared at our newest employee. "That's ridiculous. The library wasn't even here in the nineties. The lighthouse was in bad repair and locked tight."

Louise Jane didn't look at all bothered at having being caught out. "My grandmother told me the incident was hushed up."

"Your grandmother . . ." Bertie began. "Never mind. How did you know about this spare key, anyway?"

Louise Jane glanced away. "I forget."

"The day Louise Jane visited me and let herself into the library with that hidden key was the same day that I found Theodore lurking around outside," I said.

"Not him again," Bertie said.

"Did you return the key to the hiding place when you left, Louise Jane?" I asked.

"Of course I did. I wasn't planning to sneak in after hours and steal anything. Oops. Bad choice of words."

"So it's possible Theodore saw you replace it."

Bertie groaned.

"Jonathan Uppiton had a key," Charlene interrupted. "Does anyone know what happened to it?"

Bertie shook her head. "I never thought to ask."

"Sounds like there are keys to this building all over the place," Ronald said. "But there's only one key to the cabinet—isn't that right? You have that, don't you, Bertie?"

She rummaged through her bag, pulling out a ring crowded with keys of all shapes and sizes. She lifted a small bronze one. "Here."

"Then the lock was forced," Ronald said. "The police will be able to see that."

"It's locked now," Bertie said. "I tried the handle myself. It must have been locked again after *Mansfield Park* was removed."

"I suppose it's possible the lock was jimmied open, and replaced when the thief had what he wanted," Ronald said. "It wasn't a particularly secure lock."

"All this talk of keys." Louise Jane threw her hands up. "You people are obviously trying to avoid considering another possibility."

"What's that?" Charlene asked.

"That the book, the books, are being removed by someone . . . something . . . that doesn't worry about locks and keys."

"I did hear strange noises in the night. I put them down to the approaching storm," I said.

"Noises? In the library?" Bertie asked.

"Yes. And on the stairs."

"Did you investigate?" Charlene asked.

Louise Jane gasped. "That would be the worst thing she could do. Did it try to come into your room, Lucy? Did you sense a change in the temperature? Did the cat react?"

"Enough of that," Bertie snapped. "Obviously someone was here last night, after closing and before I arrived. No need to start implying ghostly influences."

"It would be foolish not to consider every possibility. I told you there are forces at work in this building we cannot comprehend. Did the cat do anything, Lucy? They're very sensitive to the paranormal."

"No," I lied. "Charles didn't hear a thing."

Charles meowed his protest. He'd taken a position across the back of the visitor's chair, the better to follow our conversation.

"He's probably used to it," Louise Jane said. "Spending all his time in here, wandering the tower at night. I bet he's even made friends with the light-house keeper's little boy."

"I said, enough, Louise Jane," Bertie snapped. "We have plenty of problems without imagining ghosts haunting the hallways."

Louise Jane shrugged. "I don't see anyone offering a better explanation. Strange noises in the night. Things disappearing from behind locked doors. I'll ask my grandmother about some charms Lucy can use to protect herself. Even if they don't mean any harm, the spirits don't know their own strength sometimes."

Despite myself, I felt an icy chill crawl across my spine. I shuddered, and Charlene threw me a worried glance.

Fortunately, that line of conversation was interrupted by the ringing of the bell. Ronald left and came back with Detective Watson and three stern-faced uniformed officers, one of whom was Butch. They were all drenched. Butch gave me a smile, but I returned a grimace. I didn't feel much like smiling.

"We're going to search this building," Watson said.

"We did that the first two times," Bertie said. "Hoping the books had been misplaced. Nothing."

"I am not," Watson said, "looking for an incorrectly filed volume. Y'all remain in here. Officer Franklin, ensure no one leaves this room." The policewoman nodded.

Watson held out his hand. "Can I have your keys, please, Ms. James. To closets, cabinets, all the rooms." Bertie passed the bunch over. "You live here, don't you, Miss Richardson? On site?"

"Yes. My room's on the fourth floor. Off the main staircase."

Watson held out his hand once again. "Key."

"Surely you don't intend to search Lucy's apartment?" Bertie said.

"I intend to search this entire building. Keys, please."

I pulled the chain out of my bag. The key to the library door, to the lighthouse apartment, my car, my parents' house, one for my office at the university that I'd forgotten to hand in, two I didn't recognize. All on a chain with a big red and white H for Harvard. I pointed out the one Watson would want, and glanced at Bertie as I gave the keys to the detective.

"I'm calling my lawyer," Bertie said. "Do not go into Lucy's apartment until he can accompany you."

"I'll go where I want, when I want."

"You need a warrant for that."

"I have one."

"Oh."

"As a courtesy to Miss Richardson, I'll wait for Amos, if you think he's necessary. Let's go, people. You know what you're looking for."

Bertie picked up her phone and dialed. She related what had happened in a few short, clipped sentences, said, "Good," and hung up. "He's on his way."

I glanced at my watch. Quarter after nine. Bertie's phone rang. She checked the display and then ignored it.

Louise Jane pushed Charles off the back of the visitor's chair and sat down. Charles gave her a vicious look but walked away, his tail high. Ronald found a place on the floor and stretched his legs out in front of him. Bertie sat in her chair, closed her eyes, folded her hands over her chest, and took long, deep breaths. Charlene and I perched on the edge of the desk, and the cop leaned against a wall. She was young, probably in her mid-twenties, shorter and rounder than she probably liked. Charles rubbed up against her uniformed leg. She pushed him away. He wouldn't be pushed. He purred and rubbed happily. Her eyes began to water, and she sniffed. She sneezed.

Charles purred some more.

The cop pulled a tissue out of her pocket. She placed her toe under Charles's belly and tried to unobtrusively edge him away. She wiped her eyes, blew her nose. Charles refused to be edged. Black and tan hairs began to collect on the hem of the woman's dark pants. Her empty hand might have twitched in the direction of the gun at her hip.

Her nose was beginning to resemble Ronald's when he dressed in his full clown costume when I finally took pity on her.

"Are you allergic to cats?" I asked, thinking that must be quite an occupational hazard for a cop.

"Yeth."

"I can put him in the staff lounge for the duration, if you'd like."

She blew her nose. "Pleath."

I scooped Charles up. He gave me a self-satisfied grin and didn't even protest at the interruption of his fun. I took him to the break room. "Won't be for long." I put the big cat on the floor and slammed the door shut before he could make his escape.

Speaking of making escapes, the cop had been so

relieved that Charles was being taken away that she'd let me walk right out of the office. I could head straight for the door, get in my car, be in Boston before dinnertime, safe behind my mother's dinner table and my father's army of eager-to-please associates.

Instead I tiptoed down the hall. I could hear books being dropped, footsteps overhead, men talking. "Lot of fuss and bother for a couple old books."

"Yes," Butch replied, "but Watson's convinced the books are mixed up in the Uppiton murder. Find out who's stealing the books, we've got our killer."

The worried-looking female cop stuck her head out the office door. "Miss Richardson, get in here!"

"Coming."

I had only just made it back to the room when a knock sounded on the office door. Officer Franklin opened it to admit my uncle Amos, blown in with a bucket of rain. "Are you folks all right?" he asked, shaking off water like a dog. My uncle was tall and lanky with sharp cheekbones, a prominent Adam's apple, and jutting knees and elbows. He walked with a slow, casual gait and spoke with a slow, soft accent full of the deltas of Louisiana where he'd been raised. The first time I'd seen *To Kill a Mockingbird*, I'd thought Gregory Peck was playing Amos O'Malley. Like Atticus Finch, my uncle was easy to underestimate, but that lazy demeanor hid one of the sharpest legal minds in the state.

Bertie said, "I don't know what's happening, Amos. Who can be doing this to us?"

"Don't worry, Bertie. I'm heading on up to see what's going on."

"They want to search Lucy's apartment."

Amos looked at me. "Why?"

"No reason," I said, perhaps too quickly. "They're searching everything."

"Try not to worry, honey." Amos left. We all settled down again.

"Shall we have some music to pass the time?" Charlene asked. Without waiting for an answer, she pushed buttons on her smartphone and we were blasted with the driving beat of rap music.

"Charlene," Bertie warned.

"If you insist." Our reference librarian sighed. She found earbuds and attached them to the phone, and all was blessedly silent once again. Charlene's head bobbed in time to the (thankfully) unheard music.

Bertie continued with her meditation, Louise Jane ate the last of the muffins, Ronald made notes on his own phone. I found a magazine and flipped pages. The cop leaned against the door, her expression indicating that conversation was not welcome.

We didn't have to wait long before we heard footsteps in the hallway and the door opened once again. Uncle Amos's face had the neutral expression of a good lawyer, but he couldn't help throwing a glance in my direction. He was followed by the police officers. We all leapt to our feet. Butch held a plastic bag in his hand containing . . .

"Thank heavens!" Bertie cried. She dropped back into her chair. "You found it. How marvelous."

Ronald and Charlene cheered. Louise Jane pouted and then put on a plastic smile.

But neither Uncle Amos nor the police looked pleased.

"Can you explain this, Miss Richardson?" Watson said.

"Explain what?" Bertie said.

"Is this the missing book?" Watson asked her. Butch held the bag up.

"Yes." Bertie said. "Where did you find it?" She reached for it, and Butch snatched it away.

"We found it," Watson said, "under Miss Richardson's bathroom sink."

"How do you suppose it got there?" Ronald—dear, innocent Ronald—asked.

"Care to tell us, Miss Richardson?" Watson said.

"You don't have to say anything, Lucy," Uncle Amos warned.

"I . . . I have nothing *to* say. I don't know. I didn't put it there."

"Your apartment door was locked. Did you leave it unlocked at any time last night or this morning?"

"No. Some people like to climb to the top for the view. So I always lock my door. Always."

"Who else has a key?"

"I do," Bertie said. "I would never dream of using it when someone is living there." She nodded to the bunch of keys in Watson's hand. "It's on that chain, with the rest of them."

"Anyone else?"

"Jonathan Uppiton, as head of the library board, had a complete set of keys. We were wondering what happened to them. Do you have them, Detective?"

"Why did no one tell me about these keys?"

"Rather than assigning blame," Uncle Amos said, "you should be asking who has the keys now."

"I have just been reminded," Bertie said, "that a spare key to the library is concealed outside." She glared at Louise Jane.

"If a random set of keys is wandering around town," Amos said, "then anyone could be responsible for this. Anyone."

"Anyone," I squeaked.

"I doubt anyone," Watson said, "would go to the bother of stealing a valuable book and then hiding it in the very building from which it was taken. We didn't find the other missing volumes. Where are they, Lucy?"

"I object," Amos said.

"I don't know," I wailed. "I didn't take them. I didn't take that one."

Bertie put an arm around my shoulders. "Of course you didn't, honey. Whoever did is clearly attempting to create confusion and sow dissent in our ranks. Now, if you have what you came for, Detective, I'd like to open our doors and get back to business. I have a library to run."

Watson hesitated. Bertie could be a formidable woman when she got her dander up.

"We can return *Mansfield Park* to the cabinet and no one need know it was taken."

"Not so fast there, Ms. James. I'm taking that book in for fingerprinting."

"You can't. It's a rare and fragile volume," a shocked Charlene protested.

"You won't learn anything," Ronald said. "We tried to insist everyone wear gloves to handle it, but, well, perhaps at first we weren't always as careful as we should have been."

"I, for one, was never allowed to touch it," Louise Jane said. "You won't find my fingerprints on it. I think the police should be allowed to do their job."

"And I think," Charlene said, "your opinion isn't needed."

"Stop," Bertie said. "Whoever's doing this is trying to put us at each other's throats."

"Tell me about the cabinet that contains the books," Watson said. "Are there spare keys for that one sticking out from under rocks also?"

"No," Bertie said. "I have the only key for the Austen cabinet."

"The lock was forced, right?" Ronald said.

"Why do you think that?" Watson asked.

"If Bertie has the only key, then there isn't another one. So the cabinet couldn't have been unlocked."

Watson gave Bertie a long look, and then he said, in a deep, slow voice. "There are no signs of the lock being forced. And it's neatly locked up now."

"That can't be!" Bertie said.

"You didn't examine it carefully enough," Charlene said. "Let me . . ."

Watson silenced her with a glare. "I'll admit that all these missing and hidden keys present a problem. I wouldn't want y'all guarding my doghouse. But I will be watching you, Bertie, Lucy. All of you. I've all I need for now. I'll return the book when the forensics folks say I can. Go ahead and open your library, Ms. James. Officer Franklin, let's go."

"You're not arresting me?" I squeaked.

"Shush," Amos said.

"Not at this time," Watson said.

He left. Officer Franklin followed, almost sprinting out the door, sniffing and wiping her eyes. Strands of cat hair seemed to have gotten into every fold of her uniform. Butch was still holding the book. "It'll be okay, Lucy," he said. "We'll get this figured out, and soon. I promise."

"Thanks, Butch."

"I'll phone Ralph at the hardware store," Uncle Amos said. "And wait here until he comes. You need new locks on all the doors. Most importantly, on Lucy's apartment."

Butch's words had made me feel a lot better, but that didn't last long. I thought about last night, about the footsteps I'd heard. I'd decided it was the storm or an enormous mouse. But now I was forced to confront my worst fears. Not only had someone been downstairs, on the first floor stealing the book, but it was footsteps I'd heard *upstairs*. And later someone had been in my apartment. I shivered. I'd go to the hardware store myself at lunchtime.

And buy a good, strong bolt and chain.

Chapter 20

"Back to work, everyone," Bertie said, once the police had gone. "We have a library to run. People who booked for the ten o'clock lecture will have to be phoned and rescheduled."

"I don't mind doing an extra talk at four," I said. "If they can come then."

"Thank you, Lucy. Louise Jane, make the necessary calls."

"I'm a library assistant, not a secretary. Why can't Lucy phone?"

"Because," Bertie said, "I told you to do it. If you've read your contract, you'll see it says something about other duties as assigned."

"Speaking of other duties," Ronald said. "I'm moving in for the duration."

"You're what?"

"Locks or no locks, strange things are happening here. Lucy shouldn't be alone in the building."

"I don't need a guard," I said.

"You might not, but the books do."

"If we change the locks . . ."

"That might put a stop to it. It might not. Are we going to wait until *Emma* is taken to find out? The books need to either be protected around the clock or returned to their owners with our apologies for losing two. I'll bring a sleeping bag and crash on the floor in the main room."

"Ronald's right," Charlene said. "But he shouldn't have to do it alone. I'll take alternate nights. We have a microwave and a kettle, a bathroom. Even a CD player. What more do we need?"

"I . . . I don't know what to say," Bertie said.

"That's a good idea," Louise Jane said. "I'll ask Andrew to take a shift, too. Having people in the building at night will help, at least until my grandmother can get here and lay some charms down. Lucy will be quite safe then. My grandmother's charms are very powerful. Although there was that time . . ." She sailed out of the room without mentioning what had happened that other time.

"Lucy, can you stay behind for a moment?" Bertie said.

"Sure."

The others filed out. Uncle Amos shut the door behind them.

"I didn't steal . . ." I began.

Bertie lifted one hand. "I didn't think for a minute that you did. But finding the book in your room means something very significant, Lucy. And I don't mean that there's a spirit playing games with us."

"What's that?"

"Teddy didn't take it."

"You're right."

"What do you mean?" Uncle Amos asked.

"Lucy and I discussed the possibility that Theodore Kowalski has been taking the books. We've had trouble with him before, and he's in here almost every day, drooling over the Austen collection."

"He was poking around on Sunday, and might well have seen Louise Jane leaving and putting the key back under the rock or wherever it's hidden."

"You didn't mention that to Watson," Uncle Amos said.

"I did! And he brushed me off," I said. "I've tried to help the good detective before. And for my troubles, I've been accused of trying to throw off suspicion."

"Sam Watson's a good cop. But he can be single-minded when he puts his mind to it. Let me worry about Watson. What makes you two so sure Teddy didn't take it?"

"If he'd stolen *Mansfield Park* . . ." Bertie said.

"He wouldn't plant it in my apartment. He has no reason to ever go up there, and he wouldn't expect me to invite him. The hidden key, if that's what he used, doesn't open my door. He wouldn't be able to get the book back. His only interest in stealing the books would be to add them to his collection."

"And even if he did have some nefarious plan, Teddy, of all people, wouldn't hide a nineteenth-century volume of that significance under a bathroom sink, of all places. Think of the damp. Imagine if a pipe sprung a leak."

Bertie and I cringed at the thought.

"Okay, so you know who didn't steal the book. Do you know who did? That's what's important now."

"Not me," I said.

"We know that, honey."

"But Watson doesn't." I turned to Uncle Amos. "I was in the police station earlier. I thought I was doing the right thing . . . heck, I *was* doing the right thing, reporting something I'd heard. And Watson practically accused me of killing Mr. Uppiton because he threatened to eliminate my job."

"The nerve of the man," Bertie said.

"Watson's clutching at straws," Amos said. "He's getting desperate. The chief and the mayor are pressing him to get that murder solved. If he wants to speak to you at any time, Lucy, call me. I want to be with you."

"You think I need a lawyer?"

"Not at the moment, no. If he thought you'd stolen *Mansfield Park* and hidden it in your room, you'd be down at the station right now. The man's no one's fool. You couldn't have done anything more likely to point the police directly at you. No, that book was planted. Whether to throw suspicion on you or just as a place to hide it for a while, I don't know. I don't like you staying here alone. Come over to the house, at least until this is over."

"Thanks for worrying about me, Uncle Amos. But I'm fine here. It might never be over."

"Not until the Austen volumes are returned to their owner," Bertie said. "I'm beginning to think I should send them back. End the exhibit early."

"They'll be safe, and I'll be safe, with Ronald and Charlene on guard."

"Not to mention Andrew," Bertie said.

We cracked nervous smiles. "See," I said to Uncle Amos. "Safe as lighthouses."

"I don't like it," he said, "but obviously you can't be convinced."

He opened the door at a knock. "Ralph's here," Charlene said.

"Good. Make sure you have my number on speed dial, Lucy." Uncle Amos left to supervise the changing of the locks.

"I'm going to pay a call on Diane Uppiton this evening," Bertie said. "If she has Jonathan's keys and is using them to break in here at night, she won't be able to do that anymore. But I want to know once and for all."

"I'll come with you."

"Yes. I think you should. This has turned personal for you, Lucy. I don't like that. Not at all."

For the rest of the day, everyone who came in was dripping with rain, shaking out umbrellas, and spreading puddles across the floor. Louise Jane was assigned responsibility for staffing the mop. She was about to protest, but something about the look in Bertie's eyes stopped her. She performed the duty, albeit poorly and with a considerable amount of ill grace.

Several patrons noticed that *Mansfield Park* was missing and asked if it had also "disappeared." Anticipating that, Bertie had instructed us to tell them the truth: the volume had been loaned to an expert for individual study and would be returned shortly.

That the expert was a police forensics lab and not an Austen scholar need not be mentioned.

Uncle Amos pulled me aside after my lecture and handed me a bright, shiny new key. "For your apartment. Bertie will get the other, and that's it. No more keys have been made. And this one," a second key followed, "is for the door to the lighthouse. One for you, Bertie, Ronald, and Charlene. Only four. No keys are to be hidden under rocks outside."

"What about the library board?"

"Under the excuse of there not being a chair of the board, Bertie has decided she won't give them one. Not to Louise Jane, either. She doesn't need to ever be here by herself."

"Thanks, Uncle Amos."

"I repeat my offer of you coming to stay at the house. Ellen would love it if you did."

"I know. But I'm fine here."

"As well as a new lock, Ralph put one darn solid chain on your door. Make sure you use it." He kissed me lightly on the cheek and went in search of Bertie.

I'd scheduled an extra lecture for four o'clock to accommodate those who'd missed the canceled morning one. The number of attendees was up because of the rain, but I rushed through the lecture, answered few questions, and we got the doors closed right on time at five.

Ronald went home to have dinner with his wife, promising to return at seven to spend the night. Charlene volunteered to remain in the library until then. "After all," she said, "I have a lot of reading to catch up on."

"You people," Bertie said, her eyes glistening with tears, "are simply amazing."

Bertie and I went to her car. She drove up the beach.

Jonathan and Diane Uppiton lived in the town of

Kill Devil Hills, in a small community of narrow winding streets and nice, although not ostentatious, houses on large lots. At Kill Devil Hills, the island widens enough that the sand dunes, beach grass, and sea oats are replaced by a maritime forest of substantial trees: live oaks, hickories, and beech mostly. Bertie pulled into the driveway of a large white home with an impressive front porch. Unlike most Outer Banks houses, this one was flat on the ground, not sitting high on pillars. The property was heavily shaded, the ground covered not in grass but unraked leaf mulch. The house next door had a formal garden with immaculate lawns, neatly planted flower beds, and groomed shrubbery. I hadn't seen Mrs. Peterson at the library today, and I wondered if she was standing behind the curtains of the large front window, armed with "birding" binoculars.

Bertie hadn't phoned ahead, not wanting to give Diane a chance to say she wouldn't be in. The garage door was shut, but a car was parked in the driveway. Not a new Corvette, but a somewhat rusty Dodge Neon.

"Is that Diane's car?" I asked.

"No. I've seen it before, but I'm not sure who owns it."

A sign was fastened to the mailbox: BEWARE OF DOG. Although the sign was so old that the letters were faded and it now read BEWARE OF OG. Several yellow Posted signs were nailed to trees at the edges of the property. I thought of the half-sawed off branch, the inquisitive little boy, his brokenhearted parents.

We parked behind the Neon, got out, and walked

to the door. I rang the bell, a dog barked, and the door was opened. Diane Uppiton's head popped out. "This is a surprise. What can I do for you, Bertie?"

"Do you have a few minutes, Diane?"

"I'm entertaining at the moment." She looked to be dressed for company—male company—in a tight black, thigh-length skirt, a teal blouse with plunging décolletage, yards of blue beads around her neck, and dangerously high stiletto sandals. The glittering polish on her toes and fingers matched the blouse.

"We won't be long." Bertie stepped forward, giving Diane no choice but to shut the door in her face or let her in. The dog, a black-and-brown miniature dachshund with a teal bow around its neck, sniffed at our feet and we entered the house in a tumble. "Princess, get away," Diane said, not very sharply. "Silly thing."

"Who is it, Diane?" A man came out of a room off to one side of the long hallway. He carried a crystal glass containing a smoky liquid tinkling with ice.

"Curtis," Bertie said, "how nice to see you."

Diane said, "Curtis dropped in for supper."

I unobtrusively sniffed the air. Nothing but cleaning fluids and Diane's perfume, applied with her usual heavy hand.

"This is a good time for a visit," Curtis said. "Seein' as to how we were just talking about the library. Isn't that right, Diane?"

"We were? Oh yes, we were."

"Come on into the study. Can I get you gals something to drink? There's white wine in the fridge. I'm having bourbon myself."

"A small bourbon would be nice," Bertie said.

"Wine for me," I said.

Curtis waved for us to go first, and Diane led the way, the little dog scampering at her feet.

Bertie and I exchanged glances. Curtis seemed to be making himself quite at home in Jonathan Uppiton's house.

I stopped dead at the entrance to the study. A wall of glass overlooked the back garden, now full of fog, the massive trees dripping rain. Everywhere else was books. Books, books, and more books. Deep mahogany shelves filled the three other sides of the room, floor to ceiling, corner to corner. A circle of dark leather chairs rested on a rich red rug, worn with age. Potted plants in concrete urns stood on tall pedestals, and spindle-legged tables, the prefect size for resting drinks and books, were beside each chair.

Particularly with the fog drifting against the windows, this room could have been at Pemberley. I glanced into a corner, dim in the fading light, and imagined Mr. Darcy seated there. A glass of whiskey at hand, fire blazing, a wolfhound resting at his feet, a leather-bound volume on his lap. And Elizabeth, Lizzie, his beloved wife, sweeping in in a flurry of skirts and laughter to tell him what her sisters had done this time.

"I'm unsure what to do with all these tedious books." Diane carried in a bottle of wine, a used glass, and a fresh one. "I suppose they're worth something."

"You're planning to sell them?" I said, accepting a glass.

"This room's so dark. It has the best view in the entire house, and what did Jonathan do with it but turn it into a dreary library. I'm going to redecorate. If I rip out those shelves, the room will be so much bigger."

I choked on the second-rate wine.

"It needs livening up—bright colors; wicker furniture, perhaps; lots of cushions; some of my own paintings."

"Diane does really good watercolors. She's sure talented, aren't you, babe? I don't know why one of the galleries in town won't carry them. Snobbery, probably."

She beamed. "Curtis is searching for a reliable secondhand book dealer, aren't you, Curtis? We want to be sure to get what the books are worth. Would the library like the leftovers, Bertie? I hate to throw them in the garbage."

I might have choked again, but by this time I'd had a look at some of the books. What on first glace appeared to be an impressive collection was no better than you'd find in any public library. A full set of *Encyclopaedia Britannica*, leather covers cracked and worn; several large atlases; modern hardcovers; and a few tattered trade paperbacks. American history, political biographies, and popular thrillers, mostly. I pulled a Linwood Barclay off the shelf and thumbed through it. The edges were creased, the pages worn. Most of the books showed similar signs of use. Jonathan had collected what he wanted to read.

I hadn't liked the man very much on the two occasions we'd met, but my estimation of him now rose considerably.

Unless the good stuff was stored someplace else, Diane was in for a big disappointment. These books might bring in a few bucks at a garage sale. Five dollars for a bagful.

"I hear the library was broken into last night," Diane said.

"Who told you that?" Bertie replied.

She waved her hand in the air. "Word gets around."

"People are talking, Bertie," Curtis said. "They're saying that without Jonathan's strong hand on the helm, the library's failing."

"Who's saying?" I asked.

"People."

"You have a strange definition of 'failing.'" Bertie sipped her bourbon. "We've never been so busy."

"You can't cope with the crowds."

"Jonathan," Diane said, "wouldn't have been so lax as to allow three volumes to be pilfered."

"Only two," Bertie said, "are temporarily missing. *Mansfield Park* is perfectly safe. It couldn't, in fact, be much safer. I'm confident the police will recover the others in due course. This is excellent bourbon, by the way. I wasn't aware Jonathan liked his bourbon."

"I brought it over," Curtis said.

"Making yourself at home, are you? How nice." Bertie sat comfortably in her chair, her posture relaxed, her tone light, sipping her drink. I was beginning to know her well enough that I could recognize the pure fury emanating from her. "Do you have a date for Jonathan's funeral, Diane?"

"What?"

"We at the library will wish to pay our respects, of course."

"Oh yeah, we've been meaning to tell you," Curtis said. Bertie's eyebrow rose at the word "we."

"The cops released the body yesterday. We'll let you know. Now, about the library. Diane and I are going to call an emergency meeting of the board soon as the funeral's out of the way. We have to choose a board chair soon. Someone has to be in command of this ship."

"Mrs. Fitzgerald is in line to take over. She is the vice chair, after all."

"Eunice Fitzgerald couldn't control a rubber ducky in a bathtub," Diane snorted. She finished her drink and poured another.

"Are you thinking of stepping into the post, Diane?"

"Oh no. Not me. I'm far too busy."

"Diane's an idea person," Curtis said. "She's great in that way, but not one for the day-to-day business of administration and managing folks. Isn't that right, babe?"

Diane preened. Her dog studied me, not liking what he saw.

"I was reluctant," Curtis said. "But at Diane's urging, I've decided to put myself up for election."

"Curtis will be wonderful!" Diane gushed. "He's owned and operated his own business for years, you know. Hugely successful, too. He could have expanded all over the state, but he's such an Outer Banks boy, he couldn't bear to leave. Isn't that right, sweetie?"

Curtis smiled modestly.

"Oh yes," Bertie said, "Gardner Beachwear, right?"

"We've six branches now. From Duck to Hatteras."

"Very impressive. As long as there isn't a board

chair at the moment, I need Jonathan's keys back, Diane."

"What keys?"

"The keys to the library."

Diane looked blank. "I don't have them."

"They would have been among Jonathan's possessions. He kept the library keys on the same chain as his personal keys. I've seen them many times. Didn't the police or the funeral-home director return them to you?"

"They gave me some keys. I am . . . rather, I was . . . his wife, you know. The cops gave me two keys. One for the car and one for the house. Jonathan changed the locks a short time ago. The key the police gave me opened the front door."

"Why do you suppose he changed the locks?" I asked. Was it possible his killing had nothing to do with the library? Had Jonathan been afraid of something—or someone?

"I have no idea," Diane sniffed.

The edges of Bertie's mouth curled up, and I understood. Jonathan had changed his locks to keep *Diane* out. "You didn't find any other keys lying around? Perhaps you didn't recognize them as belonging to the library."

"Where's this going, Bertie? The police asked about this, and now you. Diane told you she doesn't have your keys."

"I don't like to leave loose ends dangling."

"You're trying to shift blame for your mismanagement onto Diane, aren't you? Those Jane Aston books . . ."

"Austen," I said.

"Whatever. Those books are valuable. Worth a lot, so I've been told. I knew it was a mistake, leaving them sitting right out in the open for anyone to snatch. Come to think of it, Bertie, weren't you the one who found Jonathan—poor guy—dead in his own library?"

"That's not fair," I said, indignation rising.

"Quite all right, Lucy. Curtis is concerned for the library. As are we all. And about who might have murdered Jonathan. He's wondering who, after all, stood to gain by his death." Bertie looked pointedly around the room. She put down her empty glass and stood up. I scrambled to follow. My own drink wasn't worth finishing.

Night had come early as rain continued to fall. I wrapped my scarf around my neck. We got into Bertie's car and she switched on the engine.

Diane and Curtis stood at the front door, illuminated by the hall lights, watching us. Their faces were in darkness, but I knew they were not smiling. Diane held the squirming dog in her arms.

"That was a waste of time," I said as Bertie pulled into the road.

"Not at all. I learned a great deal. Diane doesn't know what happened to the key. The woman's no actress. If she were hiding it, she'd have come over all huffy and righteous at being accused."

"So we've eliminated one person as a suspect. I don't see that we're much farther ahead."

"All we know is that Diane doesn't have a key to the lighthouse. Therefore she didn't break in last night. As for Jonathan's death . . . I so hate seeing her in that house, destroying his library."

"His collection isn't worth anything," I said.

"No one ever said it was. He loved books and liked to have them around him. He'd buy new hardcovers by his favorite authors, but otherwise he got what he wanted to read from used bookstores or the remaindered bins. Diane doesn't know enough about books to understand that."

"What about Curtis? What's his interest in the library?"

"Nonexistent. Curtis is interested in Diane. Now that she's back on Arch Street, that is. Businessman? Give me a break. He inherited a grubby chain of stores from his father. It's hard not to make a profit setting made-in-China souvenirs, children's bathing suits, and beach chairs on the Outer Banks, but Curtis is doing his best to run the business into the ground. When we ask who benefits from Jonathan's death, Curtis has to be right up there. That Corvette you told me Diane was spotted shopping for? Can you see Diane, whose greatest ambition in life is to be a respected Southern matron, driving a Corvette?"

"What about him being chair of the library board?"

"I will do everything in my power to see that doesn't happen," Bertie said.

"Surely the other board members won't want him in charge?" I asked.

"If Diane found out about *Mansfield Park* going missing, then the rest of the board knows about it. Poison spreads, Lucy. Whispers are already swirling around us. Diane wants Curtis as chair of the board, and some of the other members will go along with it.

They don't want to rock the boat, and Curtis talks a good talk.

"Diane and Jonathan had a difficult, tumultuous marriage. I never thought they were suited, but that was their business. She finally gave him an ultimatum: the library or her. He chose the library, and she will never forgive him for that. I doubt she killed him, although it's entirely possible—her rage was something to see—but now, even though he's dead, she still wants her revenge. Before our well-meaning but ineffectual board knows what's happening, Diane and Curtis will be hinting to the commissioners that the library isn't viable. Idea person, my ass. Diane has one goal and one goal only: she's going to destroy not only the library in Jonathan's house, but the one he devoted a great deal of his life to. My library. Our library. I will not allow that to happen."

"Why was Jonathan upstairs that night, anyway? If we know that, we might know something about why he was killed."

"I haven't told anyone this," Bertie said, "but Jonathan and I had strong words before the guests began to arrive. As the chair of the library board, he wanted to unveil the notebook. I, well, I wanted to have that honor. I did all the work, along with Ronald and Charlene. Jonathan would hold court and accept compliments all evening, while I helped Josie with the buffet and ensured everyone's glasses were filled. I insisted on being the one to bring down the notebook. When he saw I wasn't going to give in, he grudgingly relented. Pride goeth before a fall, doesn't it? I should have been content with doing my job, but just this once I wanted a small bit of the glory for myself. I should have known Jonathan wouldn't let anyone else have one iota of the limelight. When I was delayed in getting the notebook, he scurried upstairs, figuring if he had it, I wouldn't wrestle it out of his hands in front of the whole reception. Poor Jonathan. All he wanted was to be a big man around town."

"That book of maps was on the floor beside him, remember? Had he been looking at it, do you think?"

"The police speculated he'd been trying to protect it. Someone was attempting to steal it, and when he arrived, he was attacked. The book is of some value, yes, but not worth killing over."

"We know Theodore was upstairs. I saw him go up myself. He says Jonathan told him to go back to the party. Do you believe him?"

Bertie let out a long sigh. "I don't know what I believe anymore, Lucy. I've always been secretly rather fond of Teddy, although keeping an eye on him is such a bother. I've insisted all along he would never have killed anyone for a book. But now, with everything that's happened, I don't know. Have you considered it odd that no attempt has been made to take the notebook?"

"What do you mean?"

"In strict monetary terms, the notebook is much more valuable than the first editions. After all, it's Jane's own book. In her handwriting."

"No one could ever sell it."

"No, but a fan would love to own it," Bertie said. "A rabid fan. Or a dedicated collector."

"Like Theodore?"

"Jonathan and I had kept the existence of the notebook a secret until the party, but word always gets out. Is it possible Teddy was upstairs after it? Or just snooping in his usual way? Jonathan came across him and thought Teddy was intent on stealing either the map book or the journal for his collection, and Teddy struck out. Or maybe Mr. Uppiton grabbed the map book to defend himself. That might have frightened Teddy so much, he's now afraid of touching the notebook."

"But you think he didn't steal *Mansfield Park*?" I said.

"I'm sure of it. So sure that I have to consider that if Teddy, God forbid, murdered Jonathan, then the theft of the books is an altogether separate situation."

"My head is spinning."

Chapter 21

Bertie dropped me at the library after our visit to Diane. It was just after seven, and both Ronald's and Charlene's cars were in the parking lot. The library's interior lights were all on, and as I put my new key in the lock and opened the door, I was hit by a shock wave of Eminem.

Charles was curled up on the circulation desk, holding his head tightly against his body. He lifted his head and threw me a plaintive glance. Charlene moved to her music while she watched Ronald lay out his sleeping bag in front of the Austen alcove. As well as the bag, he'd brought a pillow, a blanket, a cooler containing refreshments, a sports bag with a change of clothes, and two books. One of the books was an educational treatise on developing reading skills in grade-one students from low-income families, and the other a science-fiction paperback the thickness of the front steps with a rather lurid painting of hard-muscled men and equally hard-muscled women loaded down with futuristic weaponry.

No accounting for reading tastes.

"Hey," Charlene said, spotting me. "Welcome to the party."

"Are you really going to sleep here all night, Ronald?"

"I will protect the remaining books with my life." I wasn't entirely sure if he was kidding.

Charlene opened the cooler, and I peered over her shoulder. "At least you'll be well fed." Charles leapt down to also have a peek.

The cooler was packed full of cans of soda, sandwiches, cookies, and bags of potato chips.

"Breakfast." Ronald laid his pillow neatly on top of the sleeping bag and stood back to admire his work.

Charles curled himself into a black-and-tan ball in the center of the pillow.

"At least you won't be lonely," Charlene said. "Mind if I . . ."

"Help yourself. Nora was concerned that I might starve without immediate access to a fully stocked refrigerator."

"How about some pizza?" I said. "I have a microwavable one upstairs. I can heat it up and bring it down."

"Pizza'd be great," Charlene said.

I ran upstairs and popped the pizza into the microwave.

We sat in a circle on the floor, a pile of Ronald's snacks and the piping-hot but rather tasteless pizza between us. Charles got up from the pillow, stretched mightily, and settled into my lap with a contented purr.

"How did Charles come to live here?" I asked. "Did one of you bring him?"

"He belonged to one of the kids in my reading

program," Ronald said, tearing open a bag of chips. "The family moved to Germany for her mother's job, and it would have been too complicated to take the cat. The poor little girl was beside herself with grief at leaving him and worried over what would become of him. So I said he could be a library cat. I send her pictures regularly of him in our reading group, or posed with books I'd like her to read."

"You're a good man, Ronald," Charlene said.

He laughed and grabbed a slice of pizza.

"I thought you had dinner at home?"

"Good men always have room for pizza."

We started at a knock on the door. I was closest, so I removed Charles from my lap and got up to answer it. Connor stood there, his head and shoulders heavy with rain. "I saw the lights on and know Tuesday's early closing. Thought I'd better check."

"Come on in," I said. "Have you had supper?"

"No."

"Then you're in luck."

"You're not busy enough here?" he said, with a laugh, shaking off rain. "You're turning the library into a campground?"

We started to explain about the theft and subsequent locating of *Mansfield Park*.

"I heard about that," Connor said. "I'm afraid the story's all over town. And growing in the telling, I might add."

"That's why I'm here," Ronald said. "Anyone who wants to steal *Emma*, the next book if they're taking them in order, will have to get past me."

"And me," Charlene said.

Charles meowed, and we all laughed.

Connor dropped onto the floor beside me and accepted a can of soda from Ronald. Our mayor was dressed in a dark suit and plain tie, probably on his way home from a meeting with the board of trade or the chief of police, but he looked as though he belonged here, sitting cross-legged on the floor, eating microwaved pizza and potato chips.

We sat there for a long time, munching on high-fat snacks, drinking soda, telling our life stories, and enjoying each other's company. It was easy to forget that a man had been murdered right over our heads, that someone was stealing valuable books, and that there were people in town determined to see our library closed.

Charlene was the first to yawn and say it was time to head home.

"Fortunately," Ronald said, "I don't have far to go." He nodded toward his cozy nest.

"You're really going to bunk here every night?" Connor asked, waving good-bye to Charlene.

"While the Austen books are here, yes."

"Amazing. I'm off, too." Connor pushed himself to his feet.

I tried to stand, but my left leg had fallen asleep. It gave way under me and I staggered. I would have fallen had not Connor grabbed my arm. "That's the second time in two days I've saved you." His lovely blue eyes twinkled, and I felt myself blushing.

"I won't ask," Ronald said. "Lucy, do you want me to see you to your apartment?"

"That's hardly necessary."

"In that case," Connor said, "why don't you walk me to my car? It sounds as though the rain's let up."

Not only had the rain stopped, but most of the clouds had cleared, revealing a bright white moon. The sea was a low murmur of waves drifting onto shore. Out of sight, but not of hearing, a handful of cars moved past on the highway.

"That was fun," Connor said.

"It was."

"I'm glad Ronald's staying here. It seems silly, but it should scare our thief off."

"Charlene's going to do some shifts, too."

"Good. And not only because of the books. Are you safe here, Lucy? I don't mean to frighten you, but strange things have been happening."

"I'm fine. I got a new lock and a bolt and chain on the door to my room. To be honest, Connor, I absolutely love my apartment. I wouldn't want to leave it for the world."

"You keep your phone charged and with you at all times?"

"Yes, Dad."

"Okay, you're right. It's your decision."

"Is the library going to be all right, Connor?"

"If I have anything to say about it."

"There's going to be a new chair of the board. If it's who Bertie thinks is after the job, she's worried he's going to try to have us shut down."

"I'm not on the board, but I do have some influence in this town. The commissioners grumbled mightily about the injunction of funds, but that's what they always do. I pointed out the amount of business the library's bringing to town, with nothing but extra work to show for it, and they, still grumbling, agreed."

"Thanks, Connor."

"This business of the books being stolen, though . . . Not everyone loves Bertie or the library, and knives are coming out."

"That's ridiculous! It's hardly Bertie's fault."

"I'm on your side, Lucy. Yours and Bertie's. The Bodie Island Lighthouse Library's one of the jewels of this part of the coast." He smiled down at me. His eyes were warm, his lips full. I wondered if he was thinking of kissing me.

I wondered what I'd do if he did. Suddenly, I was that fourteen-year-old girl again, protected, innocent, having a walk on the starlit beach with the first boy I'd ever loved.

"You'd better go in," Dr. McNeil, the mayor, said. "I'll watch until you're safely inside."

"Good night, Connor."

"Night, Lucy."

I gave him a wave from the open doorway and remained there, watching as the lights of his car moved down the access road, stopped at the highway, and then sped away. While we'd been talking, the clouds had moved back in to cover the moon, but at the moment I turned to go inside, a wisp of cloud parted. A sliver of moonlight bounced off glass on the opposite side of the loop road, beneath a cluster of trees, and I could see a car, dark in color, the headlights switched off. This road led to nothing but the lighthouse, making a big circle in front of the building, providing only one entrance off the highway. Could it be a couple of lovers seeking a private quiet spot? I peered closer, willing the moon to come out in strength.

The engine started up, breaking the silence. It didn't switch on its headlights, and the dark shape glided behind the trees, keeping to the far side of the loop. Only once it turned into the highway did the lights come on. The night was too dark for me to make out the color or the model. I shivered, scurried inside, and slammed the door firmly behind me.

Chapter 22

That night I dreamt of the Cemetery of Forgotten Books as featured in the novels of Carlos Ruiz Zafón. But instead of the labyrinth being found in the backstreets of Barcelona, it was in the Outer Banks. In Jonathan Uppiton's house, to be exact. Except that Jonathan's house was on the beach, and a storm was rising and salty ocean waves were pouring into his library. They'd reached the first shelf, and no matter how hard I bailed, I was unable to turn the tide.

Mrs. Peterson peered through her curtains, telling me that her daughters were better bailers than I was.

I woke in a cold sweat. Other women's nightmares might be of monsters and giant spiders. Mine were of books being destroyed through carelessness.

Like all dreams, the images began to fade. All that was left, as I drifted back to sleep, was Mrs. Peterson waving her finger at me.

When I woke, she was still on my mind. She was such an annoying woman and so single-minded that no one paid her much attention. She was in and out of the library all the time. She was almost as much a part of the library as the furniture and books. Had she been here when the Austen books were stolen? I couldn't always place her, but she might well have been.

She'd been at the party when Jonathan Uppiton had died. She'd spent the entire night talking to Ronald.

No, not the entire night. I tried to remember what he'd said about Mrs. Peterson's whereabouts in the moments surrounding Jonathan's murder. She'd left him and gone to the ladies' room.

She said she was going to the ladies' room.

Had anyone thought to check up on that?

I leapt out of bed. Disturbed by my dreams, I'd woken early. I had time to do some poking around before I had to be at work.

The sun was touching the ocean in a brilliant orange-and-yellow ball when I drove toward town. Yesterday's rain had left everything fresh and sparkling, but I didn't pay much attention to the scenery. Mrs. Peterson was obsessed with her children. It was unlikely she'd have a job that took her out of the home. At least not in the summer when they weren't in school.

I knew where the Petersons lived. Next door to the Uppitons.

Drat, it looked like I was too late to catch my quarry at home. No car was in the driveway. The double garage doors were open, showing nothing but well-organized shelves. Two girls were throwing a ball into the basketball net attached to the garage.

They were good, their blocking movements smooth, their throws accurate.

I parked on the sidewalk and got out of my car.

"Good morning," I called.

I recognized one of the girls as a Peterson daughter. She was about fourteen, with long, tanned legs, a mass of freckles on her nose and cheeks, and hair bleached by the sun. They were both dressed in loose shorts and a UNC T-shirt and well-used sneakers.

"You're Ms. Richardson, from the library," young Miss Peterson said. "What brings you here?"

"I'm sorry," I said, "I don't know your name."

"No one does. We're just called the Peterson girls. I'm Charity."

"Pleased to meet you, Charity. I don't mean to interrupt your game. I was hoping to speak to your mother. Is she home?"

Charity's friend took a break and dropped onto the lawn, next to a bottle of water.

The blond mane shook. Charity tossed the ball from hand to hand. "No. She left bright and early. So early I wasn't even up." Her pretty face twisted.

"Gone to work?" I said.

"As if. No, she took two of my younger sisters, Dallas and Phoebe, to Elizabeth City. She managed to get them into some fancy-pants summer science camp at the last minute, and today's the first day. I bet she wanted to get out of the house before Dad was up. He wasn't exactly pleased about this camp."

"Why not?" I asked. It was absolutely none of my business, but if there was trouble in the Peterson marriage, it might have a bearing on the case. For the first time, I wondered if Mrs. Peterson and Mr. Uppiton had been "friends." Did Mrs. Peterson want more from their friendship than he was prepared to give? Or had he given it and then withdrawn it? Although it was difficult to imagine Mrs. Peterson in a fit of passion. Whether killing Jonathan or . . . doing other things.

Fortunately, there's not much more teenage girls would rather do than complain about their parents. Charity was no exception. She rolled her eyes. "Dad was absolutely furious when Phoebe told him last night they were going. Mom wanted to keep it secret, but even Dad's gonna notice when two of the kids are, like, not in the house for a week."

"Your father doesn't approve of science camp?"

"He's okay with the camp, but it's, like, really expensive, 'cause they have to stay in dorms, like, for the whole week. We can't afford it. I had a chance to go to basketball camp at UNC for a week. You can be sure Mom wouldn't have the money for that." She pouted. "But science camp. She found the money, all right. Dad was sure mad. She tried telling him that it was a good opportunity for the rug rats to get a solid grounding in science. He said that wasn't the point. The point was they couldn't afford it." She pouted again. "We haven't been able to afford much lately."

"Thanks, anyway," I said. "I might come back later. Will your mom be home this afternoon?"

"Yeah, probably. Dad gets all mad, but she doesn't really care. She only got the ankle biters into this course yesterday afternoon, and they were, like, all excited yesterday, packing and stuff."

"Why so late getting in?"

Charity shrugged. "She only got the money yesterday. I don't know where it came from. She told Dad she had her own source of funds. He said in that case, she should be contributing to running the household."

The friend hadn't appeared to be listening. But she chimed in, "Maybe your mom's turning tricks on the side."

Charity laughed.

I didn't.

Mrs. Peterson had suddenly come into enough money to send two kids to an expensive summer science camp. Money her husband didn't know about.

"Yeah," Charity went on. "That's gotta be it. 'Cause she sure didn't give it to Dad it so he could get his car fixed."

"You don't know where this money actually came from?" I asked.

"Nah," Charity said. "Who knows with my mom? She probably sold something and doesn't want to tell Dad what it is. Like his mother's antique tea set or something." She laughed again.

The friend got to her feet in one swift, clean movement. "Are we playing or not?"

Charity tossed her the ball and the girl caught it easily.

I left them to go back to their game.

I had not the slightest doubt what Mrs. Peterson had sold to get her girls into science camp.

Pride and Prejudice. Sense and Sensibility.

But how on earth was I going to prove it?

I got in my car, switched on the engine. Before I could pull away, the garage door of the house next door groaned and slid open. A brand-new Corvette, eye-catching red with glistening chrome, backed out. The roof was down, and Curtis Gardner was driving. He wore dark sunglasses, and an open-necked shirt displayed a heavy gold chain.

Diane stood in the doorway, waving good-bye. She was dressed in a pink satin nightgown. Pink slippers with a puff of pink on the toes and heels, which were higher than those on the shoes I hated, were on her feet. Why anyone would wear slippers with high heels, I never could understand. It was eight in the morning. She wasn't exactly pretending to be in mourning.

The rusty Dodge Neon was still in the driveway. It looked to me like Diane was left with Curtis's old car, while he took off in the new one, all ready to impress the ladies.

She went back into the house and closed the door behind her.

I switched off my car and leapt out. These two had benefited from the death of Jonathan. Had one of them killed him with that in mind? Had they been in it together?

I rapped on the door.

It opened a fraction. I smiled.

Diane did not smile in return. "What do you want?" she snapped. Close up, I could see that her hair was tousled, showing thinning spots. She had no makeup on, and the bright sunlight shone into her face. The fine lines around her mouth and on her cheeks were numerous, and deep circles were under her eyes. She might come to regret buying Curtis a fancy car of the sort referred to as a chick magnet. Could I exploit that, try to create a fissure between the two? Maybe see what popped out of the fissure . . .

"I was in the neighborhood," I said, "and thought I'd drop in. Check up on how you're doing."

"I'm fine."

"That's nice." I edged forward. "I'd enjoy a coffee."

"I wouldn't." She slammed the door in my smiling face.

"Eunice Fitzgerald just called." Bertie came into the staff break room as I was downing a quick glass of water prior to giving my afternoon lecture to teenagers on books to movies. No grand Victorian hat for this one. If these girls watched Jane Austen movies, they'd know all about bonnets and empire-waist dresses. "Jonathan's funeral's tomorrow. Four o'clock at his family church in Kill Devil Hills. We'll be closing the library early, out of respect and so we can all attend."

I nodded.

"You don't have to come, Lucy. You barely knew the man. And, dare I say, what contact you had with him wasn't entirely positive."

"Perhaps," I said, "I would have liked him better if I'd gotten to know him. He clearly had a great love of books and reading. Any man who reads can't be all bad."

She smiled. "True. He could be an annoying, opinionated, self-impressed fool, but he did love our library. And for that I'd forgive him anything. Almost anything . . ." Her voice trailed off. "Except for wanting to fire a librarian and use the funds to install a commemorative fountain. Of all things."

"I'll be there," I said.

My lecture turned out to be a lively one. On top of the tourists attracted by the exhibit, several local and summer girls returned. They'd obviously been reading Austen books and watching the movies and were developing strong critical opinions on the film adaptations.

Louise Jane slid up to me once the lecture was over and the girls were browsing the stacks or checking out more books. "I have some very bad news."

"You're quitting?" Charlene's head popped around a shelf.

"No," Louise Jane replied. "I wasn't talking to you, anyway."

Charlene shrugged. "We're all one big, happy library family here."

Louise Jane pointedly turned her back. Charlene, never one to take a hint, moved closer. "My grandmother has been called away. One of my aunts has taken seriously ill, and Grandmama has hurried off to Elizabeth City to be with her. "

"And just when you needed her," Charlene said. "How unfortunate."

For a moment I couldn't think of why I'd be overly concerned about the absence of the senior Mrs. McKaughnan. Then I remembered: charms against the unworldly.

Last night had passed uneventfully. No strange noises, no creaking staircases. Just a sleeping cat and a peaceful lighthouse. Peaceful, that is, except for Ronald's snores, so loud and aggressive they could be heard from the fourth-floor landing. Good thing my apartment had a thick, stout door and solid stone walls.

Not that I believed the Bodie Island Lighthouse was haunted. But under the auditory attack of a sleeping Ronald, we wouldn't need any charms to keep wandering specters at bay.

"That's okay," I began to say.

"Fortunately, I've got some knowledge of her skills, so I brought a few herbs that should help."

"I don't need . . ."

"Excuse me, but can you recommend a nice restaurant for dinner? Something kid-friendly? And give us directions? It's our first day here, and we're still not sure of what's where," interrupted a smiling woman. Louise Jane mouthed *Later* to me and took the woman to the circulation desk, where we kept a stack of tourist maps and brochures.

"Her grandmother's charms"—Charlene snorted—"exist nowhere but Louise Jane's imagination. Louise McKaughnan's known up and down the beach as one of the best bingo players around. If she's in Elizabeth City, it's because there's a big pot today. My mother told me that the matron McKaughnan carries a piece of wood to every game she plays. Salvaged from the wreck of a seventeenth-century ship, a piece of the wooden mermaid who once graced the bow. She always gives it a big kiss on taking her seat. Although, come to think of it, the mermaid didn't bring a whole lotta luck to that ship, did it?" Charlene walked away, chuckling.

The moment the doors were closed behind the last of our patrons, Louise Jane pulled a bag out from under the desk with a flourish. I'd expected something old, handwoven willow strips, perhaps, or knitted with care. But it was only a garden-variety white plastic shopping bag. Bertie had left early, saying she wanted to buy something appropriate to wear to Jonathan Uppiton's funeral. Charlene and Ronald watched, obviously interested, despite themselves, as to what Louise Jane was going to pull out of that bag.

"As I said," she said, "I am not my grandmother. This will have to do until she gets back and can lay down some proper spells."

"How come your grandmother's never done this before?" Charlene asked innocently. "Getting rid of the ghosts that live here and all?"

"No one has ever asked her," Louise Jane said, with a sniff. "And I am not *getting rid* of anything. Merely attempting to quiet them down for a while. So Lucy can sleep well at night. Don't get careless and let your guard down, Lucy. Some spirits can be very powerful. Now, where shall we begin? By the alcove, I think. Our little boy has been known to collect things."

Louise Jane slowly reached into her bag. She brought out a handful of dried green leaves and crushed them between her fingers. I smelled tones of mint and oregano overlaid with something darker, more intense.

"Are you sure that's not pot, Louise Jane?" Charlene said, sniffing the air. "We don't need a drug bust here on top of everything else."

"Your cynicism is a credit to you," Louise Jane replied. "But you'll be running to me fast enough if the lighthouse keeper's little boy gets into your map collection."

Behind Louise Jane's back, Charlene stuck out her tongue.

Louise Jane crouched down. She dribbled the crushed leaves onto the floor in front of the Austen cabinet. She swayed back and forth and quietly muttered words I didn't understand.

Charlene rolled her eyes.

Charles came out from under a shelf. He put out one tentative paw and touched the leaves. He stuck out his tiny pink tongue and licked his foot.

"As I said," Louise Jane said, "animals are highly sensitive to the paranormal. This cat's accepting the spell."

"He'd accept it even more if you mixed in some tuna," Charlene said.

Ronald stifled a laugh. "You lot can play witches and warlocks as much as you like, but I'm off home. You'll be all right here, Charlene?"

It was Charlene's turn to sleep over, protecting the Austen books. And me.

"Yup. I have a friend staying at the house with Mom tonight. See you tomorrow, Ronald."

"Night, all," he said, and he left the library.

"Your floor next," Louise Jane said, getting to her feet.

"I have some work to do," Charlene said. "I'll leave you to it."

Louise Jane and I climbed the curving iron stairs, Charles running ahead.

"Aren't you going to put anything down in front of the children's library?" I asked.

"I considered that. But I think not."

"Why not?"

"Overuse of spells ruins the effectiveness."

"Oh."

We reached my landing. Louse Jane studied the area around my door. "I've saved the most powerful herbs for here."

It was a whole lot of mumbo-jumbo, and I wondered if even Louise Jane herself believed what she was doing or was simply enjoying making herself the center of attention. I considered telling her not to bother, that I didn't want—or need—her herbs and spells. But I'd decided it best to let her think I appreciated her helping me. I didn't need to make an enemy out of Louise Jane.

"My grandmother taught me that there must be total honesty between the practitioner and the patron."

"Sounds like a good idea."

"Secrecy breeds mistrust. Mistrust breeds doubt. Doubt allows evil forces to enter."

"I thought you said the ghosts in this lighthouse weren't evil, just lost."

"Don't keep trying to trip me up, Lucy. I did say that about lighthouse keeper's little boy, and about Frances, the Lady, and it's the truth. Even the builders and the Civil War soldiers. As far as I know. I hope you're not . . . naive . . . enough to believe that the only forces at work are the ones that show themselves. No, behind them lurks a deeper, darker, far more malevolent world."

I couldn't contain a shudder. Louise Jane couldn't contain her smirk.

Charles rubbed against my leg, and I was grateful for his warm bulk. The electric white light in the landing was strong, but somehow shadows seemed to have crept into the round corners and between the iron railings.

"I'm going to lay down a protective line in front of your door," Louise Jane said. "No one will be able to cross it."

"I hope I can," I said, with a nervous laugh.

She didn't bother to answer that.

As she had done downstairs, she took herbs out of her bag and rubbed them between her fingers. She carefully laid a line of dry green leaves across the threshold to my apartment as she mumbled incomprehensible words. Again, Charles stepped forward and sampled the herbs. This time he tasted them twice.

Louise Jane got to her feet. "All done. I just hope . . ." Her voice trailed off.

"What?"

"I'm not all that experienced, you know. My grandmother believes that spell casting can only be learned with age, so she hasn't taught me much yet. Total honesty, right?"

"Yeah?"

"The spell will keep the spirits from crossing the line. I hope, well, I just hope they're not *inside* your room right now. If so, they won't be able to get out."

"What!"

"I'm sure it'll be fine. It's still daylight. I hope you opened your drapes this morning. That would keep them away."

I couldn't remember if I had or not. Knowing Ronald had slept downstairs, I'd hurried down with a cup of coffee for him as soon as I was up and dressed.

I was about to protest that I could hardly sleep in a room that *might* have a ghost trapped inside it when I reminded myself that it was all nonsense, anyway. If I didn't believe ghosts haunted the lighthouse, then I could hardly object to not being adequately protected from one.

"Yes," I said. "I opened the curtains soon as I woke up, like I always do, to check the weather. Are we done here?"

"Yup. I hope I've helped."

"I guess we'll see."

"How long will it be, do you think, before Ronald and Charlene give up playing bodyguard for you?"

"That's not what they're doing."

"Sure it is. For you, for the books. The library. Trying to integrate themselves, show how indispensable they are. Changes are coming, Lucy. There's going to be a new board, a new chair of the board. Out with the old, in with the new. Bertie can't last. She's too old-school. Diane Uppiton and Curtis Gardener have new ideas."

"The only idea they have is to close us down. Bertie's going to fight tooth and nail to make sure they don't."

"Who told you that? Bertie? Of course she did. She wants you on her side, Lucy." Louise Jane touched the side of her nose. "A word of warning. Bertie's going down. She's made a fiasco of the Austen collection. The cops are after her for Jonathan's murder. I bet the only reason they haven't arrested her is they don't have enough proof. They'll get it. And then where will you be, honey? Still, I suppose you don't really care. After all, you can go back to Boston anytime you like, can't you? Must be nice not to have roots so deep they tie you to a place, to your family."

Charles leapt onto the railing and hissed.

Louise Jane gave the cat a filthy look and walked away. Round and round, down the winding iron stairs. I hurried after her, wanting to be sure she let herself out.

The overhead lights on the main floor had been switched off. Soft yellow light glowed in the Austen alcove and from a few table lamps. Charlene was nowhere to be seen.

Louise Jane had her giant purse over her shoulder and her hand on the door. She turned and gave me that crocodile smile. "How lovely and peaceful the library is after closing. The calm before the storm, they say. Are you doing anything tonight?"

"I'm heading out to the market now. I'll pick up a few things for dinner and just stay in."

"No after-hours parties with the *favored* staff?"

So this was it. Louise Jane was jealous that we'd had our little impromptu get-together last night and she hadn't been included. Considering that it was impromptu and no one had been invited, she was being rather harsh. I couldn't be bothered to explain. "Good night, Louise Jane."

She waved her fingers in farewell and sailed out the door.

I locked it firmly behind her, and then went upstairs to change out of my work clothes and get my purse.

I stood on the wide landing at the entrance to my apartment—my beloved lighthouse aerie. I studied the line of dried plants in front of the door. Had something disturbed them in the short time I'd been downstairs?

Now I was being fanciful. Louise Jane was no practitioner of white magic. She was a spiteful, jealous woman trying to scare me out of my job and my new home.

Nothing more.

I would not be scared.

Chapter 23

Nevertheless, I stepped carefully over the supposedly protective line of herbs. As soon as I was inside, I checked the window. Despite my determination to be scornful, I was relieved to see that I'd opened the curtains this morning.

I took off my work clothes and slipped into comfortable shorts, a Harvard tank top, and flat sandals. I shook my hair out of the clip at the back of my head and arranged my curls into a ponytail. Last night's pizza had been the end of my groceries and I needed to stock up. Having such a small fridge and no stove made it difficult to plan meals in advance.

I gave the room one last glance—trying hard not to check in the corners—and left. I stepped over the herbs and locked the door.

I drove into Nags Head and picked up a few basic items. Tonight's dinner would be a Lean Cuisine, something I could heat in the microwave. I studied the little box. It had been a stressful day. Maybe I'd need two packages. A very stressful day. Into the shopping basket went a container of Butter Pecan Häagen-Dazs.

I loaded the groceries into my car and pulled out of the parking lot. I decided to drive down Virginia Dale Trail, the more scenic route along the ocean-front, rather than take the highway all the way back to the lighthouse. The sky to the east was dark as night fell over the sea, while the west was ablaze with oranges and reds. The ocean side of Virginia Dale Trail is almost all rental properties, big beach houses perched on stilts, brightly painted or gray and black with age, with outside staircases, numerous levels, and high decks to catch the view. On the land side, the houses are still mostly rentals, but the few perma-nent homes are indicated by a mailbox at the end of the drive or an attempt to make a scrap of garden in soil that's almost entirely sand. I slowed to allow a large delivery truck to turn out of a narrow street that dead-ended at the beach. Off to my right, the land side, I saw a familiar figure emerge from a small house. The house had been painted baby blue, but the paint had peeled badly in the salty wind and not been refreshed. Several of the railings protecting the deck on the second level had fallen away and been patched with plywood. The plywood was stained and cracked, indicating it had been in place for a long time. The front steps tilted ominously. The whole place had an aura of neglect and decay.

But I was more interested in the resident and what he was carrying than in the house. Theodore Kowal-ski, and a cardboard box. The sort of box, I thought, in which books were packaged and delivered. I might not have paid him any mind if not for the way he glanced up and down the street as he came out the door. He hurried to his car and shoved the box into the trunk. Then, with another furtive glance, he leapt into the driver's seat.

I was partially hidden by the truck, which was having considerable difficulty making the tight turn. Finally the truck straightened out, the driver gave me a wave of thanks, and I could carry on. Up ahead, Theodore's car was signaling a right-hand turn. Without even considering what might be the wisest course of action, I put my foot on the gas and the Yaris shot forward. I was in time to see him turning onto the Croatan Highway, heading north, back toward Nags Head, Kill Devil Hills, and Kitty Hawk. I reached the turn at the same time as there was a break in the heavy traffic and fell in behind Theodore.

What on earth am I doing? And why was I doing it? For all I knew, he was going to visit his mother and would lead me on a merry chase. I decided to follow as far as Kitty Hawk and the bridge across Currituck Sound to the mainland. If not for the furtive way Theodore had put that box into the trunk, I would have honked my horn, waved, and gone home to eat Lean Cuisine and Häagen-Dazs.

Theodore was a cautious driver; otherwise I doubt I'd have been able to follow in the heavy traffic. He kept to the right lane, going exactly the speed limit. I followed, trying to keep a reasonable distance back. I was helped by the approaching night, as long as I kept my eyes on his rear lights. My brightly colored car did not exactly blend in, but Theodore didn't appear to be watching to see if he were being followed. Cars swept past us. He signaled a lane change as we approached Kill Devil Hills, and I did the same. Soon the left indicator flashed again. He had to wait for approaching cars to clear the intersection, and I found myself sitting right behind him. I pulled down my sun visor, not knowing if that would cover some of my face or not. The approaching traffic cleared, and he made the turn into a side street, the teal Yaris almost on his bumper. Theodore drove slowly past a small strip mall and pulled into the loading area behind the shops.

A single car was there. Its headlights flashed. I glided to a stop at the side of the street. It was almost dark now, the back of the stores lit by powerful security lights. Theodore parked beside the waiting car, a gleaming black Cadillac Escalade. Interior lights came on as the two men got out of their cars. They shook hands, exchanged a few words. Then Theodore was bending into his car, taking out the box, and carrying the box to the SUV, the back of which had been popped open in anticipation. As I watched, he opened the box and lifted out a book. The other man bent to examine it.

Sense and Sensibility! Pride and Prejudice! That rat was selling the books. Bertie and I had been wrong. He must have hidden *Mansfield Park* in my room, intending to come back for it later. He'd probably offered the entire set to this . . . this . . . person, but his plans had been foiled when we changed the locks and set up a twenty-four-hour guard in the library. I was out of my car and running before I knew it. I flew across the street; an approaching car blared its horn and slammed on brakes. A woman leaned out and yelled something quite rude.

"Stop!" I cried. "Those books are stolen property."

Both men turned. Theodore saw me and his mouth went slack with shock. The other man, dressed in crisp khaki pants and a blue golf shirt, just looked confused. I had the presence of mind to whip my iPhone out of my shorts pocket. I waved it in the air. "I'm calling the police."

A head popped out from the back door of one of the shops. "What's going on out there?"

"What the hell?" the man caught red-handed receiving stolen goods said. "Who are you?"

"A concerned citizen," I replied. "Those Austens have been stolen."

"Austens?"

"Lucy," Theodore said, "go away."

"I certainly will not. Give me the books."

"I don't know anything about stolen books." The man backed up, lifting his hands into the air. "I'm not getting into that, Kowalski."

"This is all a misunderstanding," Theodore protested. He wasn't wearing his tweeds today, just a pair of jeans and a T-shirt. The ordinary clothes made him look smaller, diminished. The aristocratic English accent had been replaced by a plain North Carolina one.

"The only *misunderstanding*," I insisted, "was you thinking you could get away with it. I demand you show me the contents of that box."

"Gerry, wait right there," Theodore said. "I'll be more than happy to show this young lady what I have."

My confidence was beginning to waver. Theodore wasn't trying to bluff his way out of it or throw up a smoke screen of obstruction. He waved the book in my face. The cover was a rather dull gray dotted with, of all things, red hearts. *Casino Royale* by Ian Fleming. Underneath lay *Live and Let Die*, the cover a garish pink mess.

"Oh," I said. Despite my embarrassment, I was still able to reflect on how much cover design had changed over the years. For the better.

Theodore pulled out the books one by one, showed them to me, and put them on the clean floor of the Esplanade's trunk. Most were James Bond novels, as well as a few midcentury spy books by lesser-known authors. With every volume I felt myself deflating. Finally he lifted the box, turned it upside down, and gave it a good shake. "Do you want to search it, Lucy? Look for hidden compartments?"

"Sorry."

"So, you're not saying these books are stolen?" Gerry said.

"Uh, no," I said.

He shook his head. Theodore began packing the books back in the box. Gerry handed him an envelope. "Nice doing business with you, Kowalski. You know what I'm after: the full set of first editions. Keep me in mind if you run across any." He turned to me. "And that's not Austen, in case you're thinking of accusing me next time."

"Sorry."

With a shake of his head, he got into his SUV and drove away.

I gave Theodore a sickly grin. "Sorry."

"You thought I'd stolen the books from the library and was selling them?"

"Well, yeah." I shoved my phone into my pocket.

Theodore let out a long sigh. "I won't mention this to anyone if you don't. My ... circumstances have been somewhat reduced lately, and I'm forced to sell parts of my collection. I don't want to, but I have little choice. I went to a book show in Raleigh the other day and met Gerry. He's looking to buy, and I want ... I need to sell a few things."

"I'm sorry," I said once again.

He looked so sad, defeated almost. "I really loved those Ian Flemings. I'd prefer people don't know. It's only a temporary development, I'll be back on my feet soon."

"Your secret's safe with me."

"Thank you." He got into his car and drove away.

I started on the carton of Häagen-Dazs Butter Pecan while still parked on the side of the street.

Chapter 24

Butch came around shortly before opening Thursday morning. Bringing, we were delighted to see, *Mansfield Park*. He handed it to me with a grin and a flourish, and I held it close, just for a moment. Someone, I suspected Butch, had gone to the trouble of dusting off the fingerprint powder and whatever else the forensics lab had used on it. "Detective Watson said you can have this back. He put a rush order on the fingerprint techs."

"What did they find?" Bertie asked.

"Nothing we can use."

I took the book to the cabinet. Bertie unlocked it with much ceremony, and I placed *Mansfield Park* among its fellows. It was then locked in. I thought the set looked very empty with two missing. But at least it was only two.

Charlene had reported that nothing of interest had happened in the night.

At two minutes before nine, Bertie cleared her throat and held up one hand to capture our attention. "As I told you earlier, the library will be closing early today for Jonathan's funeral, which will be followed by a reception in the church hall."

"He was a cantankerous old goat," Charlene said, "but he did love this library. Almost as much as he loved himself as chair of the board."

Ronald and Louise Jane nodded in agreement.

"I still want to come," I said.

"We can't leave the library empty," Ronald said.

"I thought of that," Bertie said. "Ellen's sending Aaron to stand guard."

Ellen and Amos's youngest child, my cousin Aaron, was a junior in college. He played tackle on the football team, and it was said that NFL scouts were looking at him. *Mansfield Park*, *Emma*, *Northanger Abbey*, *Persuasion*, and Miss Austen's personal notebook would be perfectly safe with Aaron on guard.

Jonathan's Uppiton's funeral was a well-attended affair. His parents had been Outer Banks people; he'd lived his whole life here, active in many community institutions. Not to mention that his murder had been prominently reported in the media, and there was nothing like the hope of press attention to bring out crowds of mourners. I sat in the second-to-last row with Bertie, Ronald, and Charlene. When Uncle Amos, Aunt Ellen, and Josie arrived, they squeezed in beside us. Aunt Ellen gave me a smile and pressed my hand. Josie had come straight from the bakery and still had a whiff of yeast and cinnamon about her. Andrew had come with Louise Jane. They'd taken seats close to the front, as (Louise Jane had informed me) befitted longstanding Outer Banks families. Other than Diane and Curtis, who were probably waiting to make a grand entrance, the entire board was in attendance. Mrs. Fitzgerald was draped in what Miss Austen would have known as widow's weeds, complete with black hat and heavy veil. *She must,* I thought, *be sweltering under all that dark, heavy cloth in this far-too-full room.* Mrs. Peterson arrived, accompanied by three of her five girls. Charity, the basketball-playing eldest, looked as though she'd rather be just about anyplace else.

Two of the younger Peterson girls, I knew, were at science camp. A very expensive science camp the family couldn't afford. Mrs. Peterson spotted Ronald, seated between Bertie and Charlene, and made a "talk to you later" gesture. If I'd been closer, I might have been able to hear what he muttered under his breath.

Connor McNeil came in the midst of a group of dark-suited men and women. They took seats together near the front. Butch was also in the room. As was Detective Watson. They didn't slide into a pew but stood at the back, one on either side of the wide aisle, watching everyone as they entered.

I've read enough mystery novels to know that the police attend the funeral of a murder victim, hoping the killer will show up to gloat and give something away. The presence of the police reminded me of why—and how—Jonathon Uppiton had died, and I felt a shiver run down my back. Aunt Ellen put her arm around me.

Had someone in this room, in this beautiful, modern church, full of light and color, murdered Mr. Uppiton? Almost certainly. No one believed a total stranger had snuck into the Lighthouse Library to make their way upstairs while the party went on below. And then tiptoed out again once the deed was done. I wouldn't have recognized anyone who didn't belong unless they had a sign printed on their forehead, but Bertie and Mrs. Fitzgerald had the guest list memorized between the two of them. The police were probably here as much to see who *didn't* come, consumed by guilt, as who did.

I glanced at my watch. Three fifty-five; almost time to begin. Voices blended in a low murmur, and then, one by one, all conversation stopped as the organist took her seat and began to play. When nothing else seemed to be happening, the buzz of conversation resumed. Right on the dot of four, it died again. Everyone turned and craned their necks, and so did I.

Diane Uppiton stood at the doorway. It was a warm, sunny day, and she was framed in the yellow light streaming through the doors. She stood alone, waiting until every eye was on her.

And then she began to walk slowly up the aisle.

She was, I had to admit, perfectly turned out in a dark gray suit that was somber yet not overly dramatic (as per Mrs. Fitzgerald). Her makeup was subdued, her jewelry restrained, her plain black pumps had one-inch heels. She clutched a white handkerchief tightly in her right hand and took her place in the front pew.

A moment later Curtis Gardner slipped into the pew directly in front of us.

The music stopped. The minister, robed in a full white gown, mounted the steps and took her place behind the lectern. "Friends," she began.

I watched the back of Curtis's head. At first I

thought it was bent respectively in prayer. Then I realized his thumbs were moving as he sent a text. Diane sat alone, with no one to comfort her. Bertie had told me the Uppitons had no children, Jonathan's parents were long dead, and Diane had little contact with her family in Buffalo. Diane wiped at her eyes and twisted the handkerchief between her fingers. Her shoulders shivered as she wept. She did seem to be genuinely grieving. I reminded myself that that meant nothing. They'd been married for a long time; she had to have *some* sentiment for Jonathan. Even if as soon as the service was over she'd go back to counting his money and destroying his legacy.

Could Diane have killed Jonathan? Sure, she could. She had been furious that night at him, at me, at everyone. Furious and humiliated. Had she found him upstairs, gloating over the notebook, and struck out with what she had at hand—a beer bottle? I tried to remember if Diane had been drinking beer at the party. Unlikely. Even if she preferred beer to wine, I didn't think she was the sort to quaff beer in public, and certainly not straight from the bottle. Not very ladylike. She'd been having wine at her home the other night when Bertie and I dropped in.

Curtis, on the other hand, looked like a man who enjoyed his beer. He'd been drinking bourbon at Diane's, but bourbon wasn't available at the reception. Only wine and beer.

Was the killer a beer drinker? Had the police considered that?

He—or she—had to have brought the bottle upstairs with him or her.

Unless someone else had been up there earlier,

finished off a beer, and left the bottle behind. I shoved that thought aside. No point in adding unnecessary complications to my theory.

Mrs. Peterson certainly didn't seem like a beer drinker. Although I was now convinced that she'd stolen the Austen books, I was unsure about her being the killer. If she had murdered Jonathan, she'd had the chance to get his keys before everyone poured into the room. Had that been her objective?

Think, Lucy. Think!

I glanced about the crowded church. A few people wept and wiped their eyes, some followed the eulogy with rapt attention, one or two prayed silently. Some shifted in their seats or surreptitiously checked their phones.

But no one looked guilty.

It was no use. When my mother gave a party, she had been known to count every drop consumed, all the better to gossip about who had done what the next day. (I sometimes wondered why my father's inattention to her hadn't driven her to drink. The answer: then she wouldn't be able to check out, and comment on, everyone else.) As for me, the last thing I'd been doing the night of the reception was taking note of the partygoers' alcohol consumption. It was entirely possible Jonathan himself had carried the bottle upstairs. Maybe he'd dropped it when his assailant came in and the killer, a teetotaler or wine drinker, had taken advantage of the broken glass to do the deed.

I hadn't known Jonathan Uppiton in life, but I was getting to know him in death. And I couldn't imagine him casually taking a beer upstairs into the rare-books room to take a swig from while he gloated over the Austen notebook. After the service, I'd try to grab Theodore, ask him if he'd noticed a beer bottle anywhere in the vicinity when Jonathan had confronted him.

Aunt Ellen tugged at my arm, and I realized everyone was getting to their feet with hymn books in hand. I hurried to join them.

After the service we all trooped into the church hall for the reception. The catering was by Josie's Cozy Bakery, and my cousin had slipped out of the service early, heading for the kitchen to supervise the finishing touches. Uncle Amos spotted an old fishing buddy, and Aunt Ellen left me, saying she wanted to chat with a friend. Bertie located Mrs. Fitzgerald and dragged her into a corner, no doubt to talk about the makeup of the library board. Ronald and Charlene wandered off to mingle with the crowd.

Leaving me standing by the buffet table, balancing a glass of tea and a plate of crustless sandwiches. I'd worn black slacks and a matching jacket over a white blouse to the funeral, and for some foolish reason had slipped on those high-heeled shoes I hated but couldn't seem to talk myself out of wearing. I guess I thought the funeral would be all sitting down. I needed to talk to Theodore, but at the moment, he was deep in conversation with a white-haired, heavily bearded guy I didn't recognize. I nibbled on an egg salad sandwich. Connor broke away from the circle of what I guessed to be town and county officials.

"Who's guarding the store?" he asked me.

"What?"

"The library. The books. I thought you were going to have someone watching them all the time."

"Aunt Ellen sent Aaron over."

Connor nodded in approval. "Lucy, I was wondering if . . ."

"Mr. Mayor. I have you at last, you naughty boy." An elderly lady approached. She was about four foot five and weighed ninety pounds tops, but the grip she placed on Connor's arm was not to be trifled with. "I've called town hall again and again about my garbage collection, but no one will help me. Seven o'clock is simply too early for me to have my bins out. That man on the phone was out-and-out rude. I want him fired."

Connor threw me a grimace over the lady's helmet of steel-gray hair. "Mrs. Johnstone, let me get you some tea and sandwiches and you can tell me all about it."

"I'll have two salmon and one ham and cheese. And a couple of Josie's pecan tarts. Better get them before they're all snatched up. These people are like vultures. I'll come with you, Mr. Mayor. Now that I have you to myself, I won't risk some neighborhood busybody dragging you away with her minor complaints."

I kept my eye on Mrs. Peterson. Her daughters had spotted friends and abandoned her. She was chatting to a woman I didn't recognize. The moment the other woman excused herself, I pounced.

"Mrs. Peterson. It was nice of you to come. You brought only three of your lovely daughters. I suppose the others have summer activities to keep them busy."

She snatched my bait in her jaws. I bet fishermen wish all fish were this easy to hook. "Dallas and Phoebe are at summer camp. A very exclusive, private science camp for the brightest of young girls. Professors from UNC and Duke will be coming to spend some time with the students. I have to tell you, Lucy, that it was very hard to get the girls in. It's a highly competitive program and spaces are sought by some of the best families from as far away as New York City. Some girls"—she sniffed—"never do get in. But their parents keep trying."

"Wow," I said. "Good for them."

She beamed.

"I have a niece about the same age. I bet she'd love to go next year. It must be expensive, though."

"Very expensive. Because it is so exclusive, of course. But nothing's too much for my girls."

"You and your husband are wonderful parents. I see he isn't here. I'll phone him later and tell him about my niece."

Panic crossed her face. "Don't do that!"

"Why ever not?" I said innocently. "My sister will be concerned about the cost. Perhaps he can tell me if there are scholarships she can apply for."

Her eyes darted around the room. "My husband and I don't always agree on the importance of structured programming to the girls' future."

"That's too bad. I guess in that case he balked at the cost, eh?"

"You could say that. Now, if you'll excuse me."

I couldn't think of a single way to be subtle about it. So I asked outright. "How did you manage to pay for it, if he didn't want to?"

"I . . . came into some funds."

"You mean like rare books?" I demanded. Butch and Detective Watson were still here. I was prepared to grab Mrs. Peterson the moment she confessed and yell for police assistance.

Tears gathered in her eyes. I prepared to pounce. "Please don't tell him," she said. "Although I dare say he'll find out soon enough. I . . . I sold his golf clubs. But it was worth it. Nancy Hamm's daughter got in. Why couldn't mine go?"

That took the wind out of my sails. She wiped at her eyes. "Oh, there's Ronald. I have to tell him about the science camp. He'll be so thrilled."

She hurried away.

I went back to the buffet for another round of sandwiches. I didn't know what to think. Was Mrs. Peterson lying to me?

Unlikely. Oh, well, back to square one.

As I finished my second round of sandwiches, the white-bearded man and Theodore shook hands and parted. I dropped my glass and plate onto a table and rushed over.

"Lucy!" Theodore exclaimed. "How lovely to see you, my dear." He seemed to have decided to forget all about yesterday's fiasco, and that was fine with me. For the funeral he'd dressed in full English-intellectual mode in a belted brown Harris Tweed jacket. He wore a red sweater vest underneath, a gray cravat around his neck, and a perfectly folded red handkerchief tucked into the jacket pocket. He looked as though he were about to head out among the gorse and heather for a day of grouse hunting. "May I get you some refreshment? They aren't able to serve a decent cup of tea, but the coffee is palatable."

"No, but thanks. I wanted to ask you something about that night. The night of the reception at the library."

"Ask away." Behind the plain glass of his spectacles, his eyes shone with curiosity.

"When you encountered Mr. Uppiton upstairs, just before . . . just before he died, did you notice if he was carrying anything?"

He thought for a few moments. "Can't say as I did."

"A wineglass or a bottle of beer, maybe?"

"Why are you asking?"

"No reason," I squeaked. The police report said that Jonathan Uppiton had been stabbed. It didn't mention the weapon, and everyone naturally assumed a knife. Other than the police, only those of us—Bertie, Connor, and I—who'd been in the room knew the truth. We'd been ordered not to talk about it.

And, I suddenly realized, here I was now, talking about it. "The . . . uh . . . caterers reported some things missing when they packed up."

The look on his face clearly indicated that he didn't believe me.

I cocked my head to one side and tossed him a smile. "You're so observant, I thought you'd know." He preened. I held my smile, but it wasn't easy. The last time I'd seen that look in his small eyes, he'd been admiring the Austens.

"I'm finished here," he said. "I've paid my respects, the few that I had, to Jonathan. Why don't you and I slip away for a nice drink somewhere? An early dinner, maybe." His right eye drooped in what he might have intended to be a wink.

"Gee, that would be nice. But I have to get back to the library. I'm on duty tonight."

"You don't keep evening hours on Thursday."

I leaned toward him. He bent his head to hear better. I smelled tobacco and the acrid scent of clothing far too heavy for the climate. "We're taking shifts guarding the books. Around the clock."

"Very wise. But a young lady like you shouldn't be alone. Let me . . ."

I was digging a deeper and deeper hole for myself. "That's so nice of you, Mr. Kowalski, but Ronald will be with me."

"Theodore, please."

"Theodore. About that night? Mr. Uppiton?"

"Was Jonathan carrying anything when we had our unpleasant encounter on the stairs? He was not. I'm sure of it. He was highly agitated and waved his hands about a great deal. Mustn't speak ill of the dead and all that, but Jonathan always was inclined to be a drama queen. His hands were empty."

"Thanks."

"About that drink. You don't have to go back immediately, do you?"

"Oh, gee. Bertie's waving to me. I better see what she wants. Thanks again."

I dashed off. Bertie was nowhere in sight, but it was the best excuse for an escape I could think of. Time for me to take my leave. The crowd was building around the buffet table. Mrs. Garbage Problem was right about one thing: a funeral made people mighty hungry. *I'd better grab a pecan tart to take with me. Maybe one of those lemon squares, too.*

The oatmeal and raisin cookies looked good. They'd do for dessert tonight. (The Häagen-Dazs had somehow been finished off yesterday.) I loaded up on treats, folded everything into a napkin printed with Josie's logo, and tucked them into my bag. Through the serving hatch I could see Butch talking to Josie while he vacuumed up the sandwich tray she was attempting to refill. Detective Watson was with Uncle Amos and his fishing buddy.

Louise Jane and Andrew were chatting to Diane Uppiton, while Curtis hovered at the grieving widow's elbow. Before leaving, it would be polite for me to express my condolences. I approached the little group. "Of course," Louise Jane was saying, "the history of the Outer Banks is an awful important component of the library. . . . Oh, hello, Lucy. We were just talking about the direction Diane and Curtis want to take the Lighthouse Library."

"Sorry to interrupt. I wanted to say it was a lovely service, Mrs. Uppiton. Mr. Uppiton will be very much missed."

Diane looked at me though red, unfocused eyes. I wondered if she'd had more than a few drinks to get her through the funeral. "Who are you again?"

"I'm Lucy, the . . ."

"Librarian's assistant," Curtis said. "You remember Lucy, babe. Bertie's helper."

"I am the assistant librarian," I said, in tones reminiscent of mother chastising the employee of the flower shop for bringing salmon roses to the bridge-club charity luncheon, not peach as she had ordered.

"Not the librarian's assistant. If you're going to try to run a library board, Mr. Gardner, you need to learn the difference."

Mother managed to get twenty percent taken off the cost of the flowers. I wasn't quite so successful. "Whatever," Curtis said, with a shrug.

Louise Jane focused her crocodile smile on me. "I was reminding Diane and Curtis of how important history is to us in North Carolina, particularly in the Outer Banks. Someone with an in-depth knowledge of that history, with generations of roots planted in the sand and marsh, is much more vital to the running of the library than any outsider. Even one with a degree."

"Mr. Uppiton's death has worked out rather well for you, hasn't it, Louise Jane?" The moment the words were out of my mouth, I wanted to grab them and stuff them back. Fortunately, Diane didn't seem to have heard. She was off on her private cloud. Curtis grinned in anticipation of a catfight. Louise Jane's eyes blazed with anger.

"Who do you think you are?" Andrew said. "Take that back."

"It's all right, Andrew." Louise Jane patted his arm. She forced out a light laugh, but the look she focused on me would stop even my mother in her tracks. "Lucy's understandably upset. Poor little Lucy. So out of her depth."

I turned and walked away.

"I'm sure you'd love a glass of tea, Mrs. Uppiton," Louise Jane said. "Let Andrew get you something."

I left the ill-lit, noisy hall and walked into the hot, bright sun of an Outer Banks summer afternoon and pulled my sunglasses out of my bag. My eyes prickled, and not just against the sunlight. Tears were gathering, threatening to spill over. I wiped one away as I unlocked my car door.

I sat behind the wheel but didn't put the key in the ignition. I might as well give up, go home. Once the Austen exhibit was over, the Bodie Island Lighthouse Library didn't need both me and Louise Jane. Jonathan Uppiton was barely in the ground, and Louise Jane was fighting hard for her position. What chance did I—an outsider—have against her? She'd wear away at Curtis Gardner like ocean waves reducing a strong rock to fine sand.

Assistant, indeed.

I gave myself a mental slap. What sort of daughter of Suzanne Wyatt Richardson would I be if I gave up now? All I could do would be to keep doing the job I'd already come to love as best as I could. Surely that had to be worth something.

But right now I only wanted to go home, crawl under the covers, eat oatmeal cookies and pecan tarts, and read *The Secret Life of Bees* by Sue Monk Kidd.

I might even fortify myself with a glass of wine.

I stopped with the key half-turned. The engine died.

Wine. Beer.

Louise Jane had been drinking beer at the reception. I closed my eyes and tried to visualize the scene. Louise Jane confronting Jonathan Uppiton after he'd said he wasn't thinking of hiring Louise Jane instead of me, but intended to eliminate the position altogether.

She'd been holding something in her hand as she gestured and argued with him.

A beer.

No secret that Louise Jane was desperate for a job at the library. Desperate, but neither qualified nor needed, not that night. To my eyes, a job on the circulation desk seemed scarcely worth killing over, but was it to Louise Jane? She talked about her grandmother and great-grandmother constantly. Her family's position on the Outer Banks, the history and legacy of her ancestors.

Did Louise Jane see the library position as more than just a job—also a way to get approval from her family?

She might not have intended to kill Jonathan Uppiton. Had she followed him upstairs, found him with the Austen notebook? Did she demand he fire me and hire her in my place? Did he laugh at her? Taunt her?

Did she remind him, once again, of her family's origins? And did he, mockingly, pick up the map book and say he didn't need her? It was all in books like this one.

As if I were watching a movie, I saw it play out in front of my eyes. Louise Jane, overcome with rage, lashing out at her tormenter with the only thing she had at hand. A bottle of beer.

And then, realizing what she'd done, dashing downstairs to join the party. Afraid to call for help. Afraid she'd be accused of murder.

Or had the killing not been an accident at all, but deliberate? Had she murdered Mr. Uppiton knowing the next person up the stairs would be Bertie? Had Louise Jane killed Jonathan to set a trap for Bertie?

Bertie—the only one who stood in the way of Louise Jane getting her long-desired job.

How did that tie in to the theft of the books? First rule of detecting: ask, *Cui bono?* Who benefits? Clearly, Louise Jane. She did, in fact, achieve her fondest dream when the books began to disappear and the running of the library became more than the permanent staff could handle.

Why, then, had *Mansfield Park* been stolen and hidden in my room *after* Louise Jane started working at the library?

Did she want to get rid of me that much?

The workings of the sort of twisted mind that would kill a man in cold blood to get a job were probably not something I could fully understand.

What had Louise Jane said to me outside my apartment door, after laying the "protective" herbs? That the *favored* staff had been partying without her. The only reason she'd know about Tuesday night's get-together would be if she'd seen us. Someone, I remembered, had been parked in the dark, watching the lighthouse. Watching us come and go. That someone had driven off without turning her headlights on, although it was dark. Clearly whoever it was had not wanted to be seen. Had Louise Jane been watching the lighthouse on other nights, and when all the lights were off pulled the spare key out from under its rock and used it to get in and take *Mansfield Park*? And then, when the locks were changed, had she been forced to sit and stew in her car under cover of darkness?

I drove home very slowly, so deep in thought I scarcely noticed the RVs, camper trailers, and cars with out-of-state plates honking at me to speed up or get out of the way.

I let myself into the library and found Aaron sitting in a chair in the Austen alcove, Charles in his lap. My cousin had been reading, but both he and the cat came to attention when they heard my key in the lock and my voice calling out. He stretched those football-playing shoulders and rose to his full height. My mom and Aunt Ellen are on the short side, and I had the misfortune (I sometimes thought when standing next to the five-foot-ten, willowy Josie) of inheriting those genes. Uncle Amos is six foot two, and his children took after his side of the family.

Charles jumped down with a meow and wrapped himself around my ankles.

"Whatcha reading?" I asked, bending down to give the cat a scratch in greeting.

Aaron hesitated before holding up the book somewhat sheepishly. A paperback copy of *Pride and Prejudice,* the one with Keira Knightley on the cover.

"Enjoying it?"

"I forgot to bring a sports magazine, and the cell phone reception isn't worth much in here."

"You have to stand by a window."

"Yeah, but Mom said I was to guard the cabinet." He pointed at the picture on the front cover of the book. "She was in *Pirates of the Caribbean*, so I figured this book would be the same sorta thing."

"It's not."

"Yeah, so I noticed. But it's not bad. Once you get into the fancy language and stuff."

I hid a grin. "Thanks, Aaron. You can go now. I'll check the book out for you."

"You gonna be okay here by yourself?"

"I work here, remember? I'll stay with the books. It's almost six now. Ronald's coming by at seven to spend the night. I've some work to do, anyway."

He still looked uncertain.

"We've got this, Aaron," I said.

I was confident there wouldn't be any more thefts. Louise Jane had tried to implicate me, but that had failed. She was now taking a more subtle approach, turning Curtis and Diane against me.

I checked out the book, and Aaron stuffed it into his backpack. "Did you know today's my mom and dad's thirty-fifth wedding anniversary?"

"No. They never said anything."

"They wouldn't. You know Mom. Doesn't like people making a fuss. They're going to Owen's for dinner. Then they're spending the night in the hotel where they went on their wedding night."

"That sounds nice."

"Yeah. Well, see ya," he said.

"Thanks again. Oh, uh, would you like a pecan tart? I brought some from the funeral." I figured I could be nice and offer to share. Even though Aaron had access to all he could eat of his big sister's baking.

"Sure!" he replied. And I remembered that when it came to young men, there was no limit to all they could eat. I unwrapped the paper napkin and Aaron scooped up the tart. He looked longingly at the remaining cookie and square. "Help yourself," I said, with a sinking heart. "I had enough at the funeral."

He snatched the napkin. "Thanks, Lucy."

The door slammed behind him. I picked up the phone on the circulation desk and dialed a familiar number. It went immediately to voice mail.

"Hi, Butch. It's Lucy. I've thought of something. Something about the killing of Jonathan Uppiton that's really important. I'm at the library and plan to stay in all night. Give me a call when you have a minute. Bye!"

As soon as I hung up, I mentally kicked myself. I sounded like a teenage girl calling a guy, hoping for a date. I considered trying Watson. The last time I'd tried telling Detective Watson my suspicions, he'd pretty much turned the tables and accused me of the killing. I didn't want another chat with Watson without having Uncle Amos with me. And Uncle Amos was celebrating his wedding anniversary. No way was I going to interrupt that!

I'd wait for Butch to call, explain my reasoning about Louise Jane being the killer, and then take Uncle Amos down to the station with me in the morning. No hurry.

Charles reminded me that it was long past dinnertime.

I ran upstairs, dropped my purse on the bed, shrugged off my funeral jacket, replaced the stiff white blouse with a black T-shirt, and then returned with a bowl of cat food and my laptop. As Charles dug in, I kicked off my shoes and settled into the chair recently vacated by Aaron to do some work until Ronald arrived. I'd found a Cambridge University PhD thesis on Jane Austen's influence on the modern novel, which I'd been saving until I had time to read the whole thing.

I kicked off my shoes and settled down to read. It was a fascinating paper, and I was soon immersed in it.

The author made a reference to something in *Persuasion* that I'd missed in my own reading. I pulled my head out of the research paper and stretched muscles stiff from sitting. I went to the shelves and found a hefty hardcover of the Austen book. I walked back to my chair, flicking through the pages, looking for the reference. Only as I was about to sit back down did I realize how dark it had become. Outside, night had fallen, and the room was illuminated only by the small circle of yellow light in the Austen alcove. I glanced at my watch. To my considerable surprise, it was after nine o'clock.

Where was Ronald? I'd last seen him in the church hall, hiding from Mrs. Peterson behind a dying philodendron. I hadn't said good-bye to him or any of my other coworkers, and he hadn't said anything about not coming to sleep in the library tonight. Perhaps he'd changed his mind—it was rather a silly idea in the first place—but I would have expected him to tell me if he had.

I crossed the room in my stocking feet and peeked out the window.

Charles leapt onto the ledge to also have a look.

Rain lashed the window, and I could hear trees groaning against the wind. It had been brilliantly sunny when I left the funeral. On this narrow strip of sand sticking out in the Atlantic Ocean, the weather could, and often did, turn on a dime. When high above me the first-order Fresnel lens flashed in its two-and-a-half-second pattern, all I could see were night and rain.

A sudden deluge like this one would sometimes flood the lower-lying roads. It was possible Ronald couldn't get through. I'd give him a call. Let him know all was okay and he was not to try to come if the roads were dangerous.

I tucked *Persuasion* under my arm. My feet were freezing on the marble floor, and I slipped the killer heels back on as I went to the circulation desk and picked up the phone. It took me a moment to realize what I was hearing.

Nothing.

No dial tone. Like a character in an old movie, I pounded buttons, hoping that would help. Still nothing.

The phone wasn't working. A tree must have fallen into the lines.

I'd left my cell phone in my purse. And my purse was upstairs in my apartment. I could run up and get it, but reception was so spotty in these stone walls, I'd probably have to go outside to make the call.

In the short time I'd been living here, I'd become so accustomed to the regular pattern of the lighthouse light at night that I scarcely noticed it anymore: 2.5 seconds on, 2.5 seconds off, 2.5 seconds on, and then 22.5 seconds off. When a stream of light lit up the window and did not go off again, I went back to the window for a peek outside.

Headlights were turning into the parking lot.

Good. Ronald must have gotten through. I watched as the car pulled up to the foot of the path. It was a small, foreign compact, but I couldn't make out the model or color. The headlights were switched off, and a moment later the thousand-watt light of the lighthouse went into its 22.5 second dormancy. I strained to peer outside, but it was as dark, as if this coast were still lit by nothing other than homemade tallow candles and sputtering oil lamps.

A knock pounded on the door.

Ronald must have forgotten his key.

I peered out into the night. And then, for some unknown reason, I remembered the night of the reception. The night Jonathan Uppiton had died. Louise Jane had been drinking beer, all right. But Louise Jane never did anything for herself. Not when she had Poor Andrew at her beck and call. "Get me a drink," she'd ordered him. He'd brought her a beer. But it had been in a glass, not straight from the bottle. She'd finished that one and had still been holding her empty glass when I ran past her and up the stairs in answer to Bertie's cry.

She had never gotten a new beer because the person who had grabbed her the bottle never poured her the drink. Instead he had gone upstairs with the bottle of beer he'd started to get for his dear Louise Jane in his hand.

I sucked in a breath.

It was Andrew. Andrew who'd attacked John Uppiton.

Andrew who'd stolen the precious books.

Thank heavens Ronald had arrived. He could

guard the library while I drove to the police station to tell them what I'd figured out.

As I turned away from the window, Charles hissed and spat and dug his nails into my hand very hard.

"Hey! Stop that. I wouldn't have thought you'd be afraid of a little storm."

I headed for the door. Charles leapt off the ledge and threw himself under my feet. I stumbled, cursed, and nudged the cat aside with my foot. His fur was standing on end, his eyes were narrow yellow slits, and his lips curled back to reveal his little teeth. He hissed once again as I, wondering if he'd heard an animal outside, unlocked and threw open the door.

Not Ronald, but Andrew. He'd taken off the tie he'd worn at the funeral and undone the top buttons of his shirt. His fair hair was mussed, as though he'd raked his fingers through it over and over.

"Oh, hi," I said, trying to sound calm. "Louise Jane isn't here."

"I know that. She went home after the reception. She was very tired."

"So am I. Absolutely beat. It's late. Why don't you come back tomorrow?" I tried to close the door, but I was too slow. He was inside the library. "I need to talk to you, Lucy. I'm worried about Louise Jane. I think . . . I think she's in trouble. I want do to the right thing, but I'm afraid for her."

"We can talk about it tomorrow."

Charles spat.

"Tomorrow," Andrew said, "will be too late."

He slammed the door shut behind him and

twisted the lock. His boyish face was set into hard lines, his shoulders tight, and his fists clenched. He didn't look much like harmless, mild-mannered, sycophant Andrew anymore.

I realized I hadn't seen the car's interior light come on when the driver got out in the 22.5 seconds the area was in pitch-darkness. It had been intentionally switched off. So I wouldn't know it wasn't Ronald coming up the path.

Rainwater dripped off his shoulders and began to puddle at his feet. "You should have gone home, Lucy. Back to Boston, where you belong. You can't just come here and take other people's jobs, you know."

My mouth was dry, my tongue overly large. I took a step backward. "I realized that myself. This afternoon, at the funeral. Diane and Curtis intend to shut the library down. There won't be jobs for anyone, not me nor Louise Jane. I phoned Bertie a couple of minutes ago. I told her I quit. She was angry. Told me to get out and not bother filling in my notice."

"You phoned Bertie?"

"Yup."

"How?"

"Huh?"

"The landline's out. The wires are down."

Until now I'd been hoping I was misinterpreting Andrew's voice and gestures. It was possible that the interior light in his car was burned out. But this I couldn't fail to understand: how did Andrew know the phone wasn't working? "The storm?"

"The storm. With some help. I heard what you said at the funeral, Lucy. You suspect Louise Jane killed Jonathan. Well, she didn't. I can't let you start spreading rumors that she did."

"I won't." I squeaked.

"No," he said. "You won't."

"Why don't you tell me," I said, trying to force out a smile, "why you had to do it. I know you must have had a good reason." *Keep him talking. Keep him talking.* Ronald was bound to get here soon.

"Uppiton had no intention of hiring Louise Jane. Even if they got rid of you, he didn't think the library needed her. He didn't realize how valuable an employee she would be. None of you did. So I killed him. I should have killed you, too. But no, I was too weak. Too kind. I thought if I stole those stupid books and made it look like you were a thief, they'd realize they had to get rid of you and hire Louise Jane." He gave me a sickening smile. "It worked, didn't it?"

"Totally. Louise Jane must be very proud of you."

"Oh, she doesn't know anything about it. She doesn't know what I'd do for her. What I've done for her. But I don't mind. If she's happy, then I'm happy."

Charles leapt to the floor. His back arched and he hissed.

"I'm so glad it worked out," I said. *Where the heck is Ronald?* "I won't tell her if you don't want me to."

"Oh, I don't want you to, all right."

All of a sudden, without my noticing where it had come from, a knife was in Andrew's hand. It wasn't much of a knife, just an ordinary kitchen thing, used for slicing vegetables, probably. But I had no doubt it could do serious damage to more than carrots and turnips.

I bolted. Andrew was between me and the door, so I headed for the stairs. If I got to my apartment, my lighthouse aerie, I could barricade myself in. I'd grab my iPhone and hope I could get a signal. If I had to, I'd break the glass on the window and lean out as far out as possible. I'd get soaked, but the phone should work then. I thought of Louise Jane's story of the lighthouse keeper's young wife throwing herself out that window. Would they find me below and think her ghost had driven me to do the same?

My foot hit the first rung of the twisting iron stairs. I felt Andrew behind me. The light from the alcove didn't reach here, and everything was as dark as can be. I scrambled up the stairs. He grabbed at my ankle. I lashed out and felt the pointed heel of my shoe make contact with something soft and yielding. He yelped and I was free. I reached the first landing. The steps shook with the impact. When the great lamp came on and some light burst through the window, I dared to glance over my shoulder. Those killer heels had gotten Andrew full in the face. He'd been knocked onto his butt and was rubbing his left cheekbone. He looked up at me. He pushed himself to his feet as we were plunged into darkness when the light switched off. I couldn't remember if I'd locked the door to my apartment. I always did during the day when we were open to the public, but sometimes I didn't bother if I went down to the main library after hours. If I had locked the door, I was doomed. My keys were a weight in my pocket, but I wouldn't be able to find the right one among the bunch in the dark. Never mind fit it successfully into the lock. Any hesitation, and Andrew would be on me.

If he kills me, I thought, *the police should have enough evidence—this time—to arrest and convict him.* The thought did nothing to comfort me.

Second floor. I flew past the children's library. Plush toys, soft-covered books, blankets and comforters, and brightly colored plastic games. Nothing I could use as a weapon there. Behind me, Andrew got to his feet. I heard his deep breathing, the pounding of his feet on the stairs.

I zigzagged from one side of the stairs to the other, knowing he wouldn't be able to see my legs in the dark. Thank heavens I was wearing black slacks and a black shirt.

The third floor. Charlene's research collection. No help there.

"You can't run forever, Lucy," Andrew said as the light burst on once more. "There's nothing at the top but a long, long way down." He made another grab for my ankle, but didn't have a strong grip. I twisted free and his fingers fell away. I ran on, higher and higher. Around and around.

I was almost at the fourth floor. My door. *Please, God, I hope I haven't locked it.*

I was used to walking these stairs in the near dark. I knew exactly where the door was. I reached it, grabbed the knob. Twisted.

Locked.

My key was buried somewhere in a pocket of my pants. Andrew's harsh wheezing breath followed me as he came up the stairs.

No time, no time.

The light was approaching the apex of its dark period. I had about fifteen seconds to get ready.

I whirled around, placed myself at the edge of the top step. I planted my feet firmly apart and bent my knees. I braced myself. I would not simply let him kill me.

The light came on. Andrew stood no more than a foot from me. He was one step lower, making his face almost level with mine. He was so close, I could have reached out and touched him. I screamed and my courage fled. I leapt backward.

"Got you now," he said. He raised the knife as the light died.

In the total darkness, the silence was broken by a howl of feline rage. Andrew screamed in pain. The light flashed and I could see again. Charles had leapt onto Andrew's chest and raked his claws across his face. Andrew swung the knife toward the cat, but Charles jumped nimbly away and the blade slashed at empty air. Andrew stood on the edge of the step. I screamed to give myself strength, lifted my hand, and lashed out. I struck him on the side of his head, hard. He stared at me through wide, surprised eyes. It went dark, and I heard him fall.

It was a terrible sound. He rolled down the steps, the iron clanging at every impact. He came to a stop at the third-floor landing with a final hard thud. I held my breath, but all fell quiet.

When the light flashed once again, I could see Andrew where he lay on the landing, outside the reference room. His body was very still. Charles perched on the railing above him, flashing his claws and spitting in anger.

I took a long, deep breath. For the first time I became aware that I was holding something. I tightened my fingers around the solid bulk of the Austen hardcover I'd picked up so long ago. I'd clung to it without thinking all this time. *All he needed was a little* Persuasion.

Chapter 25

At last my shaking hands found my key and put it into the lock. I opened the door, ran into my apartment, slapped on the kitchen light, slammed the door behind me, kicked off my one remaining shoe, tossed *Persuasion* onto the table, and swept up my purse and a good, sharp kitchen knife.

I then opened the door, peering out, half expecting Andrew to leap out from behind . . . something. Fortunately, there was nothing on the landing that he could use for concealment.

The line of protective herbs Louise Jane had laid across the threshold was undisturbed. I rubbed the ball of my right foot through it.

Then I made my way cautiously down the stairs, knife at the ready. Andrew remained where he'd fallen. Charles had leapt off the railing to stand guard beside Andrew's head. The knife lay beside his outstretched hand. Keeping my eyes firmly on his face, I kicked the weapon over the edge. It made a distant clatter as it landed on the bottom floor. Andrew's chest was moving and, despite all, I was glad to see it.

The landings were wide and by keeping my back pressed against the wall, I could pass Andrew without bringing myself into range. Just in case he was faking being out cold.

Then I dashed downstairs, Charles at my heels.

I intended to run for my car, lock myself in, call 911, and wait until the police and ambulance arrived. I reached the main floor, unlocked the door, and stumbled out into the night.

A car was coming up the road, moving fast. Its headlights reflected off the pouring rain and trees swaying with the wind. A second car pulled in close behind the first. The cars pulled to a stop, water spraying under the wheels. Butch's Focus. Connor's BMW.

Both men burst out of their vehicles, leaving the doors open, the headlights on, the wipers moving, the engines running. They ran toward me, reached me at the same time.

"Lucy! Are you all right?"

"What's happened? Lucy, thank heavens."

"What are you holding?"

"Lucy, you're safe. Put the knife down."

"There, I've got it." A large, strong, warm hand gently pried my fingers off the hilt of the knife.

"Andrew," I said. "It was Andrew. He killed Mr. Uppiton. He stole the books. He tried to kill me. *Persuasion* saved me. Jane Austen and Charles saved me."

"Charles the cat?" Connor said.

Butch pulled out his phone and spoke rapidly

into it, while Connor asked, "Where's Andrew now?"

"Inside. He fell. I don't think he's dead."

"Take her to your car, Mr. Mayor," a grim-faced Butch said. He reached under his jacket and pulled out his gun. "I'm going in to have a look. Help's on the way."

A siren broke the quiet night. Then another. Soon the road was full of flashing blue and red lights and men and women in uniform.

I sat in Connor's car and began to shiver. He turned the heat up high. We watched as police officers ran into the lighthouse, guns at the ready. Butch soon came out, sliding his weapon into the holster. He waved for the paramedics to come in. They were back minutes later and put their loaded stretcher into the back of the ambulance. It sped away under lights and sirens.

Rain continued to fall.

I opened the car door.

"I'm taking you to the hospital," Connor said. "You need to be checked out."

"I'm okay. I can't leave Charles alone."

A police car was blocking the entrance to the parking lot. A car pulled up beside it. The officer bent down before waving it through. Bertie.

She saw Connor and me and ran toward us. "What's happening? Ruby at the police station phoned to tell me there'd been a call to the library."

"It was Andrew," I said. "Andrew, responsible for it all. The killings, the thefts."

"Let's see if they'll let me inside," she said.

Watson met us at the door. "This is a crime scene, ladies, Mr. Mayor. You can't come in."

"But . . ." Bertie said.

"No *but*s about it, Ms. James."

"Let me get the cat. Please," I said. "He saved my life. He'll be so frightened. All you people stomping around."

"Very well. Just you. Get the cat. Then I'll need you to come down to the station with me to make a statement."

I found Charles curled up in the chair in the Austen alcove.

Fast asleep and purring.

Bertie said she'd look after Charles tonight. She then called Uncle Amos, over my protests, dragging him away from his anniversary dinner. Connor drove me to the police station, where my uncle met us. Uncle Amos remained with me while I made my statement to Watson, who was polite to me for a change. I told my story, and then Watson said I was free to leave.

"Have you heard anything from the hospital?" I asked, as we got to our feet. "About Andrew?"

"He's concussed and has a broken leg and collarbone, as well as two broken ribs. He regained consciousness before they took him into surgery and insisted he be allowed to call a lawyer."

"Well, it won't be me," said Uncle Amos.

Uncle Amos wouldn't hear of taking me back to the library to spend the night on my own. Neither would Watson, who said the stairs to my apartment were off-limits. So Uncle Amos drove me to his house, where Aunt Ellen had the guest room freshened up and ready.

I was exhausted, but my mind was in such a whirl, I knew I wouldn't be able to sleep. I allowed Aunt Ellen to make a fuss over me and tuck me in as she had when I was a little girl visiting for the summer. "I'm sorry," I said, snuggling under the covers.

"Sorry for what, honey?"

"I ruined your anniversary."

"I'd say it was Andrew who ruined our anniversary. Never mind. Amos and I plan to have plenty more. I'll call your mom, tell her you'll talk to her in the morning."

I was asleep before she shut the door.

Chapter 26

I woke to brilliant sunlight pouring through my window, and the steady, rhythmic pounding of waves on shore. For a moment I didn't know where I was, and then it all came back.

Andrew. Mild-mannered, whiny Poor Andrew had almost killed me.

He would have killed me, if not for a big Himalayan cat and a reissued classic novel.

I made my way down the hall to the bathroom. When I came out, Aunt Ellen was waiting by my bedroom door, wreathed in smiles. "I checked on you during the night several times. Not a stir."

"I guess I was tired."

"Ready for coffee?"

"Oh yeah."

"Get dressed and go into the breakfast room. I'll bring the coffee, and you can call your mother from there. Josie still keeps some of her clothes here, so I put a few things out in case you don't want to put your work clothes back on."

I dressed quickly in jean shorts and a blue T-shirt.

The shirt was, ahem, far too large in certain places, and the shorts were tight across my hips and came down to my knees. But I didn't mind. I wasn't dressing for company.

When their children left home, Amos and Ellen sold their big, rambling house and bought their dream place: a small beach house. In typical Outer Banks style, it was perched on stilts, narrow and high, with multiple levels jutting out in a jumble. The house floated on the edge of the dunes, with a view stretching all the way to Spain. The outside was painted cheerful yellow; the inside walls were white, the house decorated in a riot of blues and yellows. I went through the French doors leading off the modern steel-and-glass kitchen into the breakfast room, a big, half-covered deck. It was on the second level, facing east, looking over the beach and the sea. Morning joggers ran past, a few families scoured the tide line for washed-up shells, fishermen set up their chairs, and sandpipers darted in and out of the surf. The rising sun was a happy yellow ball in a cloudless blue sky. No traces of last night's storm remained.

Aunt Ellen brought me coffee and a phone. I called my mom, assured her that I was safe and being well looked after. And, no, I didn't think this was reason for me to come home. They did have crime in Boston, didn't they? She said that my father was concerned about me, but he had an important meeting this morning and couldn't be disturbed. Oh, and Ricky was seen having dinner with that totally unsuitable Collins girl. Clearly he was on the rebound, and everyone knew he was waiting for me to come back.

I told my mom I loved her and hung up.

I leaned back, smiled to myself, and watched gulls circling overhead. Nice to know some things never change.

My suspicions rose when Aunt Ellen began setting the table with far more cutlery and plates than would be needed for the two of us. The doorbell rang, and voices called out greetings.

Josie was first, carrying a box from her bakery. Charlene and Ronald followed. Bertie brought up the rear, bearing a squirming furry bundle. Charles. "I brought him out to say hi," Bertie said, "but I'd better lock him in the house. Let him have one look at those birds, and we'll spend the day chasing him up and down the beach."

I gave my hero a hearty scratch behind the ears. He struggled to get out of Bertie's grip. She went into the house with Charles and came back with the coffee tray. Aunt Ellen brought out platters piled high with scrambled eggs, bacon, and sausages. Connor followed, carrying butter and pots of jam. "Nice to see you looking so well, Lucy. You gave us all quite a fright last night."

I remembered. "Ronald! What happened? Why didn't you come to the library?"

His mouth twisted. "I was snagged by Mrs. Peterson at the funeral reception. She must have nattered on for half an hour. Everyone else was gone when I finally got a word in edgewise and escaped. I was on my way to the library when I got a call. From Nora. She'd been in an accident."

I gasped. "What happened? Is she okay?"

He opened the box and selected a plump croissant. "She's fine, thank heavens. Her car was side-swiped on the road to our house and crashed into a tree. Fortunately, she wasn't going fast, and the air-bags deployed. She was a bit bruised, quite shaken up, but nothing more serious. The car's a mess, though. She was calling me from the side of the road, waiting for the police."

"That can't be a coincidence."

"No. The car that hit her sped up and disappeared before she could gather her wits about her. She didn't get the plate, but did notice that it was a blue Corolla."

"Andrew drives a Corolla," Josie said.

"His car's been towed to the lot." Butch came out of the kitchen. He pulled up a chair, and Aunt Ellen passed him a plate. "Fresh damage to the front bumper. Mornin', all." He piled eggs and sausages, and accepted a muffin from the box.

"He took the chance of hurting Nora, perhaps killing her, just to keep Ronald away from the library?" Josie said.

"Yup."

"What a . . . not-nice person," Charlene said.

"You both"—I nodded to Butch and Connor—"arrived in the nick of time. What made you realize something was wrong?"

"Not quite the nick of time," Connor said, adding a healthy dose of cream to his coffee. "If you and Charles hadn't subdued Andrew, we would have been too late."

"Don't even talk about it," Aunt Ellen said.

"I got a call shortly after you left the funeral

Lucy," Butch said. "A punch-up at a bar, an almighty mess. When we finally cleared the scene and hauled the participants off to jail, I checked my phone. Only then did I get your message. I tried calling you back. The library phone was out of order, and that worried me. We had no reports of any phone lines down, so I called Bertie."

"And I," Bertie said, "had just heard from Ronald, phoning from the hospital to say he wouldn't be able to go to the library as planned."

Connor said, "Bertie and I went for a drink after the funeral to talk about the future of the library. It wasn't hard to guess that something was wrong, so I thought I'd better check. Butch and I arrived at the same time."

I smiled at the two men who'd rushed to my aid.

"Tell Lucy what else you found, Butch," Bertie said.

"The keys to the library in the glove compartment of Andrew's car. He must have figured he might have a use for them, and took them off Jonathan after he was killed."

"Pretty cold-blooded," Connor said.

Butch nodded.

"Not that!" Bertie said. "Tell her what *else* you found."

"The books. *Sense and Sensibility* and *Pride and Prejudice*. In the trunk of Andrew's car."

"That's great! Are they okay?"

"Fine," Bertie said. "He even had the courtesy to wrap them in plastic bags."

"More likely to keep his prints off, I'd imagine," Connor said, "than to protect them."

"When can we have them back?" I asked.

Bertie smiled as she speared another sausage. "I've already been down to the police station. Detective Watson decided he didn't need them for evidence."

"Sounds like y'all had a busy night," Josie said.

"Not as busy as Lucy's," Connor said.

I shivered in the warm sunshine and cradled my mug in my hands. Aunt Ellen served me eggs, and Josie placed a muffin on the plate.

"Andrew's been charged with the murder of Jonathan Uppiton as well as theft and the attempted murder of Lucy," Butch said around a mouthful of egg.

"Why do you suppose he stole the books?" Josie asked.

"To cause trouble, muddy the waters, distract us from the murder investigation," Butch said. "And to get Louise Jane what she wanted. The job."

"That worked," Connor said. "But it still wasn't enough for Andrew. Louise Jane was only hired temporarily. At the end of the summer she wouldn't be needed anymore. He had to get rid of Lucy so Louise Jane would be able to stay on. Thus, he tried to have Lucy arrested for theft. And when that didn't work everything began spiraling out of control."

"Why do you think he stole the books in the order they were written?" I asked.

"I have absolutely no idea," Bertie said. "He might not have even known that was the case. He wasn't at all interested in the exhibit."

"Maybe he was trying to make it look like an inside job," Charlene suggested. "He figured that would be more likely to point the finger at Lucy."

"What's Louise Jane's role in all this?" Connor asked.

"She was questioned last night. Said she had no idea."

Charlene snorted.

"I believe her," I said. "Last night, Andrew was adamant that she didn't know."

"Louise Jane loved having Andrew trotting around after her," Bertie said. "I'm sure she simply considered his adoration to be her due and didn't realize the lengths he would go to in order to make her happy."

"Is that all it was?" Josie said. "Nothing was in it for Andrew?"

"Poor Andrew, indeed. What does he have to say for himself?" I asked.

"That he's innocent. That you went nuts and shoved him down the stairs for no reason," Butch said.

I half rose from my seat. "What!"

"Don't worry, Lucy. He doesn't have a leg to stand on." Connor counted off Andrew's offenses on his fingers. "His car drove Nora off the road. He had the stolen books in the trunk. He can't explain why he was in the lighthouse—which is, after all, Lucy's home—when he had no reason to be here."

"One thing I'm not understanding," I said. "How did Andrew get into the Austen cabinet?"

This time it was Bertie's turn to snort.

"Along with keys to the library," Butch said, "Jonathan Uppiton had a key to the cabinet."

"That rat," Bertie said. "The cabinet was custom-made for the exhibit. Jonathan organized it. He told me he'd only had one key made and handed it to me. I should have known he'd hold one back."

"Andrew's a cool one, I'll give him that," Butch said. "He got the cabinet unlocked, the books snatched, the cabinet locked again in a crowded library while everyone's backs were turned. The third time he broke in at night, and that upped the risk even more. If he'd been caught prowling around the library in the dark, he wouldn't have been able to explain it away as curiosity."

"Was there a key to my apartment on him?" I asked.

"Yup."

"Another one Jonathan shouldn't have had," Bertie said.

I thought back to the morning after the night *Mansfield Park* had been stolen. Louise Jane had arrived for her second day of work. Andrew followed, bringing treats. Bertie had ordered him to leave, and the staff went into her office to wait for the police. No one had thought to make sure Andrew did leave. Earlier, he must have either hidden the book somewhere in the library or brought it in with him. And then, once our backs were turned, he went up the stairs, unlocked my door, hid the book, locked the door, and went out again.

I shivered. Connor noticed and threw me a smile over the rim of his coffee mug.

"Well, I, for one, am glad all that's over," Bertie said. "And we can get back to the business of running a library."

From the pantry, Charles reminded us that once again, he'd accidently been locked in.

Chapter 27

The letters VR "shot" into the red wallpaper was a nice touch. I took a step back and admired my handiwork. The silly bit of decorating I'd done to make the third-floor room, where we would be holding the book club, resemble the parlor of 221B Baker Street was in place. We were reading *The Moonstone*, not Sherlock Holmes, but Holmes's sitting room was so iconic, I hoped the club members would enjoy it. I'd bought a single roll of red-and-gold wallpaper from the discount outlet and punched the holes in it before draping it over one of the shelves. I'd placed a pipe and deerstalker hat from Ronald's collection of costumes onto a shelf arranged to resemble the mantel of a fireplace and taped a picture of a roaring wood fire beneath.

We'd brought chairs upstairs and arranged them in a circle. I'd plugged in the coffeepot and laid out cookies Josie had brought, leftovers from the bakery

"Everything looks just great, Lucy," Bertie said. preened.

At long, long last, the evening of the inaugura

meeting of the Bodie Island Lighthouse Library classic novel reading group had arrived. I was expecting twelve attendees, rather a lot for this small room, but we'd make space somehow. We always did at the Lighthouse Library.

Mrs. Fitzgerald had proved to be more stubborn than anyone had expected and mustered enough support to be elected chair of the library board. When it came for a vote, only Diane Uppiton and Curtis Gardner opposed. Whereupon Mrs. Fitzgerald had rapped her cane on the floor and said that any idea of closing the Lighthouse Library was an abomination. When the applause died down, she presented the first order of business: raises all around for the staff. Next, she had declared that the rare-books room would be renamed the Jonathan Uppiton Collection, and she would, at her own expense, have a bronze plaque prepared to that effect to hang beside the door.

The Austen collection—the full and complete Austen collection—was still on display downstairs, but the rush had died off. We'd been overwhelmed when word got out that the two stolen books were back, but at last it seemed as though every Austenite in the eastern United States had been satisfied. We were getting only one or two bus tours a week now, the shops had gone back to displaying seashell art and paintings of piers and lighthouses, and the restaurants had taken afternoon tea off the menu.

My lectures had been reduced to three a week, Charlene's visiting English scholars were happy, and Ronald was talking about taking some vacation time. We were managing fine without Louise Jane.

She had professed herself to be mortified at what Andrew had done. Her protestations of innocence might have been somewhat melodramatic, and somehow she'd managed to turn herself into the victim in all this, but I believed her.

She might be arrogant, self-absorbed, willfully blind, but she hadn't killed anyone, nor had she stolen any books.

We'd remained closed the day after Andrew's arrest, but were open again bright and early the next morning. Louise Jane had shown up for work on time, chin up, face forward, shoulders set. Bertie called her into her office, and when Louise Jane slunk out fifteen minutes later, she told us that an aunt in Raleigh had taken ill and Louise Jane was needed to care for her.

But we were not to worry; she assured us that she'd soon be back.

I heard that Louise Jane had left the Outer Banks without bothering to visit Poor Andrew in jail.

"Nervous?" Josie asked me.

"More like excited. I'm really looking forward to this group. They were supposed to have read *The Moonstone*. Do you suppose they did?"

"I did," Josie said. As well as pastry, Josie had brought her friend Grace, and introduced her to me as an ardent mystery lover. "It was great," Grace said.

"All the copies we had were checked out," Bertie said. "People'll be arriving any minute. You wait here. I'll go downstairs and show them up."

Josie and Grace chatted while I fussed with the decorations, pulled the chairs into a tighter circle, arranged the cookies. Ate a cookie. Charles studied the fake fireplace with an expression that indicated he wasn't impressed. I ate another cookie.

I leapt away from the treats table at a burst of laughter on the stairs. Mrs. Peterson sailed in first, accompanied by the elder two of her daughters. They were followed by the visiting English postdoctoral students. "We want to hear what a Yank has to say about Wilkie Collins," one of them said.

"Yanks!" Grace said, with a laugh. "Careful there—we're Southerners."

My cousin Aaron arrived, to the obvious delight of the oldest Peterson girl. Then several women I knew as keen patrons and avid readers. Mrs. Fitzgerald made it up the stairs to the third floor, enjoying the assistance of Theodore Kowalski.

"Thought I'd be needed to keep an eye on you, Lucy," Theodore said. "What do you young people know about the classic novels, anyway?" He helped Mrs. Fitzgerald to a seat.

An attractive woman in her early forties, casual clothes accented by good jewelry and a colorful scarf, approached me, hand extended. "I'm CeeCee Watson. Pleased to meet you, Lucy. I've heard so much about you."

"You have?" *Watson?*

"I do believe you know my husband. Sam doesn't entirely approve of my mystery-reading habit, but I'm afraid I'm an addict. I read modern stuff almost exclusively, and it was a joy to discover Mr. Collins. Now that I've read a nineteenth-century novel, I'm hooked. I'm looking forward to hearing everyone else's opinion." She gave my hand a pat. "Is that the hero cat I've heard so much about? I adore cats, but

Sam won't let one in the house." She crouched down and held out her hand. Charles accepted her praise.

About the last person I expected to join my group was Louise Jane. But here she was, broad smile, outstretched arms. She enveloped me in a big hug. "You've done an awful nice job on the room, Lucy. Shows what can be done with a small budget and not much imagination." I stepped out of the hug, wondering whether I'd been insulted. "My relatives in Raleigh wanted me to stay on longer, but I hurried back so I could be here tonight. I want to hear what you have to say about *The Moonstone*. From an academic perspective, I mean. I hope you don't make it sound too dull. Oh good, there's Mrs. Fitzgerald. I haven't had a chance to tell her about my haunted-island exhibit." Louise Jane hip-checked Grace, who was about to take the seat next to the elderly lady, and plunked herself down. "Eunice, I was simply thrilled to hear you'd taken over as board chair."

As everyone came in, I invited them to help themselves to cookies and coffee and find a place to sit.

Soon only two empty chairs were left.

"I guess we should start," I said. "I hope you all had a chance to read the book."

They nodded.

"After you, Mr. Mayor," said a voice from the landing.

"After you, Officer" was the reply.

Connor and Butch stumbled into the room together.

They both grinned at me, and I smiled back.

"I, myself," Theodore said, adjusting his spectacles, "have read *The Moonstone* many times, of course. Although I prefer the *The Woman in White* for its biting social commentary and . . ."

I smothered a laugh. Oh yes, living and working at the Bodie Island Lighthouse Library was not going to be boring.

ACKNOWLEDGMENTS

Writing this book has been nothing but fun, from visiting the Outer Banks to scout out locations to actually doing the writing. In particular I'd like to thank Mary Jane Maffini for her friendship, support, and encouragement. And Barbara Sweet, librarian extraordinaire. I also thank my agent, Kim Lionetti, for taking me on and believing that I could do this, and Laura Fazio, my marvelous editor at Obsidian, who came up with the concept and provided encouragement and much-needed advice in bringing it to fruition.

Read on for a sneak peek at the next
adorable cozy mystery in Eva Gates's
Lighthouse Library Mystery series,

BOOKED FOR TROUBLE

Available from Obsidian in September 2015

I love my mother. Truly, I do. She's never shown me anything but love, although she's tempered it by criticism perhaps once too often. She believes in me, I think, although she's not exactly averse to pointing out that I'd be better off if I did things her way. She's a kind, generous person. At least, that is, to those she doesn't consider to be in competition with her for some vaguely defined goal; for those she does—watch out: she'll carry a grudge to the grave. She may be stiff and formal and sometimes overly concerned with observance of proper behavior, but she's also adventurous and well traveled. And above all, her love of her children knows no bounds.

I do love my mother.

I just wished she wasn't bearing down on me at this moment, face beaming, arms outstretched.

"Surprise, darling," she cried.

It was a surprise, all right. My heart sank into my stomach, and I forced out a smile of my own. I'd been living in the Outer Banks of North Carolina for a short time, making a new life for myself away from the social respectability of my parents' circle in Boston, and now here she was.

"Hi, Mom," I said as I was enveloped in a hug. It was a real hug, too. Hearty and all-embracing, complete with vigorous slaps on the back. When it came to her children, Mom allowed herself to forget she was a Boston society matron. I loved her for that, too.

I pulled myself out of the embrace. "What are you doing here, Mom?"

"I've come for a short vacation and to see how you're settling in." She lifted her arms to indicate not only the Outer Banks, but the Lighthouse Library, where I worked and lived. "Isn't this charming? I haven't been in this building since it was renovated."

"You were here before it became a library?" I asked with some astonishment. When the historic Bodie Island Lighthouse had no longer been needed for its original function as a manually operated light, it had slowly crumbled into disrepair. Then, in a stroke of what I considered absolute genius, it was renovated and turned into a public library. High above, the great first-order Fresnel lens flashed in the night to guide ships at sea, while down below it books were read and cherished.

"Of course I was," Mom said. "Oh, I can remember some wild nights, let me tell you. Sneaking around in the dark, trying to break into the lighthouse. Up to all sorts of mischief." She must have read something in my face. "I was young once, Lucy. Although it sometimes seems like another lifetime."

She looked so dejected all of a sudden that I reached out and touched her arm. "It's nice to see you, Mom."

"You must be Mrs. Richardson." Ronald, one of my colleagues, extended his hand. He was a short man in his mid-forties with a shock of curly white hair. He wore blue-and-red-striped Bermuda shorts, a short-sleeved denim shirt, and a colorful tie featuring the antics of Mickey Mouse. "The resemblance is remarkable," he said. "Although if I hadn't heard Lucy call you Mom, I'd have thought you were sisters."

Mom beamed. I didn't mind being told I looked thirty years older than I was; really, I didn't. Ronald was our children's librarian, and a nice man with a warm, generous heart. He'd only told Mom what she'd wanted to hear. And, I had to admit, Mom looked mighty darn good. Weekly spa visits, a personal trainer, regular tennis matches, and the consumption of truckloads of serums and creams (and, perhaps, a tiny nip and tuck here and there) only accented her natural beauty. She was dressed in a navy blue Ralph Lauren blazer over a blindingly white T-shirt and white capris. Her carefully cut and dyed ash-blond hair curled around her chin, and small hoop earrings were in her ears. Her gold jewelry was, as always, restrained but spoke of money well spent.

I, on the other hand, looked like the harassed librarian I was. Only horn-rimmed glasses on a lanyard and a gray bun at the back of my head were missing. My unruly mop of dark curls had been pulled back into a ragged ponytail that morning because I hadn't gotten up in time to wash it. I wore my summer work outfit of black pants cut slightly above the ankle, ballet flats, and a crisp blue short-sleeved shirt, untucked. I hadn't gotten around to washing the shirt after the last time I'd worn it and hoped there weren't stains so tiny I hadn't noticed—because Mom would. I made the introductions. "Suzanne Richardson, meet Ronald Burkowski, the best children's librarian in the state."

"My pleasure," Mom said before turning her attention back to me. "Why don't you give me the grand tour, dear?"

"I'm working right now."

She waved her hand at that trifle.

"You go ahead, Lucy," Ronald said. "My next group doesn't start for fifteen minutes. I'll watch the shop while you take your mom around the place. But," he added, "don't go upstairs yet. I want to show her the children's library myself."

Mom laughed, charmed. Ronald smiled back, equally charmed.

I refrained from rolling my eyes as she slipped her arm though mine. "Come on," I said. "I'll show you the Austen books and then introduce you to my boss."

"Is he as delightful as your Ronald?"

"He's not my Ronald, and Bertie is a she." I liked Bertie very much, but if there was one thing she was not, it was delightful.

I proudly escorted Mom to view the Bodie Island Lighthouse Library's pride and joy: a complete set of Jane Austen first editions. The six books, plus Miss Austen's own notebook, would be on loan to us for a few more weeks. They rested in a tabletop cabinet handcrafted specifically to hold them, tucked into a small alcove lit by a soft white light. The exhibit had proved to be successful beyond the wildest dreams of Bertie and the library board—not to mention the local craftspeople and business owners when crowds of eager literary tourists began flooding into the Nags Head area.

"I'd love to have a peek at Jane Austen's notebook," Mom said. "Written in her own handwriting—imagine."

"I'll get the key when we meet Bertie. I'm sure we can make an exception in your case." We'd learned the hard way to keep the cabinet locked at all times and to secure the only copy of the key on Bertie's person. She'd told me that if the library caught fire in the night, I had permission to break the glass and grab the books. Otherwise, only she could open it.

Bertie was in her office, chewing on the end of a pencil as she studied her computer screen. I gave the open door a light tap. Bertie looked up, obviously pleased by the interruption. I knew she was going through the budget this morning. Charles, another of our staff members, occupied the single visitor's chair. He stretched lazily and gave Mom the once-over.

Neither he nor Mom appeared to be at all impressed by what they saw.

The edges of Charles's mouth turned up into the slightest sneer and he rubbed at his face. Then, very rudely, he went back to his nap.

"Oh," Mom said, "a cat. How . . . nice."

Bertie got to her feet and came out from behind her desk. I made the introductions, and the women shook hands.

"I hope you're taking care of my only daughter,"

Mom said. Behind her back, I rolled my eyes. Bertie noticed but she didn't react.

"Lucy's taking care of us. She's a joy to work with and I consider myself, and the library, very lucky to have her."

Mom smiled in the same way she had at parent-teacher interview day.

I'm thirty years old and have a master's in library science, but to Mom I'm still twelve and being praised for getting an A-plus on my essay on the Brontë sisters. I felt myself smiling. In that, she was probably no different from most mothers.

"Are you staying with Ellen?" Bertie asked, referring to Mom's sister.

"I'm at the Ocean Side." Mom always stayed at the Ocean Side, one of the finest (and most expensive) hotels on this stretch of the coast. "I haven't been to the hotel yet, Lucy. I wanted to stop by and let you know I'd arrived. Why don't you come with me and help me check in?"

"I'm working," I said. Work was a concept with which Mom pretended to be unfamiliar.

"Go ahead, Lucy," Bertie said. "Take the rest of the afternoon off. You've been putting in so many extra hours, you deserve it."

"But—"

"I'll take the circulation desk."

Between Mom's wanting me to come with her and Bertie's wanting to escape budget drudgery, I could hardly say no, now, could I?

Not wanting to be left alone, Charles roused himself and leapt off the chair. He rubbed himself against Mom's leg. She tried to unobtrusively push him away.

Charles didn't care to be pushed. At thirty-some pounds, he was a big cat. A gorgeous Himalayan with a mass of tan fur, with pointy black ears and a mischievous black-and-white face. We walked down the hallway, with Mom trying not to trip over the animal weaving between her feet.

"Did you drive all the way down today?" I asked. Mom loved to drive, and she'd often jump into her car and take off for a few days, giving the family no notice. "Me time" or "road trip," she called it. As I got older I'd begun to realize that me time usually corresponded with my dad's dark moods.

"I spent a couple of days in New York. I left there this morning."

"New York," Bertie said, almost dreamily. "I haven't been there for ages. How was it?"

"Marvelous," Mom said. "I did some shopping, saw a play."

I grabbed my bag from the staff break room, leaving Mom and Bertie to talk about the delights to be found in New York City.

When I reappeared Ronald had joined the conversation. He was from New York and had been a professional actor before giving that up to become a librarian. *Broadway's loss*, I thought. Ronald loved nothing more than putting on dramatic presentations for the kids. Ronald's children's programs were one of the most popular things at the Lighthouse Library.

Bertie unlocked the Austen cabinet with a great flourish. I handed Mom the white gloves used to handle the valuable books and indicated that she could then pick up the notebook. It was, of course, a precious and fragile thing, about four inches square and an inch thick, with a faded and worn leather cover. Mom opened the book. The handwriting was small and had been faded by the passage of years. Mom smiled. "How marvelous." She carefully returned it to its place, and Bertie turned the lock.

We stood quietly for a moment, no one saying anything. Then Mom shook the sentiment off, almost like a dog emerging from the surf, and said, "We'll take my car. I'll bring you back."

Mom's eye-popping silver Mercedes-Benz SLK stood out among the sturdy American vans and practical Japanese compacts pulling into the parking lot, bringing kids for the summer-afternoon preteens program. Since she'd been in New York for a couple of days, she'd probably done a *lot* of shopping. More than would have fit into the suitcase-sized trunk of the two-seater convertible. She must have told the stores to send everything to the house.

"How's Dad?" I asked.

"Busy. Some silly deal with some silly Canadian oil company has run into problems."

My dad was a lawyer, a partner in Richardson Lewiston, one of Boston's top corporate law firms. My dad loved two things in life: his law practice and Laphroaig. Unfortunately he dealt with the stress of the former by retreating into the whiskey bottle that held the latter.

"You know your father. Always working." Mom gave me a strained smile. In the light of the brilliant North Carolina summer sun, I could see the fine lines edged into the delicate skin around her eyes and mouth.

I climbed into the passenger seat of the car and we roared off in an impressive display of engine power.

I knew perfectly well that Mom had not come for a visit, or to see that I was settling in nicely. She'd come to try to take me home.